DEAD LAW

A Cass Leary Legal Thriller

ROBIN JAMES

Chapter 1

"You'll never make it," Miranda said.

"I'll make it," I countered, my fingers clacking across the keyboard. One more paragraph and the thing would be done. Not my best piece of writing, but it got the point across.

"You missed a space." Miranda stood over my shoulder. "Right there. After the wherefore."

I made the correction and hit print.

"You're gonna lose," Miranda said, hustling over to the printer in the other room. She shook her head with disapproval as she gathered each sheet of paper when they spit out of the front of the machine.

"Thanks for the vote of confidence," I said. "How much time do I have?"

"Not enough," she answered. "You're due in Judge Castor's courtroom at 9:00 a.m. and Judge Wentz's courtroom on the Chaney hearing at 9:15."

"How do you expect me to be in two places at once?"

"You'll work it out. Just check in with Nancy. She'll go up and stall Judge Wentz."

Miranda stapled my brief with gusto.

"My bag?"

"On the step."

I grabbed my well-worn leather messenger bag and heaved it over my shoulder. Before I could put a hand out, Miranda swooped in and tucked my brief in the outside pocket.

"Your jacket," she said. She took my black blazer off the chair and held it out so I could slip my arms into it.

"I need my ..."

"Coffee," she said, handing me my silver insulated mug.

"Where'd I put my ..."

"Keys," she said, dangling them in front of me. Smiling, I took them from her.

"Thanks."

"Your breakfast," she said.

"No time."

She gave me no choice. As I headed for the back door, Miranda grabbed a glazed donut off the plate on the counter and stuffed it in my mouth.

"Fanks," I mumbled while chewing.

"You can't keep going like this," she said.

"Mmmmpf."

"Come back here straight after. I'll order your lunch."

"No time." I swallowed and mumbled as I pushed my way through the door.

"Make time or I'll come find you!"

I waved behind me as I ran to my car, slid behind the wheel, and peeled out of my parking spot. It was 8:53 a.m. Seven minutes to be late in two different courtrooms.

It was Monday morning. I knew my week would only go downhill from there.

Two minutes racing down First Street. My tires squealed as I made the hard turn into the courthouse parking lot. It earned me a death stare from Ernie, the attendant. I gave him a sheepish expression and a wave.

"Park in the sheriff's spot," he called out. "Then throw me your keys!"

"I love you!" I yelled. Ernie just saved me a precious three minutes. I pulled into the spot, then tossed my keys underhanded in a high arc. Ernie palmed them and shot me a wink. Then I ran as fast as I could in heels. Down the hall. Up a flight of stairs. Down one more hallway then I burst through the solid oak double doors, brushing the donut glaze off my blouse.

"All rise!"

I barely made it into Judge Felix Castor's courtroom. My newly printed counter-motion and brief in response was still warm in my hands as I slapped a copy on Rafe Johnson's table and walked the judge's copy up to his clerk. She glared at me, stamped it, then put it on Judge Castor's bench just as he walked in from his chambers.

"You're cutting it too close, Ms. Leary," Judge Castor said.

"Your Honor," Rafe said. "I haven't even had a chance to look at Ms. Leary's brief in response."

"Then you should have served your motion on me in a timely fashion," I said. "I only got it the day before yesterday. I'm doing the best that I can."

Judge Castor stared at Rafe down the barrel of his reading glasses. He picked up my responsive brief and scanned it.

"Your Honor," I said. "In light of the untimeliness of the state's motion, and in order to give this Court a proper amount of time to review my counter-motion and response, I respectfully ask for a continuance on this matter."

"You've had three of those already," Castor said. "Mr. Johnson, Ms. Leary's point is well taken in one regard. You know better than to file an evidentiary motion like this at the eleventh hour. We're in trial next week. Your motions were due four weeks ago."

"Your Honor, some new evidence has come to light. It was beyond my control."

"Be that as it may, I've cleared my docket. We're going to trial next week. Period. Ms. Leary, no more continuances."

The doors opened. Nancy Olson, the Circuit Court clerk, poked her head in. She gave me a wide-eyed, impatient look. Judge Wentz was waiting for me two floors up in Probate Court. He had a lethal reputation for sanctioning attorneys who kept him waiting. He also didn't tend to like me very much in general. It's why I avoided Probate Court at all costs. Only now, with Tori, my associate, still in the hospital, and Jeanie, my partner, recovering from hip surgery, I was a one-man band for the near future. At the rate things were going, the Leary Law Group was in danger of sinking. That is, if I could make it out of this courthouse today without getting slapped with contempt charges.

"Fay," Judge Castor said to his clerk. "What's my docket look like this afternoon?" I tried to check my watch without being obvious about it. It was 9:17. Wentz's hearing started two minutes ago.

Nancy came up behind me. "Judge Wentz's about to rule on your petition, Cass. His clerk sent me down to find you."

"I'm dancing as fast as I can, Nancy," I whispered through gritted teeth.

"Judge," Fay the clerk said. "You've got a sentencing hearing at eleven-thirty. A settlement conference at one-thirty on the Walling matter."

"Fine," Castor said. "I expect both of you back here at 12:45. Ms. Leary, if you're even a second late, I'm granting Mr. Johnson's motion and assessing costs on your side."

I still hadn't unclenched my jaw. There were about five reasons why he couldn't do that. But I'd take my small victories where I could.

"Thank you, Your Honor," I said, gathering my things. I shot Rafe a look. He wouldn't meet my eyes. Then I walked out right behind Nancy.

"How angry is Judge Wentz?" I asked.

"Scale of one to ten? I'd say a solid six. But he idles at five so there's that."

"He's still holding my DNA against me?" I said as we headed for the stairs together. No point waiting for the ancient elevators in the Woodbridge County Courthouse.

"He's a snob," she said. "But he's fair when it comes down to it. Still, when's Tori coming back?"

"I don't know." There was more I couldn't say. I didn't know for sure whether Tori would ever be able to come back like she was. She had suffered a closed head injury in a nasty car accident eight weeks ago. She had a long road ahead of her. She struggled with short-term memory loss and brain fog that might never go away. But she was young. Strong. And she had something special to fight for. She and my brother Matty had given birth to a baby. Born a preemie, he was now a beautiful, healthy boy named Sean, after Tori's father. He was coming home from the hospital tomorrow.

"Soon, I hope," I said.

"Good," Nancy said as she pushed the third-floor door open. "Though ... when she and Matty tie the knot, she might want to keep her maiden name, at least professionally. You know. For Judge Wentz's sake."

I couldn't tell whether Nancy was kidding or not. I didn't get the chance to ask. The courtroom doors swung open and Judge Wentz's bailiff confronted me.

"She's right here, Your Honor!" he bellowed.

"Good luck," Nancy whispered. "You're gonna need it, honey."

Finding my biggest smile, I stepped into the lion's den of Judge Michael Wentz's courtroom, pretending I wasn't wearing meat underwear.

ONE HOUR LATER, I was still sweating when I came back out. It wasn't pretty. Judge Wentz spent almost ten minutes lecturing me on punctuality, legal ethics, the state of the economy, and my various other shortcomings. But in the end, he granted my— or rather, Tori's—motion to approve the Louis estate's final accounting. There had never been any doubt that he would. The man just wanted me to suffer for it for sport. Fine. I played the game.

As I headed back down the hall, I got a text from Miranda. She reminded me of two client meetings I had later this afternoon. One, a potentially lucrative personal injury matter. The other, a new divorce client. A friend of Jeanie's. If she felt up to it, she was supposed to sit in. Both were matters the firm sorely needed if we were going to make payroll for the quarter. We'd burned through our last big retainer far faster than I hoped and with Tori down, I'd had to turn work away.

"Don't forget," Nancy said. The woman just seemed to materialize out of thin air, startling me. "Judge Castor wants you at 12:45."

"Right," I said. I texted Miranda back, asking her to shuffle all my other appointments back an hour. She answered with an angry face emoji.

"Also," Nancy said. "There's someone looking for you. I told her where to find your office, but once she realized you were here in court, she said she wanted to wait. She's sitting on the bench next to my desk."

"A litigant?" I asked as we made our way back downstairs.

Nancy didn't answer. Instead, she pointed me to the bench against the wall. A young woman sat there. Early thirties, maybe. She had dark hair and a pleasant, round face. She rose when she saw me, clutching her purse against her stomach.

"You're Cass Leary?" she asked.

"She is indeed," Nancy answered for me. She gave me one last smile and left me.

"Can I help you?"

"I hope so," she said. "I'm Zoe. Zoe Paul. I heard ... well ... everyone says you're the best."

"Ms. Paul, I'm flattered. But I'm due in another courtroom in about twenty minutes. Would you like to make an appointment? I'll give you my card." I rifled through the outside compartment of my bag.

Zoe Paul rushed toward me. She looked like she was about to fall over.

"Maybe we should sit down," I said. She did, sinking back to the bench. I retrieved my card and handed it to her. She had an envelope in her hand. With shaking fingers, she held it out to me.

"I don't know what to do with this," she said. "And they told me you're the best."

Puzzled, I took the envelope from her. It wasn't sealed. One end had already been torn open. Zoe nodded as I tilted the envelope and let its contents fall out into my other hand.

The paper was old. Yellowing. But it was an uncashed cashier's check dated over sixteen years ago. I read the amount and my eyes popped. It was written for two million dollars.

Chapter 2

An hour later, after suffering through a different judge's temper, I ran up the back steps and burst into the office.

"Is she here?" I said to Miranda. She was standing in the kitchen, blowing steam off a fresh mug of coffee. Bless her, she'd brewed a fresh pot. I quickly refilled my insulated travel mug.

"She's here," Miranda said. "They both are."

"Both?"

"Jeanie showed up. She's in her office and driving me crazy."

"She's supposed to be in bed," I said. I peered around the corner. Zoe Paul sat in the waiting room, clutching her purse to her chest again. Now that I knew the contents of it, I didn't exactly blame her.

"Nancy called me by the way," Miranda said. "This one better be quick. You can't be late for Judge Castor."

"I'm aware."

"He's gonna grant Johnson's motion anyway. I don't know why he's putting you through the torture of coming back. He could just do it on briefs."

"Because he enjoys the torture. I seem to be every judge's favorite voodoo doll today."

"Well, that one looks like she's gonna be sick. You want me to send her up to your office?"

"No," I said. "I'll take her to Jeanie's. I wouldn't mind her take on this one."

"Bless you!" Miranda said. She pulled me into an embrace and kissed my cheek. "Anything you can do to keep Jeanie out of my hair for a little while. She's making a menace of herself."

I took one last swig of coffee and handed Miranda my mug.

"Ms. Paul?" I said brightly as I walked around the hall and into the waiting room. "Sorry to keep you waiting."

"I don't mind. I'm just grateful you could squeeze me in. I know how strange it was for me to ambush you in court. I just ... I didn't know what else to do."

Behind me, I heard Miranda mutter. "You could have called. Emailed. Made an appointment like a normal person."

Her voice was low enough that only I could hear. Still, I batted a hand behind me, waving her off.

"Come with me," I said to Zoe Paul. "I'd like to bring my partner in on this anyway. Her office is just through that door." Jeanie had the biggest first-floor office. I knocked on her door and poked my head in.

"You decent?" I whispered.

Jeanie stood in the center of the room white-knuckling a walker. Her face contorted with both pain and determination as she took slow steps to the leather armchair in the corner of the room.

"I've got a potential client out here. Can I bring her in?"

"Thank God," Jeanie said. "I'm out of my mind, bored. Miranda's no fun at all."

"She says the same about you." I looked over my shoulder. "Come on in and have a seat, Ms. Paul."

She did. Still keeping a death grip on her pink purse, she said a nervous hello to Jeanie then took a seat on one of the leather couches by the fireplace. I took the second armchair.

"Okay. How about you start from the beginning. Show Ms. Mills what you showed me."

Zoe Paul opened her purse and took out the envelope. She stood up and handed it to Jeanie. Jeanie slid her readers on. A new development. At seventy-five, she'd always had eyes like a hawk. She kept a stony expression on her face, but I knew her blood pressure jumped just as mine had when she read all those zeros. With a steady hand, she placed the check on the table between us.

"Who's Marilyn Paul?" Jeanie asked. It was the same question I had. The sixteen-year-old cashier's check had been written out to her, not Zoe.

"She's my grandmother," Zoe said. "She's been in a nursing home since August of '06."

I leaned forward and read the date on the check again. It meant the check had been written three months before Zoe's grandmother went into nursing care, if she was telling the truth.

"What's that check for?" Jeanie asked. "And why on earth didn't she cash it?"

"I don't know," Zoe said. "That's the whole thing. I don't understand any of it." Her face flushed. She was starting to sweat.

"Okay," I said. "Just tell us what you do know. We'll go from there."

"It's cash though, right? That's a cashier's check. They don't expire. That's what I read online. So ... is that like two million dollars of cash sitting on that table?"

"Maybe," I said. "Maybe not. Where did it come from?"

Zoe nodded. "Okay. Okay. See, I found it a week ago. I just ... found it. My grandma ... um ... Marilyn Paul. She raised me. My mom's never been in the picture. She was an addict. A junkie. In fact, I was born addicted to heroin, they told me. And my dad, um ... his name is Bradley Paul. Or it was. To be honest, I don't even know if he's alive anymore. He had his own issues and ran out when I was like two. I barely remember him growing up. He's just floated in and out. Mostly out. Anyway, my grandma is the only person who ever really cared about me. She took me in when I was a baby and raised me. That is ... until her accident."

"What happened?" I asked.

"Right after my senior year in high school ... um ... sixteen years ago, she was in a really bad car accident. She wrapped her Honda Accord around a telephone pole out on a country road. Broke both her legs. Ruptured her spleen. Fractured her skull. That was the worst of it. The closed head injury. She's been in a

14

nursing home ever since. She's almost non-verbal. Like a two-year-old, they say. She's at Maple Valley."

"We know it well," Jeanie said. She'd spent time there herself after recovering from cancer treatments a few years ago. Blessedly, she was in remission.

"So, you've been on your own since you were eighteen?" I asked.

"I'm all she really has. She's all I really have. She's got a brother but he's never been really nice to her. My grandpa died, gosh, thirty-some years ago. They'd just gotten a divorce. He ... he was against her raising me."

My throat went dry. Zoe Paul's childhood didn't sound much different from my own. We'd lost my father to alcohol for most of my growing up. My own mother had died in a car accident when I was just a teenager. I'd essentially raised my younger brother and sister. It had been Jeanie who fought for us and kept them out of foster care.

"You have to understand," Zoe said. "I had nothing. We had nothing. My grandma ... I mean, before her accident. She never made a lot of money. She worked as a secretary for a while. I think a bank teller at one point. But it was always paycheck to paycheck. And this?"

Zoe reached forward and picked up the check. "I never knew anything about this. Nobody did."

"How did that come into your possession?" I asked.

"I kept my grandma's house. It's nothing special. A three-bedroom, one-bathroom bungalow on Hyde Street. Over the years, I've been fixing it up. I've been paying the mortgage on it since I was twenty. It was rough financially for me for a while after my grandma's accident. But I got the house out of foreclosure. I went to court and got myself appointed my grandma's guardian and all of that after her accident."

"The check though," Jeanie said.

"Well, have you been down Hyde Street lately? It's all turned around. Those houses are being flipped and it's nice again. I've had like a dozen offers from home remodelers and real estate agents to sell the thing. It's my home. The thing is, all the money I'd get from it would end up paying for Grandma's care anyway. I think she'd rather I just stay there. Anyway ... I was starting to redo the bathroom. It's just got old pink tile from the sixties. When I ripped up a section near the sink, I found this cigar box hidden under this patch of loose tile. The envelope was in there. It had never been opened."

"My lord," Jeanie said.

I picked up the check and looked at it again. There was nothing extraordinary about it. The memo line was blank. There was no note indicating it was void after a certain time like some cashier's checks I'd seen. There was nothing remarkable about it except for the staggering amount.

"Delphi Savings Bank," Jeanie said, reading the payor bank in the top corner. "They don't even exist anymore. They were bought out by First Bank. And they aren't even around anymore. I wanna say you're looking at three or four mergers over the past sixteen years."

"It could be Knight Bank now," I said. "At least that's what's in the old Delphi Savings Bank building downtown here. I can solve that with a quick phone call."

"Is it still good though?" Zoe asked. "Two million dollars. I have no idea where this was from. Why it was written to her. Like I told you. We were living hand to mouth before Grandma's accident. And she would have done anything for me. I just don't understand why she would have held on to something like this. Why she would have hidden it from everybody. It's two million dollars!"

"I'm afraid I have more questions than I can give you answers right now, Zoe," I said. "Banking law isn't my expertise. But it's not like a personal check that would go stale. Generally speaking, cashier's checks are like cash."

"If it went uncashed," Jeanie said, "the bank probably would have had an obligation to report it to the state. Have you ever gotten any notices in your grandmother's name about unclaimed funds?"

"No," Zoe said. "Nothing that I remember."

"Have you talked to your uncle or your father about this?" I asked. "Have you talked to anybody?"

"I asked a couple of friends. But like I told you, I'm not close with any other members of the family. I don't even know where my dad is. My grandma's brother moved to Florida a few years ago. But I can tell you, if he knew about a two-million-dollar check, he would have said something. He would have tried to figure out a way to get his hands on it. I can guarantee you that."

"Well," Jeanie said. "I can look at the probate file for your grandmother. See what's what."

"She had a will," Zoe said. "Sixteen years ago, when the school legal clinic helped me out getting the guardianship and things, they recommended I file it. She left everything to me."

"That's good," I said. "But as far as her will, it's not the controlling document while she's still alive."

"Do you think they'll still honor this though?" Zoe asked, pointing to the check.

"I can make a call to the bank," I said. "See if I can figure out if this was ever reported as unclaimed. Do you mind if I make a copy?"

"I'm hoping you'll keep it," Zoe said. "That's why I'm such a wreck. Carrying the thing around. I mean ... my God. It was under the bathroom tile! A hundred people have been through that house over the years. There could have been a fire. What if I'd never found it?"

"I can do that," I said. "I can put it in my safe deposit box for now until we can figure out what to do about it."

Zoe's shoulders drooped as if a giant weight had been lifted from them. "Thank you! So you'll help me? You'll take this case?"

Before I could answer, Jeanie heaved herself to her feet. Pain or no pain, the six zeros on that check worked on her like a magic elixir.

"Oh, we'll take your case, honey. We love a good mystery around here."

The moment she said it, a chill went through me. It seemed like the kind of thing we might come to regret. But I rose with her and shook Zoe Paul's hand.

Chapter 3

At nine weeks old, Sean Matthew Leary fixed his big blue eyes on me, scrunched up his face, and farted.

"Well done, little man," I whispered, kissing him on his downy forehead.

I loved the solid weight of him in my arms. He'd been just a pound at birth. Scrawny. Bird-like. Now, I traced the curve of his tiny shoulder and felt the beginnings of baby fat there. He tensed his round belly, flailed his arms and legs, and let out a burp. Pleased with himself, he curled his tongue, yawned, and fell promptly asleep with a smile.

"He really is something," Eric said. He stood behind the couch over my shoulder.

He almost didn't make it here. Three days after his birth, my nephew developed a respiratory infection that nearly took his life. He fought back though. Hour by hour, painstaking day by day. A week ago, he left the hospital, hopefully for good.

"I'll be right back," Eric said. "Your brothers just pulled up in the truck."

It was moving day. Matty and baby Sean had been staying with me since Sean was released from the hospital. Yesterday, my brother finally closed on a house just across the lake from me. I bought it for him with part of the proceeds of another house I'd just sold up in Helene, Michigan. My last tie to Killian Thorne. I hadn't wanted anything to do with it, but in the end, Eric had been the one to convince me to take the money and do something good with it.

This was my something good. Matty and Tori had protested, promised to take out a mortgage and pay me back. I didn't want it. So, we compromised. The house would stay in a trust for Sean. And I got to have my brother close by for the rest of our lives.

"Well, we're westsiders now," Matty said as he and Eric burst through the open front door carrying a couch.

"There goes the neighborhood," my sister Vangie called out. She had busied herself setting up the kitchen. I was handling the very important baby-holding duties.

Matty wanted everything to be perfect for when Tori came home. If all went according to plan that would be in just a few weeks. She'd made excellent progress in rehab. In the last two months since her car accident, she'd relearned how to walk. A fighter, just like her son.

"Where do you want it?" My older brother, Joe said to Matty.

"Against the east wall," Vangie answered him. Tori had given her explicit instructions on how she wanted everything arranged. Matty would make sure her home was perfect for her the moment she walked ... yes ... walked in.

Slowly, silently, I stood. Sean's nursery was the first thing we'd set up this morning. The house had two bedrooms on the main floor, two upstairs. For the first few weeks after Tori got home, she wanted Sean in the bassinet beside her. I took him there now. He'd be close enough for us to hear him, but tucked away enough he could get some sleep.

I gently set him down on his side and covered his feet with a light blanket. A cool, summer breeze came in from the window. Tori and Matty's room faced east. They would have a gorgeous view of every sunrise over the lake.

I walked out into the kitchen just as Jeanie arrived. She'd appointed herself lunch duties for the day. She carried two stuffed grocery bags. Eric swooped in and took them from her. The smell of Cubby's Sandwich Subs filled the house. My stomach growled. I set out to find the box with all the paper plates.

The men took a break and we all gathered around the giant farm table Matty had refurbished. It sat twelve people. Tori was determined to host the next Leary holiday here. With Thanksgiving just three months away, it gave her another target to reach.

Jeanie sat beside me, smiling. She liked watching my brothers eat. I took a bite of my turkey avocado and reached for the two-liter of Vernors.

"So," Jeanie said, after Matty, Eric, and Joe left to bring in the mattresses. "I had a chance to look at the probate file for Marilyn Paul."

"Any surprises?"

Jeanie wiped mayonnaise from the corner of her mouth and shook her head. "She has no listed assets other than the house. The granddaughter has been paying the taxes and mortgage on it since she was twenty years old. Before that, like she said, it was almost foreclosed on. There was a small checking account at one time, but that's long since been drained."

"Was there a settlement or anything due to her car accident?" I asked.

"Just a first-party PIP claim. There were no other drivers involved. Her insurance has been paying for her care."

"Well," I said. "That's the one good thing about Michigan no-fault, I guess."

"So," Jeanie said. "Barring any unforeseen complications, if we can get the bank to honor that cashier's check, Marilyn Paul could become a millionaire."

"I just can't see it," I said. "There has got to be an explanation for how that check got there. What it was for."

"What's your game plan?" she asked.

"Well, first I'm meeting with Zoe at her grandmother's house later this week. She said she's kept all of Marilyn's things in a back bedroom. I'm going to go through some of it with her and see if we can shed any light on what was going on in her life in those last few months."

"What are we thinking? An inheritance? A settlement check? Blackmail?"

There was a twinkle in Jeanie's eye when she said it.

"You know, your guess is as good as mine. As far as inheritance though, Zoe insists nobody in their family had anything."

"I peeked at her divorce file from Zoe's grandfather. There wasn't anything there either. Looks like her old man was broke. He filed for bankruptcy during the proceedings. So, that check wasn't from him either. Maybe she had a kindly aunt who won the lottery or something."

"Who won the lottery?" Vangie called out.

"Nobody!" Jeanie and I shouted together.

"How do we even know who to present the check to?" Jeanie asked.

"That's another thing on my to-do list. Miranda's going to call Knight Bank and see if they acquired Delphi Savings Bank's assets after multiple mergers."

"I pity whatever poor teller's going to have to try and sort that out when you march up there with a two-million-dollar check."

"I'll be back," Joe said, poking his head in. "I've got to run to the hardware store. You okay watching the little guy?"

"Go!" Vangie called out. "We need more box cutters."

"I've got one in the truck!" Matty called out. He and Eric were taking a beer break on the lawn, staring out at the lake. The previous owners had left the dock in. It was an older, clunky, wooden one with six sections; one of them was currently dipping almost underwater. Matty was already coming up with ideas how to fix it.

"It's going to do Tori a world of good coming home," Jeanie said. "It's killing her not to be near Sean."

"Matty and I are taking him to see her later this evening," Vangie said. "And I promised her we'd FaceTime in about an hour. She's got physical therapy at three."

"We should go visit her," Jeanie said. "This Marilyn Paul case would have been hers to handle if ..."

If, I thought. If Tori hadn't gotten behind the wheel of my car two months ago and taken a curve too fast. I still couldn't shake the feeling that it was my fault.

"What's with those two?" Vangie said, wiping her hands on a dish towel. I looked back out the window. Matty and Eric had their heads practically locked together. Eric had a scowl on his face that seemed more serious than a crooked section of dock.

"I don't know," I said. My stomach twisted. Vangie's observations were right. There was something going on.

"I'll be right back." I handed the receiver for Sean's baby monitor to my sister and headed out the back door.

"You have to tell him," I heard Eric say.

"Tell who what?" I asked.

When my brother turned to face me, my throat ran dry. His brow was deeply creased, and he looked positively pained. He and Eric shared a look.

"Let's take a walk," Eric said. "You should tell Cass too. But you already knew that, or you wouldn't have said anything. Vangie and Jeanie don't need to know. Yet."

"What's going on?" I said, lowering my voice. I walked with Eric and Matty up the driveway and safely out of earshot of the house.

"It's Joe," Matty said. "Or … um … it's about Joe."

"Matty, what?" I said, practically shouting. "Is he okay? What happened?"

"I think there's trouble with Katie. Something he's not telling the rest of us."

I took a breath. Joe's wife Katie was the one person who was conspicuously absent today. Joe had said something about her feeling under the weather and I hadn't pressed.

"What do you know?" I asked.

Again, Matty looked at Eric.

"Don't look at him," I said. "Look at me. Tell me!"

"Cass," Matty said. "I think Katie's cheating on Joe. I saw her. I had a job last week out at the Renaissance Suites. A roofing job. Anyway, I saw her coming out of one of the units with another guy. It wasn't casual. They were … um … together."

"The Ren's bread and butter is clandestine affairs, Cass. Every unit has its own garage so nobody can drive around checking license plates."

I took a step back. It felt like someone had punched me. Katie. Joe's Katie. They'd had their issues over the years, but this couldn't be true.

"Cass," Eric said. "I didn't want to say anything. I'm not one to spread rumors. But they're going around. One of the guys at the department said something to me. He ran into Katie and another guy having dinner in Ann Arbor. This was about three weeks ago."

"Why didn't you tell me?" I asked.

"I wanted to be sure it was true," Eric said.

"He doesn't know. We're sure Joe doesn't know?"

"I'm not sure of anything," Matty said. "But I don't think she's really sick. I think they're in trouble and Joe just hasn't told any of us."

"We have to tell him," I said. "Ugh. No. I have to talk to Katie. Let me do that first. If you're wrong. If there's some other explanation, she deserves the benefit of the doubt, doesn't she?"

"Does she?" Matty said, rage coloring his words.

"Let me just ... I'll talk to her," I said. "Then we'll figure out what the hell to do. Okay?"

Matty nodded. Eric put a light hand at the small of my back.

"Matty?" Vangie called from the house. "Sean's waking up again. You want me to feed him?"

"No!" Matty yelled. "I'll do it." He gave me a tight-lipped smile, then ran up the walkway.

"Shit," I said looking back out at the lake. "What do you really think?"

"I think ... you're right. Take a day. Talk to Katie if you want."

"You've already drawn your own conclusions, haven't you?"

Eric kissed me. He wouldn't answer. A minute later, my brother Joe's truck rounded the corner and pulled into the driveway. I took a deep breath, steeling myself. Joe could always read my face. I put on a smile and walked back up toward the house.

Chapter 4

For two days, my sister-in-law Katie refused to answer my calls or texts. That alone confirmed my worst fears. There was something going on. Something bad. So, at dinner tonight, my little brother and I decided we would tell our oldest brother about what Matty saw. An intervention of sorts, he might think. Mainly, I just wanted to make sure Joe was in a safe place when we delivered the news that would blow up his life.

For now, though, I would spend most of my day trying to reconstruct a different life. Marilyn Paul's.

I met Zoe at her grandmother's house on the very south edge of Woodbridge County. She had been right. Hyde Street had undergone a remarkable transformation over the last five years. Dilapidated homes were either torn down or rebuilt and remodeled. New trees planted. The old park nearby had a new ADA-compliant jungle gym and tennis courts. The latter were currently being used for Pickleball.

I pulled into the driveway of 312 Hyde Street. Zoe waved from the front window. Roofing tiles were stacked up on one side of the driveway. She had contractors coming out to do the tear-off later this week. But she'd stopped all interior remodeling after pulling up the infamous bathroom tile.

"Sorry, everything's such a mess," Zoe said. She was more at ease today, smiling as she opened the screen door and let me in. When she did, a wave of nostalgia hit me. Marilyn's house had been built in the same era as the one I'd lived in until I was ten years old—it was a 1930s-era bungalow. I felt certain the same builder had constructed it. I recognized the crown molding, the oak floors with three-inch baseboards, the now unnecessary telephone nook carved into the plaster wall in the living room.

"It's adorable in here," I said.

"It's home, anyway. Come on. I've kept all my grandma's things upstairs. It's three bedrooms but I only use two. One for me, one for a home office."

I followed Zoe up the curved staircase, running my fingers along the wrought iron railing. We had one just like that too in my parents' house on Manchester Street.

Zoe led me to the first bedroom on the left. There was nothing in it now but stacked Bankers Boxes and an old roll-top desk.

"This is it," she said. "Everything that was left. I've brought it all down from the attic."

"Has anyone else lived or stayed here since your grandmother's accident?" I asked. I went to the desk and opened it. Zoe had a wooden chair in front of it on giant casters. I took a seat.

"Just me for the most part. There was a little while in the beginning where I went and stayed with friends. I didn't think I could manage living in a house by myself. It was vacant for maybe a year. Then my Uncle Roy, my grandma's brother, moved in. It got kind of complicated though. After I filed the papers to be made Grandma's guardian, I had to kick him out. The court said he needed to pay rent and he refused. We haven't spoken since."

"Your grandma raised you alone?"

"Yeah. I think I told you. My grandpa was never keen on the idea. He was ... abusive to my grandma. She kicked him out when I was little. It was bad when he was here. I remember her putting makeup on to hide her black eyes. When the worst of it happened, she'd send me down the street to stay with the neighbor. Frieda Jones. She's been like a second grandma to me. She was my grandma's best friend."

"Does she still live down the street? I wouldn't mind talking to her."

"She does. I'm sure she'd be happy to talk to you."

I turned back to the desk. Marilyn had stationery, thank you cards, blank birthday cards, some old family photos, and other bits and pieces — but nothing that would immediately shed light on how or why someone would write her a two-million-dollar check.

Zoe slid a Bankers Box toward me. "She kept her tax returns in here. She would do them herself with online software. These are ten years' worth. That's all I could find. And then there are these."

She handed me a gallon-size freezer bag. Inside of it were at least a dozen old check registers.

"This is good," I said. "This could be helpful. At least I'll be able to see who she might have been doing business with. Where was your grandmother employed ahead of her accident?"

"She worked a couple of jobs. She was a bus driver for Delphi Public. That was part time. Three days a week, I think. Then she worked weekends and two days during the week at corporate for Valentine Pizza. Secretarial stuff. Before that, I think I told you, she worked as a teller, as a clerk for one of the utility companies. She kind of went from job to job."

"Who would you say knew her best?" I asked.

"That would be Frieda, our neighbor."

"Did she date?"

"Oh yeah. Nobody she considered serious. She was upfront with me about that. She said she'd never bring a man here. Not while I was growing up. She used to say that maybe someday, when I went off to college, she'd settle down again. But I think she really liked her life, you know? She wasn't looking to get married again."

"Can you remember any names of men she might have dated?"

"Gosh. It's been so long. And like I said, she didn't bring them around me. When she did go out, she'd do it on nights I went on sleepovers with my friends. Or I'd stay over at the Joneses down the street."

"Is Frieda one of the people you told about the check?" I wasn't sure what I wanted Zoe's answer to be.

"I didn't tell her the amount," Zoe said. "I just asked her if my grandma ever mentioned anyone owing her a large amount of money. She said no. But also that she couldn't be sure whether my grandma would have told her something like that. You can talk to her though. I told her there's been some estate stuff that has come up and that I've hired you to handle it."

I smiled. I was still trying to figure out how to bill her if it got that far.

"That's helpful," I said. "What about a computer? I know it's been a long time, but did she have one? Is it here?"

"No computer," she said. "Not anymore. She had an old Mac that she hated. But that's long gone. There's this though."

Zoe reached around me and opened the bottom desk drawer. I peered inside. It was a graveyard of old tech. A pager. A palm pilot. Two different cell phones, one of the flip variety. I pulled them out. They'd long since lost their charge, but there was another baggie in the bottom of the drawer containing various power chords.

"Have you looked at any of these?" I asked, holding up the phones.

"Nope," Zoe said. "But the red one is the one she had on her the day of her accident."

"I'm glad nobody got rid of it," I said. "There might be something useful on it. I should at least be able to figure out who she was talking to in the weeks before she had the accident. Though no guarantees it'll help."

If I could get the phones charged and powered up, I planned to call in a favor and ask Eric to do reverse lookups on any numbers we found.

"So, what do we do now?" Zoe asked. "How do you even begin to figure out if that money is out there?"

"It's out there," I said. "The question is whether there's a bank on the hook for honoring it. The first step is trying. Jeanie, my partner, figured out that Knight Bank is the one who might be obligated. They bought out the bank who bought out Delphi Savings five years ago. So ... tomorrow morning, we're going there. Bring a copy of your letters of authority under the conservatorship."

"Are we just gonna march up to the teller and ask to cash it?"

"That's exactly what we're going to do. If it comes down to having to sue the bank, we have to present the check first. Give them a chance to honor it. If they won't, then you may have standing to sue. But I hope it doesn't come to that. I've got a bit of research to do. I'm trying to figure out what duties the bank had when that check was never cashed."

I took the cell phones and power chords and tossed them into the box containing Marilyn Paul's old check registers.

"Can I take these back to the office with me?" I asked.

"You can have whatever you want. Anything."

I opened another desk drawer. It contained a small voice recorder, the kind Marilyn might have used in dictation. It had a small cassette still in it. When I hit the play button, nothing happened. The batteries were likely long since dead. I tossed it into the box with the phones. There was one thing left in the drawer, a dusty cordless phone strapped to its base with an old telephone cable.

"Are there messages still on this?" I asked, pulling the entire thing out of the drawer.

"I don't know. I never thought to check. There might be."

I tossed it into the box with everything else and replaced the lid.

"This is a good start," I said, rising. "I'll see what I can find out from all of this. We'll present the check to the bank tomorrow.

Then we'll go from there. I wish I could give you a solid answer on whether you'll ever see a dime."

"It's possible though?"

"It's possible, yes. What bothers me is there's no listing of any unclaimed funds in your grandmother's name with the state of Michigan. We need to know why."

Zoe picked up the other Bankers Box containing her grandmother's old tax returns. We walked downstairs together, and Zoe helped me load my trunk. Once again, my heart twisted thinking about Tori. This was exactly the kind of project she would love sinking her teeth into. After our meeting at the bank, I planned to go visit her at Maple Valley, and perhaps pay a visit to Marilyn Paul herself.

I said a quick goodbye to Zoe and got behind the wheel. I never made it out of the driveway before my phone rang. It was Joe.

"Cass!" he yelled as my Bluetooth speaker kicked on. "She's done it. I need you. She can't do this!"

"Who? Do what?" I asked, and instantly regretted it.

"Katie," he said. "She's changed the locks. She's got all my clothes in boxes in the driveway. She's trying to kick me out of the damn house!"

I blew out my breath. "Just … stay put. Don't do anything. Don't lose your temper. I'll be right there."

I gave a last wave to Zoe Paul then headed for the next fire I'd need to put out.

Chapter 5

THE SECOND I pulled into Joe and Katie's driveway, a sheriff's deputy pulled in behind me, tapping his siren once to let me know he was there.

My brother Joe paced up and down the sidewalk, smoking a cigarette, something he hadn't done in over ten years. He turned toward the house and yelled at the top of his lungs. "You can't do this, Katie, it's against the law! See?" He gestured wildly toward the sheriff's cruiser, only I knew they weren't here for Katie.

"Joe," I shouted. I got out of my car and raced toward him. I put up my hand in a stopping gesture directed at the deputy. From the corner of my eye, I recognized him as Jeff Steuben.

"Joe, stop shouting," I said as I got to my brother. "Just ... stop."

"I told you!" Katie hollered from inside the house. She stood at the bay window, partially shielded by curtains. She had her phone to her ear. If she hadn't been the one to call the cops, I'd lay bets it was one of Joe's neighbors. Plenty of them peered out of their own windows, enjoying the spectacle.

"She can't lock me out of my own damn house, Cass."

"What happened?" I said.

"She's gone crazy. A mid-life crisis. Some sort of breakdown, I don't know. She won't talk to me."

Another car pulled in behind Deputy Steuben. My sister Vangie got out.

"No," I said. "Oh no. Not you too." Vangie didn't have the best track record when it came to her involvement with cops. She had a mean streak in her and a mouth that got her into trouble.

"Cass," Steuben said. "I need to talk to Joe."

"I've got nothing to say to you," Joe fumed. "You're on my property. You're trespassing. There's nothing going on that's any of your business."

"Well, now, Joe. Katie is saying she doesn't feel safe. She feels threatened."

"What?" Vangie and I spoke in unison.

"I haven't done anything," Joe said, flapping his hands in frustration. "I just came home from work. She locked me out and put all my stuff out in boxes. She can't do that. This is my house too. My name's on the mortgage. Cass, tell him she can't do that."

"Just stay here," I said. "Don't do anything. Don't say anything. Just ... stay put."

I walked over to Deputy Steuben and gently took his arm. He glared at me but came with me more or less willingly.

"Jeff," I said, when I knew we were out of earshot. Still, I kept my voice low. "You and I both know how this is going to go. This is a civil matter."

"Cass," he said. "I got a call about a domestic disturbance. I need to talk to Katie. Get her side of it."

"Fine," I said. "You do that. After you're done, I'd like to talk to her."

"That's up to Katie. Right now, I don't like the odds. Three keyed-up Learys against one."

"Give me a break, Jeff," Vangie said, approaching us. "Joe hasn't done anything wrong except come home from work. You know my brother. Whatever this is, it's a misunderstanding. Just go home and let us deal with it as a family."

"I can't do that, Vangie."

My sister batted her eyes at Jeff Steuben. It had been a long time ago, but Vangie had gone out with him once upon a time. If memory served, she'd been the one to call it off. Something about Jeff getting too serious too fast. But that had been Vangie's MO through most of her twenties.

"I'm going inside my own house!" Joe shouted. He stormed up the driveway. Steuben ran after him.

"Jeff!" I yelled. "Just hold on!"

From inside, Katie pounded on the window. "Go away, Joe! He's menacing, Deputy Steuben. You can see it for yourself."

"What is wrong with you!" Vangie shouted. She went right up to the window and smacked her palm against it, making Katie jump. "Joe's never done anything to you but keep this roof over your head and put food on your table, Katie. He doesn't deserve this. It's tacky. It's low class. You're better than this. He certainly is."

"Vangie," Steuben said. "You're not helping. Just go on back to your car. You too, Cass. Joe, is there someplace else you can stay tonight? I think everybody just needs to cool off. Katie, I need you to let me in. You called me out here. We need to talk."

"Just you," Katie said. "The rest of you need to get off my property."

"Your property?" Joe roared.

"Stop!" I grabbed Joe's arm and pulled him back, away from the front door. "Joey, stop. Have a seat in my car. We'll sort this all out."

I wished Matty were here. Though he wasn't the calmest soul when it came to entanglements with law enforcement either. Still, I had no idea if he'd said anything to Joe about his suspicions. The way Joe was acting, I'd bet he had no idea Katie might be stepping out on him. I could only pray that news wouldn't break while we were standing here. De-escalation was the goal.

"Come on," I begged Joe. "Give Jeff five minutes. Take a breath."

Joe jerked his arm out of my grasp but did what I asked. He walked to my car and threw open the passenger side door. He plopped himself down and lit up another cigarette.

"Really?" I said. Joe's glare told me this might not be the best battle to pick right now.

"Fine," I muttered. "But you're paying to have my car detailed."

As I turned, Katie had opened the door and let Deputy Steuben in.

"Stay there," I said to Joe. "Don't you dare move or I'm gonna let Steuben have his way with you."

Joe flicked ash out the window. At that moment, his resemblance to our father couldn't have been stronger. Belligerent. His eyes lit with rage. I gritted my teeth and walked back up the sidewalk to where Vangie stood trying to hear what Katie and the deputy were saying.

"What happened?" I asked. "Have you talked to Katie today? What is she thinking?"

Vangie looked back toward my car. Joe was currently focusing his ire on the next-door neighbors. They'd been rubbernecking the whole show since I got here.

Vangie stepped off the sidewalk and headed for the row of mailboxes on the other side of the street. With Joe out of trouble for the moment, I went with her.

Vangie whirled around. "Does he know?" she whispered.

"Know what?"

"About Tom Loomis."

My head spun. "Who's Tom Loomis?"

"The guy Katie's been screwing for the last four months."

"You knew about it? I mean ... it's for sure true?"

Vangie's shoulders dropped. "I wish it weren't. Believe me. I'd been hearing rumors for a few weeks. I ran into Tom at the grocery store the day before yesterday. I went up and asked him."

"You what? Who even is he?"

"Tom Loomis? Sis, have you been living under a rock?"

"Apparently."

"Tom Loomis. He's the new Eye on Sports guy for Channel 23."

She pulled out her phone, tapped the screen, then foisted the thing in my face. She'd pulled up a publicity still for the Channel 23 Action News team. Tom Loomis with his surfer-blond hair and his perfect capped teeth smiled back at me. I grabbed the phone from her.

"This guy? What is he, twenty-five?"

I looked over my shoulder. Joe was puffing away at his third cigarette since I rolled up. He had his face in his own phone but didn't seem at all concerned about what Vangie and I were talking about.

"Joe doesn't know," I said. "He would have found the guy and tried to castrate him."

"Yep," Vangie agreed.

"What is she thinking?"

"Come on, Cass. Things have been shaky between Joe and Katie for a long time."

"They've been through a lot. But I thought things were okay."

"Katie has been quiet-quitting her marriage for over a year now. At least."

"I'm going up there," I fumed, handing Vangie's phone back to her. "Stay here. Or ... stay with Joe. Do *not* let him follow me."

Just as I made my way up the sidewalk, Deputy Steuben started to come out.

"Perfect," I said. I charged up and caught the screen door before he had a chance to close it.

"Cass," he said. "Now don't go making things worse."

"Who, me?" I said. "Katie. Come out here. Talk to me."

"Are you okay with that?" Steuben asked.

"Jeff," I said. "You know Joe isn't a threat to her or anyone else. Katie knows that too. Don't you?"

Katie stayed against the wall, half hidden in the shadows.

"Katie?" I said.

"I told him to leave," she said.

"It's his house too."

"No," she said. "I mean I told Deputy Steuben to leave. I wasn't trying to get anyone in trouble. I didn't call the cops. That had to be some busybody neighbor." She was lying. Steuben said she'd called the cops herself.

"I'll leave," Steuben said. "On one condition. Joe needs to find someplace else to be tonight. That's non-negotiable. Then the two of you can work this out in family court if that's where you're headed. I just want to keep the peace."

"Thank you," I said. "We all appreciate that."

"Now," Steuben said. "I just wanna have a word or two with Joe."

I resisted the urge to warn him to keep out of Joe's strike zone. I just prayed my brother could keep his temper. As Steuben started walking toward him, I glared a silent warning to my brother. He waved me off at first, then gave me a sharp nod. Vangie moved in. I wasn't sure if that would make things better or worse.

"There's nothing you can say, Cass," Katie said. She'd stepped into the light and stood in her living room, arms folded. But she was no longer refusing to let anyone else in.

"What are you doing, Katie?" I said. "What's all this?"

"It's over," she said.

"Since when?"

"Since ... it just is, Cass. I'm done. I want Joe to move out. We'll sell the house if we have to. I'm not trying to bleed him dry or anything. I can be fair."

"Fair," I said. "Emma lives here too last time I checked. You kicking her out too?"

Katie's lips quivered. "She's not my daughter, Cass. Something she makes sure to point out."

"Katie, come on. Emma loves you. You're her family too."

"She doesn't live here anymore. She's got her apartment near campus. She barely comes home. She's got her own life. I've done everything I can for her. I need to figure out who I am now."

"Is Tom Loomis helping you do that?" I asked, my tone biting.

Katie blinked rapidly. "You should leave," she said. "I haven't taken anything from Joe. All his stuff is neatly packed."

"Katie, this isn't you. This isn't you and Joe. If you want a divorce, fine. We'll figure that all out. But throwing him out on the literal curb? Has he done something? Tell me."

"You're only going to take his side," she said. "You Learys all stick together."

"Last time I checked, you were a Leary too."

"No," she said. "I know what I am to you."

"What? You're blaming me for whatever this is? Katie, you've been like a sister to me. I've always treated you that way. I love you. You must know that."

"Just go. Please?" Katie started to sob. "I can't do this anymore. This hasn't been easy. But it's what I want."

"You don't think there was a better way to go about it?"

"I've tried," she said. "I've been telling Joe how unhappy I am for months."

"Did you tell him you were having an affair? Because everyone seems to know but him. He should hear it from you, Katie. I can be there. I can make sure ..."

"Cass?" Deputy Steuben walked back up. "Joe's calm. He understands the situation. But I still can't leave until I know he's going to. Katie, if you're not willing to let him back in ..."

"There's no reason," she said, wiping her nose on the back of her sleeve. "I told you. All his stuff is packed. There's nothing in here for him."

"He can come stay at my place," I said. "For tonight. But Katie, we're going to handle this as a family. The right way. Do you understand?"

Joe walked up the drive. Katie straightened her back.

"Can we talk?" he asked. My brother's tone broke my heart. What in God's name had happened to make things get so bad between them?

"No," Katie said, letting her tears fall. "I'm done, Joe. There's nothing left to say."

"Joe," Steuben said. "I'm sorry, but your wife just doesn't want you here right now. Cass says you can go stay with her tonight. I strongly recommend that you do."

Vangie came up. I didn't like the fire in her eyes. If she were part dragon, she would have incinerated Katie by now. While I understood the sentiment, I couldn't help just feeling sad for both of them.

"Yeah," Joe said, reading Katie's expression clearly for the first time. "I'll leave with my sister. But I'll be back in the morning."

"I'll be with him," I said to Steuben. "We have this under control."

Steuben pursed his lips. "Yeah. Sure. Okay. I'm well aware how the Learys take control."

"What the hell does that ..."

I grabbed Vangie's arm before she launched herself at Jeff Steuben. Behind me, Katie slammed the door and engaged the deadbolt.

"Come on," I said to Joe. "Start grabbing boxes. We'll sort this all out tomorrow." But as my brother and sister picked up the totes closest to them, I had the sense that this mess was too big for even me to fix.

Chapter 6

"I'M SORRY, you want me to what?"

Her name was Ashlee with two Es. She had long, straight, dark hair and still wore braces. The poor kid barely looked old enough to drive let alone handle banking transactions. But the window number 4 teller at Knight Bank had a ready smile and a crooked name tag as she read the zeros on Marilyn Paul's creased cashier's check.

"I want you to honor it," I said.

"That's two million dollars. It's … we aren't Delphi Savings Bank. I don't even …"

"We'll wait for the manager," I said. Zoe stood beside me, apprehensive and quiet. I picked up the check along with the copy of Zoe's letters of authority from the Probate Court. We sat in the waiting room while poor Ashlee tried to explain to the assistant branch manager what the heck we were doing there.

"You don't think they're just gonna let me deposit it into my grandma's trust account, do you?"

"I absolutely do not," I said. "But like I told you, we can't sue them for payment if we don't give them a chance to honor the check first."

A moment later, the manager beckoned us over to her cubicle. Her equally crooked name tab read Lucille Manning. She looked to be about seventy years old with striking white hair and chic tortoise-shell, horn-rimmed glasses perched on the end of her nose. I had Zoe put the check and the probate letters on Lucille's desk.

"Well," Lucille said. "This is a new one."

"I figured it would be," I said. "I made some calls. Knight Bank has acquired the accounts of Delphi Savings Bank. So, you're on the hook for this one."

Lucille gave me a stern look. "I can't say I agree with you. This check is sixteen years old. It's two million dollars. I've made calls of my own. I've been instructed not to honor it."

I pulled a legal pad out of my bag. "Can you write down the name of the person who gave you those instructions? And their number?"

Without hesitating, Lucille did as I asked. "I really do wish I could help you. You understand why I can't."

"I understand why your supervisor doesn't want to touch this," I said. "Can I ask you a couple of questions though?"

"By all means."

"How long have you worked at this branch?"

"Twenty-two years," she said proudly. "I'm fighting to hang on for three more years before I retire."

"So, you were here when this was the main Delphi Savings Bank branch."

"Honey, I was here when they broke ground on the building."

"I don't suppose there's any chance you remember Marilyn Paul banking here?" I asked. "This is the branch closest to her house. She had four accounts."

"Of course I remember Marilyn," she said. "Nice lady. Very polite. I'm so sorry for what happened to her. After her accident, this is where people dropped off their donations to help your family, Zoe."

"I don't remember that," Zoe said. "People brought a lot of lasagnas over. I don't remember there being money donated."

"Oh, we raised about ten thousand dollars, I think it was. Your Uncle Roy ... um ... what was his last name?"

"Lockwood," Zoe answered.

"Well, he was in charge of distributing it. My understanding was it was to pay for the mortgage on your grandmother's house. Or for any portion of her care that wasn't covered by her car insurance."

"The house ended up in foreclosure," Zoe told her. "He never told me a thing about any fundraiser."

"Hmm." Lucille shot me a look.

"You can tell us what you're thinking," I said. "I'm investigating what was going on with Marilyn in those months before her accident. Her financial situation is part of that."

"Oh, I don't know anything," Lucille said. "And of course, with your conservatorship papers, Zoe, you can have access to all your grandmother's records that still exist. I doubt there are many. I just ... I don't have a very high opinion of your Uncle Roy. I told you; Marilyn was just the sweetest lady. Roy was rude to my tellers. He wasn't a nice man."

"No," Zoe said. "He still isn't. But I haven't talked to my uncle in years. He moved to Florida a while ago."

"Well, I'm glad you're looking after Marilyn now. And you too, Ms. Leary. I know things will be done right. Marilyn deserves that. I just wish I could help you more today."

She slid my legal pad back to me after she wrote down her supervisor's contact information.

"Thank you," I said. "You've been helpful enough."

Zoe and I said our goodbyes and walked out into the parking lot. We'd driven separately. I had a day of dry research ahead of me. Zoe was going to visit Marilyn. She went once a week just to sit with her. Next week, I planned to go with her.

"I was kind of hoping they'd surprise us and just cash the thing," she said.

"Me too. But I knew this case wasn't going to be easy."

"What's next?"

I slid the papers and pad back into my bag. "First, I'm going to get this check back into my safety deposit box."

"Good. It freaks me out having it out in the world. I have nightmares about it under the bathroom tile for all those years."

"Zoe, what about what Ms. Manning said about your uncle?"

"Yeah. Uncle Roy was never the most popular guy around town."

"Is it possible your grandmother put that check under the floorboards to hide it from him?"

"I don't know," she said. "Those donations she was talking about. I'm telling the truth. I never knew a thing about that. People knew my grandma was raising me on her own. Do you think … what if my uncle stole it? Is there any way we can figure that out? I know the chances of him paying any of it back are zero. I'd just like to know."

"So would I," I said. "I'd like to talk to him. Do you know how to get a hold of him?"

"I've got a phone number and an address in my grandma's things. It's been years since we had any contact. But I'll find what I have and get it for you."

"Good," I said. The idea that Roy Lockwood could have embezzled money from his ailing sister when she was the sole support for teenage Zoe turned my stomach. If it were true and Marilyn knew her brother's true character, it could provide the explanation for why she hid such a large amount of money. It also meant the minute the existence of this check became public record, I could expect Roy Lockwood to come crawling out of the woodwork.

"But Zoe," I said. "Do me a favor. Don't tell anyone else about this check. Not until I tell you differently. Okay?"

Her face lost a little color, but she nodded. "Okay. Do you think … will someone try to say the money belongs to them instead?"

"I just know that nothing brings out bad behavior in people more than greed. So, for now, it needs to stay a secret."

A look passed through Zoe's face, as if she wanted to tell me something but changed her mind.

"Zoe? Is there something wrong?"

She shook her head. It was a little too forceful, a little too quick. I instantly knew she was lying. I just hoped whatever she was hiding wouldn't make more trouble for me than I already had.

Chapter 7

In a tucked-away corner on the third floor of Great Lakes University is a room hardly anyone uses for its intended purpose. At one time, all law school libraries had a place like this. In my law school days at a different university, we called it the Dead Law Room. Where outdated statutes come to die. Or more specifically, where the librarians stored older, obsolete bound volumes of various state and federal statutes when the publishers printed the latest versions. Nowadays, nobody does research this way. We do it online. But for me, for this kind of project, I wanted to hold a book in my hand.

It isn't to say this room wasn't used at all. To the contrary, it was the quietest place in the library. Perfect for introverted legal scholars to do their research in peace. Also perfect for amorous students to get up to no good. Tonight, though, it was only me.

I worked my way through the stacks until I found the maroon and gold bindings of the Michigan Compiled Laws Annotated. I headed straight for the Bs and pulled out the volume on banking.

If Tori were here, she would have rolled her eyes. "You can do this in ten seconds with Lexus, Cass."

When I told her I preferred the smell and feel of an actual book, she'd say "Okay, boomer," just to affectionately piss me off. I would remind her that I was technically a millennial elder statesman, thank you very much.

I missed her. Deeply. In two weeks, if everything went according to plan, she would come home to Matty and her son.

It took two hours, but I found the items I needed. I made my way to the copy machine in the next room and started scanning.

With the exception of Gordon the librarian, who'd worked here longer than I'd been a lawyer, this section of the library might as well have had tumbleweeds rolling through it. It made me sad. It also made me feel old. For now, though, I had the entire floor to myself. I'd left Gordon smiling at his desk one floor below me.

"Okay, boomer," I whispered to myself, smiling. "Tori. I swear. You're gonna love this case when you get back on your feet."

When I finished, I took the books to a cart near the front desk. It was library policy not to return books to the stacks where you found them. The librarians kept data on which tomes were used and how frequently. It helped them allocate funds by understanding which subscriptions for physical books should be maintained. I had every confidence I was the first person to crack these particular books since they'd been sent back to Dead Law. I probably could have walked out with them and nobody would have stopped me.

As I turned back, the hairs stood up on the back of my neck. There was something. A shadow. A feeling. I whipped around, looking back at the shelves directly behind me. I saw a pair of men's leather sneakers through the space in the bottom rack.

I hadn't heard anyone else come back here.

I slipped my copies into the outside compartment of my messenger bag and looked around the stacks. But there was nobody there.

I was losing it. Plain and simple. Jumpy. I walked further down the row. Had I imagined it? Who else would come back here?

I stood next to the shelves containing twenty-year-old editions of the United States Code.

There was someone here. I smelled pungent, skunky marijuana.

"Hello?" I called out.

Nothing. I clutched my bag tighter to my body.

A footstep fell on the tile floor toward the door. By the time I came around the corner, the heavy steel stairwell door clanged shut.

Shaking, I waited. Then I collected my wits and headed for the elevators. The thing slowly lurched its way downward. When the doors opened, Gordon stood behind his desk, smiling at me.

"Find everything you need?"

"Yes. Um … was someone else up there though? I thought I heard someone."

Gordon gave me a curious head tilt. "Actually yes. A gentleman came in right behind you."

"Did he tell you what he was looking for?"

"Nope. Barely even acknowledged me."

"What did he look like?"

Gordon shrugged. "I didn't pay much attention. Middle-aged, I think. But older than you."

I winced at the reference. Middle-aged. At forty-one, I supposed I was.

"White guy," Gordon continued. "He had a hat on. A ball cap. A windbreaker jacket. Blue. Sorry, that's about all I can remember. Was he bothering you?"

"No. No. Nothing like that. It's just ... well, I think he left through the emergency exit. He didn't come back down this way?"

"Nope. Huh. That is strange though. Opening that door's supposed to set off an alarm. I'll have to have maintenance come out and check it."

"Sure. I figured you'd want to know."

"It's odd. Nobody's asked to be let into the archive section room in over two years. Tonight, I got two customers."

"Huh. That is odd," I said. Smiling. It could be nothing. Just a coincidence. Though every cell in me told me it was anything but.

Chapter 8

"WELL," Jeanie said as she stood over the conference room table. "It's something."

I'd covered the space with highlighted printouts from my hunt in the Dead Law section last night. Once I got back, I couldn't sleep.

"You did all this last night?" Jeanie asked.

"Total adrenaline rush," I said. "Felt like law school."

Jeanie laughed. "Your brothers would call you a nerd for that."

"Well," I said, picking up the most highlighted printout. I handed it to Jeanie. "Zoe and I have been all over the state website. In sixteen years, there has been no report of any unclaimed funds in Marilyn Paul's name. Delphi Savings Bank or whatever incarnation they've become did not report this money. It never escheated to the state. They were legally required to turn it over."

"It's two million dollars," she said. "How is that even possible?"

"Who knows? Negligence. Sloppy reporting."

Jeanie put the printout down. "So, what's that mean for the bank?"

"It means they are liable for the full amount of the check if Knight Bank assumed Delphi Savings Bank's debts and accounts. I'm fairly certain they did. Though if it comes down to it, I'm sure they'll push back. We can get all that in discovery though."

"It's gonna get messy and take time then," Jeanie said. "The bank has the resources to fight. Does Zoe?"

"The thing is, look here." I picked up another printout showing a different section of the statute.

"The law is clear. We go by the statutes in effect when the check was drawn. Not what's in effect today. That's why I needed the old books. The penalties for failing to report unclaimed funds to the state are severe, Jeanie. They could be on the hook for major fines. And it's based on the amount of the check. Each quarter they fail to report is a separate violation. We've got a decade of them after the initial deadline."

"Well, hot damn," Jeanie said. "So, it'll be a lot less bother for the bank to simply honor this check than to fight it."

"I hope so," I said. "I'm working on a complaint and a demand letter."

"What'd you work out with Zoe in terms of our fee?"

"You sound like Miranda," I said. "I won't take this on contingency. I'm afraid that feels like a conflict of interest. I'm just going to bill Marilyn's estate at my hourly rate. I've got a good feeling about this. The bank's gonna pay it."

"Then what?" Jeanie said. "It's not like Zoe can use any of these funds. They belong to Marilyn. She's still very much alive."

"Zoe's just hoping she can get her grandmother into a better facility. She hasn't been happy with the care Marilyn's receiving at Maple Valley. That's another thing I may have to help her with."

"Well, good work," she said. "I can't believe how quickly you found an answer for her."

I'd made a copy of the cashier's check. It sat on the table with my research. I picked it up, running my fingers over the watermark.

"It doesn't feel like an answer. We still have no idea what this money was for."

"Who cares? Zoe hired you to make the bank pay it. Is the rest any of our business?"

I heard the front door open. Eric's voice rang out as he said hello to Miranda. He said something that made her laugh. A moment later, she knocked softly on the door.

"Eric's here, Cass. You want me to set him up in your office?"

"No," I said. "Let him in."

Miranda waved Eric in. He made her blush as he smiled down at her and brushed past her.

"Hey, Jeanie!" he said. He crossed the room and gave Jeanie a peck on the cheek. "You're looking good. How are you feeling?"

Jeanie waved her cane in the air. "Hurts like a son of a bitch. But my leg feels a lot more stable."

"Good. When do you get the other hip done?"

"They said two months."

"How's your ramp working out?" Eric and my brothers had modified Jeanie's front porch, installing a wooden ramp. She hated it, but finally admitted she needed it.

"Makes me feel old."

"You're not old," he said. "You're just ... vintage."

Eric's eyes went to my printouts on the table. "Well, this looks ... mind-numbing."

"Have a seat," I said. "I was just telling Jeanie. I think I've solved Zoe Paul's case, at least from a banking law standpoint."

Eric reached into his pocket and pulled out a small notepad. He set it on the table. He had a thin file folder tucked under his arm and set that out too.

"Well," he said. "I don't know if I've solved anything for you on that other front. But I did find some stuff."

"What's all that?" Jeanie asked.

"I asked Eric to see if he could do a reverse look-up of the frequent numbers we found on Marilyn Paul's old cell phone. I want to know who she was talking to around the time of her accident and when that check was written."

"I've got her accident report too," Eric said. "It was done by Woodbridge County."

I reached for the file folder and started leafing through it. "Any surprises?"

"Not really," he said. "There were no other drivers involved. The weather was good. No rain. Broad daylight in August. The woman just swerved off the road and hit a tree."

"Any witnesses?" I asked, paging through the report. I found a statement as Eric answered me.

"Two. There was a guy driving behind her. He told the deputies she didn't seem to be speeding. Accident reconstruction report supports that. She was traveling at fifty miles an hour in a forty-five. The second witness was looking out his front window and saw the whole thing. The driver behind her said she slammed on the brakes and swerved to avoid a squirrel. Lost control, hit a big oak tree."

"Geez," Jeanie said. She looked over my shoulder as I reviewed the photographs in the file. They were hard to look at.

Marilyn's blue Honda Accord hit the telephone pole head on, smashing the engine into the front seat. The car was a mangled mess. The deployed airbags were covered in blood. More blood had spilled out the front door and into the street where the emergency responders had cut Marilyn out.

"All that for a squirrel," Jeanie said.

"The eyewitness driver was pretty shook up," Eric said. "I spoke to Deputy Horack. He's still working in traffic for the sheriff's department. He remembered this one. Said it was one of the worst accidents he'd ever seen where the victim survived."

"Survived," I said. "Barely."

My throat ran dry as I looked at the photographs. My hands started to shake. I put them down. Just a few short months ago, I'd looked at similar photographs involving my own car. Guilt washed over me as it often did. I shouldn't have just given Tori my keys. I should have driven her home.

Eric met my eyes. He knew what I was thinking without asking. Letting out a breath, he sat in the chair beside me.

"Marilyn's at Maple Valley too?" he asked.

I nodded.

"I'll leave you two to talk," Jeanie said. "I've got PT in a half an hour over at Brentwood."

"Do you need a ride?" Eric said.

"Nope," she said. "Miranda's taking me. We're gonna grab dinner after."

Jeanie patted me on the shoulder as she limped her way toward the door. Miranda was already standing there waiting for her. She shot me a wave as the two of them headed for the parking lot, leaving Eric and me alone.

He turned to me. "Tori still set to come home soon?"

"As far as I know," I said.

"She's a fighter, that one."

"She is. It helps that she's got something big to fight for."

"How is the little guy settling into his new house?"

Warmth flooded me. "Baby Sean and his daddy are doing great. I mean, really great. Matty has stepped up, Eric. I was so worried."

"You always worry." He smiled. "Speaking of that, how's the other family crisis?"

My head started to pound. "I don't know. Joe won't talk about it. He just goes to work, comes home, and seals himself off in the guest house. I've offered to have coffee with him in the morning. Make him dinner. Just ... talk. He wants nothing to do with me or anybody else."

"Give him time," Eric said. "He's had a lot to process."

"I just can't figure out what Katie's thinking. Joe has always been crazy about her. He's worked his tail off giving her everything she needs. Being a good dad to Emma."

"Emma isn't Katie's daughter," Eric said.

"It doesn't matter. She's the only mother Emma really knows. She's raised her since that girl was three years old. They're a family."

Eric didn't say anything. He just frowned.

"What? Do you know something? Eric ... Katie's the one who's been cheating on Joe. Not the other way around. I'm sorry. But I'm having a really hard time seeing her side of this thing. Whatever that is."

"I know," he said. "And I'm not saying Joe's in the wrong. I'm just saying ... you never know what goes on behind closed doors. There are two people in that marriage."

He was right. It was still hard for me not to be angry with Katie. When the dust settled, I was Team Joe forever and always.

"I don't want to talk about it anymore," I said. "It gives me a headache. What else do you have for me?"

Eric reached across the table and picked up the notepad he'd tossed there. "I've got a couple of interesting hits off Marilyn's cell phone. Looks like there were seven numbers she called most often. One's Zoe's. One's to her neighbor, Frieda Jones. But you said Zoe said those two were tight."

"She did," I said. Eric showed me one page in his notebook. He'd written Frieda's name next to a number.

"The week of her accident, she called Frieda Jones almost every day."

"Zoe told me if Marilyn worked late, she'd have Zoe head over to Frieda's house for dinner. Zoe said her grandmother was working a lot in the weeks before her accident. She was saving up to get a new air conditioner."

"Yeah," Eric said. "That's what makes no sense. If she had that two-million-dollar check sitting around, why would she need to work extra hours to pay for an air conditioner?"

"What's that number?" I asked. "The 313 one. That's the one that seemed newer."

"That," Eric said, "belongs to someone I actually know. He's a retired detective. Ned Corbett. You know him?"

"Detective Corbett," I said. The name didn't ring any bells. "I don't think so."

"I'm trying to get a hold of him. It looks like Marilyn called him on his personal cell on a regular basis. Then there are a few calls to the department. She was calling him at work."

"You think they were dating?" I asked.

"I'm gonna find out. I don't know Corbett very well. He retired from the Bureau a year or two before I got promoted. I've got a text in to one of the guys from the union. Trying to see where Corbett retired to. If he's still local."

"Zoe said her grandmother dated a lot. But nobody she ever felt comfortable bringing around the house."

"We don't know what their relationship was," Eric said. "Give me a day or two and I'll find out for you."

I smiled. "You're good at this, you know. Almost like a real private investigator."

It was a running discussion between us. I'd been bugging Eric for over a year to retire and come work for me. He smiled but didn't answer.

"Come on," I said. "You're finding this fun."

He shook his head. "I think you're the one finding this fun." He gestured toward my stacks of highlighted printouts.

I didn't mean to, but my smile faded as I thought about what happened at the law library last night. I hadn't meant to let it show on my face, but Eric caught it quick enough.

"What is it?" he asked.

"It's nothing. I mean, it's probably nothing."

"But ..."

"But ... when I was at the library last night, I think there was someone else interested in what I was researching."

His scowl deepened. "What do you mean?"

"Probably nothing. Like I said. It's just ... Gordon, the librarian? He mentioned something about how odd it was that he had two customers searching in the Dead Law books that night. I'm probably just jittery, but ... I don't know. You made me swear to mention to you if there was anything strange going on after Tori's accident. Well, this seemed strange."

Eric chewed his lip but didn't answer.

"I shouldn't have mentioned it," I said.

"Yes. You should have. But you're right. It's probably nothing. So, what's next for you on this?"

"I'm headed to Maple Valley in the morning. Jeanie thinks Tori might like getting looped in on this case. If she were here, she'd be helping me with it. It's a probate matter after all. While I'm there, I thought I'd pay Marilyn Paul a visit. I know she isn't verbal, but I'd like to meet her."

"You want me to go with you?"

"If you'd like," I said. "I know Tori would like to see you."

Eric leaned in and kissed my cheek. "How about I pick you up at eight? We can go before I've got to be in the office."

"Sounds good," I said. I touched his face. I didn't like the worry I'd put into his eyes. "I'll see you first thing in the morning. And thanks for all of this. It helps, Eric."

He nodded. He was still scowling as he left. I hoped my fears were for nothing. Only I couldn't shake the feeling that someone had been watching me last night.

Chapter 9

"Cass, this is something. I mean ... it's *something*."

Tori Stockton had been with me for years now. We'd found each other when she needed help to prove her father's innocence in a decades-old murder case. After that, she'd become an essential part of my law practice and later, my family. Now, she looked frail, but stronger. Her long blonde hair had just been washed and brushed to a shine. She sat in a wheelchair facing the window, my notes and highlights in her lap. She got tired easily. Her brain fogged up on her and sometimes she forgot a word she needed, but slowly, achingly, she was coming back to a new normal.

"I think so," I said. "I just can't see how this doesn't end in major trouble for the bank if they truly dropped the ball and failed to turn these funds over to the state."

"That's what I'm seeing too," she said. She closed the file folder I'd given her and set it on the small table near the window. The sun was out. It shone on Tori's face, making her glow.

"Thanks for bringing this," she said. "It's the perfect distraction. Matty's been great, but he thinks I'm fragile."

"He doesn't think that at all," Eric said. He sat on the register just behind me. "He's just worried."

"I am too. I know I'm going to need help. But I need to be home. I need to be the one taking care of Sean."

"You will be," I said. "Just a few more days. And we'll all be there for you for whatever you need."

"Did you see him today?" she asked.

Smiling, I took out my phone. "I stopped over on my way here." I pulled up my camera roll and played the video I'd taken of baby Sean while Matty changed his diaper.

"He's getting great at it," Eric said. "Like a NASCAR pit crew but smellier."

In the video, my little brother cooed and talked baby talk to his small son as he efficiently wiped his bottom. Sean windmilled his legs the second Matty let go of them. I got in close. It was brief, but as Sean focused on his father's face, he cracked a smile.

"Is that ...?"

"It sure is," I said. "He's been doing it more and more."

"I missed it!" Tori said. "I hate that I missed it."

"You're exactly where you need to be. You're doing the very best thing for Sean. You have a lifetime to take care of him. You'll be his world. I promise."

"He's already mine," she said. She laid her hand flat on the file folder. "But this. I want to come back to work too."

"Work can wait. And that'll be there for you too."

"No. I mean now. And when I get out next week. I want to be part of it. I *need* to be part of it. I want to use my brain."

"Tori, I don't think ..."

"I do," she said. "I'm not talking about coming back full time. Or even truly part time. But this case. I want to help you investigate it. You're going to have to file a lawsuit in Probate Court if the bank doesn't honor that check. Let me help you with that. Please?"

"Of course. We'll take things one step at a time. But yes. I need you."

I couldn't stop myself. I moved in and hugged Tori. She was skin and bones, but I could feel a quiet tremor of strength go through her.

"Thank you," she said. "For everything. For the house. For ... just ..."

"Shh. You're family and that's the end of it."

Tori got quiet. "Matty told me about Joe and Katie. I didn't see that coming."

"None of us did. Not even Joe."

"How's he holding up?"

"I'll leave you two to talk," Eric said. "I'll be down in the lobby."

I reached up and touched Eric's shoulder, thanking him. He said a quick goodbye to Tori and left the room. I turned my attention back to Tori.

"Joe's been living in my guest house," I said. "So far, he refuses to talk. He just goes to work, comes back. He won't have dinner with me. He won't even come to the main house and grab a cup of coffee."

"Poor Joe. Katie was texting with me for a while. But lately, not so much."

"Everything is just ... fraught."

We sat in silence for a moment. Then Tori picked up the file folder again. "What's the next step?"

"Actually," I said. "She's here. I'm not sure if you knew that. Marilyn Paul is in the long-term care wing. I asked Zoe if I could meet her."

"Is she verbal?"

"Not according to Zoe. I mean, she talks. But Zoe says it's random. She says she seems to know when Zoe's here. She reacts to her. But she hasn't really said anything meaningful since the accident."

Tori's gaze went back to the window. "I was lucky."

"Yes."

"When do you meet with her?"

I checked my smart watch. "In a few minutes."

Tori nodded. "You mind stopping back after you're finished? I'd like to hear how it went. I could use the distraction."

"Absolutely," I said. I reached for the file folder.

"You mind leaving that? That is ... if you have other copies."

"Of course. For sure."

"Would you happen to have a spare legal pad in your bag? I wouldn't mind taking some of my own notes. I'm sure you've thought of every angle, but just in case ..."

My heart swelled as a look came into Tori's eyes I hadn't realized I missed. It meant her brain was starting to buzz in a good way.

I fished out a pen and paper from my bag and set it on the table. "Give me an hour," I said. "Then I'll let you know what Zoe had to say. And how Marilyn seemed."

I gave Tori another hug. Her grip was strong as she hugged me back. She would be okay. Different. But okay. And I knew nothing else in this world would matter.

Chapter 10

I MADE my way to the stairwell and up one flight. Zoe had texted me with her room number. Marilyn was at the end of a short hallway. She had a room to herself.

"That's not happening!" I heard a male voice shout. To my left, a nurse came running. She rounded the corner, heading in the direction I was.

"Just leave!" another voice shouted. This one I recognized. It was Zoe.

"Call security!" another nurse shouted. They were all heading the same way I was. I started running too.

When I got to Room 328, a small crowd had formed. Zoe stood just inside the doorway, her face flushed. An older man advanced on her, pointing a finger in her face.

"You're finished," he shouted. "I know what you did. What you've been doing. It ends now."

"Sir!" the nurse said. She stood further in the room. Behind her, I saw Marilyn Paul for the first time. I knew she was only in her early seventies. And yet, she looked at least a hundred years old. Pale. Thin. Her hair had gone completely white and hung past her shoulders. She sat in her hospital bed, mouth slack, staring in my direction, but not really seeing.

"She's a thief!" the man said.

"Cass," Zoe said as tears filled her eyes. "This is my lawyer."

"You have to leave," the nurse said. "You all have to leave. I will not have you upsetting my patients. Take your arguments outside."

"What's going on?"

The man turned to me. Red-faced, he advanced on me, pointing his finger in my face now. I stood my ground.

"You're the lawyer?"

"Yes."

He reached into the back pocket of his jeans and pulled out a folded stack of papers. "Consider yourself served."

I took the papers but didn't look at them.

"She has no right to be here anymore," he said to the nurse. "I'm taking over my sister's care."

Sister. So, this was the Uncle Roy Zoe had mentioned, the one who had briefly stayed in Marilyn's house and neglected to pay the taxes on it.

"Enough," the nurse said. Behind me, two security guards showed up. One looked big enough to muscle Roy Lockwood if necessary. The other just looked scared. Behind *them,* Eric arrived. He looked ready to murder Roy Lockwood for me.

"You better step away from her," Eric said. He flashed his badge. Roy Lockwood scowled but took a step away from me.

Zoe spoke up. "I'm my grandmother's patient advocate. I'm the one with the right to be here. This is my uncle. He's not authorized to have anything to do with Grandma."

From the bed, Marilyn Paul let out a sound that was part moan, part shriek. She clutched the side rails of her bed and started kicking her feet.

"The nurse asked you all to leave," the larger security guard said. He shot a look at Eric, sizing him up. "All of you."

"We're going," I said, putting a protective arm around Zoe. "Is there some place we can talk?"

"There's a family waiting room down the hall. If you can talk quietly," the security guard said.

"Perfect."

I ushered a distraught Zoe out of the room. I frankly didn't care if Uncle Roy followed us or not. He did though. He jutted his chin at the security guard and stormed ahead of us. I took a quick glance at the papers he'd shoved at me as we went down to join him. They were file stamped just an hour ago and captioned, Petition to Remove Guardian and Conservator.

"What's it say?" Zoe whispered.

"Just let me do the talking. And try not to lose your temper." That last bit was good advice for me.

As we walked into the waiting room, Roy Lockwood whirled around and started jabbing that finger again. This time, Eric got between us and backed the older man into the wall.

"You get within ten feet of either of these ladies again, I'm going to put cuffs on you."

"You can't do that?"

"Try me."

Roy narrowed his eyes at Eric but seemed to believe him. His shoulders dropped and he plopped himself into the nearest chair.

"She's a thief," Roy said. "That kid has been bilking my sister's estate for years. It ends today. I want a full accounting of what's been happening. And I'm taking over her care and her finances."

"The hell you are," Zoe said, ignoring my advice. "And you're the thief. You want to tell me what happened to the funds the bank raised for Grandma's care after her accident? You haven't even seen Grandma in what, eight years, ten?"

"That's your fault," Roy yelled. Pointing at her, he turned to me. "That's her fault. She wouldn't let me see my sister. I didn't even know where Marilyn was until three days ago."

"What? She's been here for fifteen years. You absolutely knew where she was. I've never kept you from seeing her."

"You can iron it out with my lawyer," Roy said. "I'm done playing nice. The rest of the family has been on me for years to intervene. I should have listened. Whatever she's told you? Don't believe it. Zoe is an opportunist. A sociopath. I promise you, whatever she's told you is a damn lie."

"Okay," I said. "You've filed your petition. Whatever you're asking for, it'll be up to the court to decide. You're certainly not helping your case by charging in here and upsetting your sister and half the staff."

"I'm taking her out of here," Roy said. "That's the first thing. I'm hiring specialists. For all I know, these people have been keeping my sister zoned out on medication she doesn't need for over a decade."

"What?" Zoe burst into tears. "Cass, he's crazy. This is crazy."

"Okay," I said, turning to her. I didn't want her to say any more.

"It's not just me," Roy said. "Read my petition. The entire family is on my side, including Zoe's own father."

Lord. So much for my grand plan to manage the emotions in the room. Zoe became almost inconsolable. Her face turned purple, and she began to hyperventilate.

"Have a seat," I said. "Just ... breathe. Mr. Lockwood, I think we're done here. You've said what you needed to say. I have your petition. You have an attorney representing you?" I quickly glanced at the final page of the petition. Sure enough, it had been filed by an attorney with a firm in Southfield.

"Yeah. One that's going to argue circles around you. I'll spare no expense when it comes to my sister's well-being."

I had to bite my tongue past the retort I wanted to make. Funny how Roy Lockwood came out of the woodwork only when there was real money at stake. That would be my first question to Zoe as soon as her uncle left.

"Goodbye," I said. "We're done here. I'll speak to your lawyer. It's not appropriate for us to be having any further conversation."

Roy gave me the same testosterone-fueled chin jerk he'd given to the security guards and Eric. He vaulted to his feet and puffed out his chest. Eric once again got between him and me. Roy mustered up one last snarl then he barged out of the room and disappeared down the hall.

"This can't be happening," Zoe said. I gave her a tissue from a box on the nearest table.

"Zoe," I said. "Who else did you tell about the cashier's check?"

"I told a couple of friends," she said. "I said something to Frieda. She's the one who suggested I come to see you."

"You didn't say anything to anyone from your family?"

"There was no one else from my family," she said. "I haven't seen Uncle Roy in years. And my father? Did he really sign that petition?"

I looked at the name of the petitioners. Sure enough, Bradley Paul was listed right after Roy.

"It appears so."

"I haven't seen or spoken to my dad in thirteen years. Cass, he abandoned me when I was little. When Grandma had her accident, nobody came forward for me. Nobody helped me with anything. Just Frieda. I told you all of this. I was eighteen years old. I was still a kid. I'm the only one who has stuck by my grandma and cared about her and for her. I swear. And this is how they choose to make contact?" She pointed to the petition. "I don't understand."

I did. And I knew it would bring her no comfort. I would need some time to read through the court papers and see what grounds they were claiming for Zoe's removal. But the end result was clear. The Paul family saw dollar signs now. This thing was about to get very, very ugly.

Chapter 11

"He'll talk to you." Eric stood in the doorway of my office, a detective's badge swinging from a chain around his neck. It was lunchtime. We were supposed to meet at a new Mexican restaurant that had just opened downtown. But he'd judged the tone of my voice when he called this morning. I was knee-deep in paperwork.

Eric came further into the room. As he did, the delightful smell of sesame chicken filled my nostrils.

"You good with Chinese?" he asked. "We'll try El Dorado next week. Mexican food never travels well in Styrofoam in my experience."

"Good man," I said as he handed me a set of chopsticks. I was hungry enough to eat my way through the cardboard box.

We both turned our heads at the sound of a thunk at the top of the stairs. Jeanie had climbed her way up, brandishing her cane like a weapon.

"What are you doing?" I said. "We could have come down to you."

"I need the exercise. You gotta move if you wanna move. Scoot over and hand me some chopsticks."

Eric did as he was told. The three of us moved to the sitting area in the corner of my office, keeping our rice and noodles far away from the growing stacks of papers I'd spread out all over my desk and half the floor.

"Anyway," I said. "You were saying. He'll talk to me?"

"Who?" Jeanie asked through a mouthful of General Tsao's.

"Ned Corbett," Eric answered. "Marilyn Paul was exchanging a lot of calls with him in the weeks before her accident."

"Did he tell you anything?" I asked.

"Said they were acquainted. Also said it was a million years ago so he wasn't really sure how much he'd be able to remember."

"Did you get the sense they were more than friends? Like romantically involved?" I asked.

Eric pulled an egg roll out of the bag and bit into it. "Hard to get a read on him over the phone. He wasn't too keen on talking to you at first. Corbett's pretty old school. Has a standing beef against defense attorneys in general. I explained the situation though. If you've got time tomorrow morning, he said he'd meet you."

"I've got time," I said.

"Heard you had a party out at Maple Valley," Jeanie said.

I reached over and picked up one of the copies I'd made of Roy and Bradley Paul's petition. I handed it to Jeanie. She skimmed the first page, her frown deepening.

"Cass, is this true?"

She'd come to the fifth line of the factual statement of the petition.

"I'm meeting with Zoe again tonight after she gets off work. But I'm worried she hasn't been completely honest with us. Eric, by the way ... consider yourself my non-lawyer assistant on this one. Nothing we say leaves this room."

"Does that make me like your unpaid intern?"

I swirled my chopsticks at him, then reached over and purloined a chunk of his sesame chicken.

"Hooo boy," Jeanie said as she got to the last page of the petition. "You think there's any truth to this?"

"What're they saying?" Eric asked. He took Jeanie's copy of the petition and started reading.

"Marilyn's brother claims Zoe is trying to defraud her estate. He says he's got a copy of a letter Marilyn wrote a few months before her accident expressing concerns and fears she had about Zoe."

Eric leafed through the paperwork. "He didn't bother to attach a copy."

"I'm skeptical whether these documents even exist."

"Or they're fake," Jeanie said. "I'm sorry. I feel like I'm a pretty good judge of character. Zoe has come across as earnest to me. She's lived in that house since she was a kid. She's never gotten a dime from Marilyn's estate. Until now, there hasn't been anything in it. Everything's been paid for by Marilyn's auto insurance. There was no third-party claim."

"She lied to us, Jeanie," I said. "If paragraph sixteen of that petition is true, Zoe withheld a critical piece of information."

Eric flipped through the pages. He started reading paragraph sixteen aloud. "Petitioners have recently learned that the protected individual, Marilyn Paul, has been diagnosed with stage IV pancreatic cancer. It is incurable, inoperable, and Ms. Paul is not expected to live longer than six months."

"They're going to argue that the timing of Zoe's discovery of this check is no coincidence. That she's been sitting on it all this time."

Eric shook his head. "That makes absolutely no sense. It's two million dollars. Why would anyone do that?"

"Because it's not Zoe's," I said. "The check is written to Marilyn. She's still very much alive. It can only be used for her benefit."

"Unless she's dead," Jeanie said. "Then it becomes part of her estate and distributable to her heirs."

"And her brother and deadbeat son are saying that's them," Eric said. He let out a low whistle. "But wouldn't that be true even if she had no will? Wouldn't her next of kin be set to inherit, even without this petition?"

"They think there's more money out there," I said. "They think Zoe's been hiding it. She's been in the house. She's had access to Marilyn's things. But ... Zoe filed a statutory will she found in Marilyn's things at the same time she petitioned to become her legal guardian sixteen years ago. She left everything to Zoe and named the neighbor, Frieda Jones, as successor guardian if Zoe could no longer serve."

Jeanie threw her chopsticks down in disgust. "It's just so obvious what's going on. Zoe made one mistake. She talked to one too many people about this check she found. It got back to her deadbeat dad and uncle. Now they're trying to worm their way back into the fold with their hands out."

"How well do you trust this neighbor, Frieda?" Eric asked.

"I haven't met her yet. But why?" I said.

"Well, this petition is filled with a lot of facts that shouldn't have been common knowledge. The existence of the check, Marilyn's recent grim prognosis. You said Zoe's always looked to Frieda Jones as a second grandma. Apparently, Marilyn did too at one point. So, what I'm wondering, she'd be the one who'd have been privy to this new information. You sure she isn't stabbing Zoe in the back to her relatives? Maybe for some promise of a kickback?"

"That's cold," I said. "And diabolical."

"But possibly true," Eric said.

"Yeah. Possibly true. It's just ... well. The other person or people who would know about the existence of this check are the ones who wrote it to Marilyn. So far nobody has come forward with an explanation. I think it's going to matter. I think no matter what, Judge Wentz is going to want to hear evidence on the source of the funds."

"I just don't like it," Eric said. He stabbed his chopsticks into his now empty cardboard box. "Somebody is pulling strings behind the scenes."

Jeanie shot him a look of confusion. I tried to get Eric's attention. He was heading into territory Jeanie didn't yet need to know about. I hadn't told her about my suspicions of being watched or followed at the law library.

"This is just typical family drama," she said. "More money, more problems. Nothing we haven't dealt with before. It's most certainly worth a conversation with Zoe. A heated one. She should have told us about Marilyn's prognosis. The one thing Uncle Roy has going for him is that appearance of impropriety. It just won't be enough to upend Marilyn's estate, I don't think."

Jeanie was on her feet. Eric rose, offering to help her. She quickly waved him off.

"I can handle myself. If you hear a great thud, come running. But beyond that, I'm okay."

Eric grumbled. "If I hear a great thud, it'll already be too late, Jeanie. You're just being stubborn."

"Yep. And stubborn is what's keeping me on my feet, kiddo." She looked ready to stab him with her cane. Eric kept his distance, but he refused to let her traverse the stairs without being right there. She swore up a blue streak, but Eric could be every bit as stubborn. It was only when she hit the ground floor that he relented and left her alone.

When he came back up, his scowl had deepened. I knew his stubborn streak would now be directed at me.

"I don't like it," he repeated. "Why do you always manage to march headlong into trouble?"

"It's a probate case," I said. "I'd say this thing is pretty tame by my standards."

"Cass, somebody followed you to the law library the other night. Your instincts on that stuff are as good as mine. Maybe better. Now somebody's feeding Marilyn Paul's greedy family information. I just have a bad feeling about this one. It feels like ..."

I went to him. On my tiptoes, I pulled his head down to mine until our foreheads touched. "Like what?"

"Like it has the makings of one of your capers. They never end well."

I kissed him then pulled away. "It's not a caper. It's a probate matter. Boring. Dry. Nothing but legal briefs and evidentiary hearings. I promise."

"Hmmm. Well, I'm going with you when you meet with Ned Corbett."

"Wouldn't have it any other way," I said as I started to gather the copies of the petition and put my paperwork into stacks. To anyone else, it looked like a hoary mess. To me, it was how I started organizing and immersing myself in a case.

"People don't generally go talk to cops when things are going well, Cass. What if Marilyn was worried something bad was going to happen?"

I went back to him and slid my hands up his chest. "I can think of at least one other reason why people spend time with one cop in particular." I kissed him again. "They were dating. That's my strongest instinct. Marilyn wasn't calling Ned Corbett at work. She was calling his personal cell. Right?"

"Cass ... Ned Corbett might not tell you the truth. I need you to be prepared for that."

"Why wouldn't he?"

Eric let out a hard breath. "Because. There's one little critical detail about what was going on in Corbett's life sixteen years ago. If you're right about their relationship, anyway."

I stuffed some papers into my messenger bag so I could take them home. "What's that?"

"Sixteen years ago, when Marilyn Paul was communicating with Corbett, he was a married man."

I froze mid paper-stuff.

"You think that check was blackmail money?" I asked.

Eric raised a brow. "I don't know."

"You think Ned Corbett had two million bucks laying around?"

"No. It's just ... something doesn't sit well with me about all of this."

I slipped my arm through the shoulder strap of my bag. I wouldn't say it. I didn't want to fuel Eric's overprotectiveness. But I was beginning to feel like Marilyn Paul's secrets could be a powder keg about to explode.

Chapter 12

"HE'S OUT BACK."

The current Mrs. Ned Corbett peered up at us from behind the porch screen. She had a beehive of cotton-like red hair on top of her head. She was yoga-instructor fit, wearing a tight pink tank-top with a giant red heart emblazoned on the front. Her platform flip-flops smacked as she turned away from the door without offering to let Eric or me in.

We turned to each other. "He's out back," I whispered.

"This should be good," he grumbled.

I followed Eric down the sidewalk and around the back of Ned Corbett's brick ranch house. He lived in one of the older neighborhoods in Delphi, boasting a two-acre lot with tall pines forming a natural barrier between his yard and the neighbors'. Even so, he had a seven-foot privacy fence sectioning off half the yard.

"Corbett?" Eric called out as we reached the gate.

No answer, but we heard a splash. Eric unlatched the gate and held it open for me.

Ned Corbett, tanned to a leathery glow, emerged at the shallow end of an Olympic-sized pool. Water dripped from his bald head as he grabbed a towel from the deck and hoisted himself up the cement steps.

"Corbett?" Eric said again. "It's Eric Wray."

"Right," Corbett said, wiping off his face. His belly glistened with droplets of water. He put the towel around his neck and walked over to the shaded area of the patio. There, he took a seat at a long, wrought iron table with a red umbrella sticking through the middle of it.

"Can I get you a beer?" Ned asked. "I can have Daisy bring out some lemonade. Ice water?"

"None for me, thanks," I said. Ned gestured toward the open patio chairs around the table. He sat wide-legged on one and rubbed his head vigorously with the towel.

"Suit yourself," he said. He had a small cooler beside him. He opened it and took out a bottle of Corona. Eric and I found dry chairs around the table and sat.

"Thanks for carving some time out for us," Eric said. "I know this is going to seem like a strange conversation."

Ned screwed off the bottle cap and took a sip of beer. "I'm sure I've had stranger."

"Nevertheless," I said, reaching over to shake his hand. "I'm Cass Leary."

"I know who you are," Ned said. He reached across to shake my hand but seemed a little put out by it.

"Looks like retirement is treating you well," Eric said. "I'm counting the days myself."

"You should," Ned agreed. "Get out. Don't let them tempt you with DROP. You can't put a price on peace of mind."

"That's what I hear," Eric said.

"So, what case did you want to talk to me about?"

Eric shot me a look that conveyed a nonverbal message. He wanted me to let him take the lead.

"Not a case, exactly. I'm helping Cass with a probate client she's got. It's nothing criminal. But the client is a relative of a woman named Marilyn Paul. I think she might have been a friend of yours."

Eric had a photograph of Marilyn taken the Christmas before her accident. Zoe gave it to me. Marilyn sat on her fireplace hearth, a big smile on her face. Ned took the photo and squinted at it.

"I can't see shit," he said. "Daisy! Can you grab my readers off the kitchen counter?"

A moment later, Daisy Corbett walked out and handed her husband his glasses. She said not a word to any of us. She simply flip-flopped her way back inside while her husband admired her rear end in her tight pants.

Ned took another look at the photo.

"Marilyn Paul," I said. "She was ..."

Eric pushed his hand downward. I bit my bottom lip.

Ned tilted his head to the side, studying the photo. "Hmm," he said, tossing it onto the table. "Yeah. I remember Marilyn. I knew her a little bit. That might have been twenty years ago though. Maybe more."

"Ned," Eric said. He pulled Marilyn's old cell phone out of his pocket. "Here's what's going on. This lady was in a bad car accident a number of years ago. There's some family drama surrounding her will. It's the kind of thing that'll require us to reconstruct what was going on in this woman's life the last few months beforehand."

"Yeah. I knew that," Ned said. "That she was in a car crash, I mean. I didn't think she survived it though. She's still alive?"

"She's been in nursing care ever since," I said. "Severe brain damage. I don't know if I'd call what she has much of a life."

"Man," Ned said. "Yeah. I sort of remember that. What's this got to do with me again?"

Eric put the phone down on the table between them. "We're just trying to figure out who she was talking to in the weeks before her accident. Your numbers are among the most frequent ones she called in the weeks prior."

Ned picked up the phone. He flipped it open and pressed the power button. Eric and I waited while he scrolled through the numbers.

"This was how long ago?" he asked.

"Sixteen years," I said.

Ned put the phone down. "Yeah. Sorry. I can barely remember who I talked to last week, let alone sixteen years ago. I remember Marilyn though. She played Bunco or something with my ex-wife, Sherise."

"Look, I know it's a long shot," Eric said. "But would you happen to remember what all these calls were about? Was there a case you were working on that involved her?"

"I honestly don't remember talking to her all that much. I gotta be honest, seeing these numbers surprises me."

"How close was your wife, Sherise, to her?"

"Who knows. They were friends. I'm trying to remember back. Marilyn was a sweetheart. I know that. A single lady. Kind of a flirt. She didn't have a man in her life and she kind of attached herself to different people."

"In what way?" I asked.

Ned kept his eyes on Eric. "She kinda thought of me as her Pet Cop."

"Her what?" I started.

"Yeah," Eric said. "I've gotten a few of those over the years. Cass, you know what he means. Like when people figure out you're a lawyer. Wanting free legal advice every five minutes."

"Exactly," Ned said.

"She had legal questions for you?" I asked. "Do you remember what they were?"

Ned shook his head. "I don't know. I think there was one where she might have fallen for some phishing scam. You know, when you get a call from someone claiming to be the IRS and there's a warrant for your arrest? That kind of stuff. And I wanna say she had a kid. A teenager. Got in trouble in school or something. It was just little, piddly stuff. I think I was just trying to be nice to make Sherise happy."

Ned started to laugh so hard he made himself cough. He took a sip of his beer. "Sorry. I just forgot about all of that. Fat lot of good it did me trying to keep that woman happy."

"So, you're saying it was your wife who encouraged you to talk to Marilyn Paul?"

"Yeah. Probably. But what I'm saying is that I don't remember all that much."

"Did you ever go to her house?" I asked.

"Might have. Actually, yeah. That was one of the things she wanted advice on. She got an alarm system and wanted me to show her how to use it. Yeah. I do remember that. She had a house over on Hyde Street, right?"

"She still does," Eric said. "Her granddaughter lives there."

"Granddaughter, yeah. That's what it was. Yeah. She asked me about that too. It's kind of coming back now. Was there some kind of custody deal?"

"There was some family drama," I said. "Do you happen to remember what Marilyn's relationship was with her granddaughter?"

Ned looked skyward for a moment. "You know, I wanna say it wasn't good. Marilyn was what, late fifties, maybe sixty at the time? I think she got saddled with raising her deadbeat son's kid. Is that right?"

"It is," I said.

"Yeah. Okay. I think at one point Marilyn wanted advice on how she could find her son. He owed her child support, I think it was. Yeah. She asked me if I could run a search for him. I think that might have been the last time I had contact

with her, come to think of it. Wray, you know how that goes.
You had to have had a million questions like that. Some
neighbor wants you to do a background check on his
daughter's new boyfriend, that kind of thing. People think
we've got some magic database we can access with all the
answers. We don't. It's not like that. And that kind of thing is
illegal. Yeah. That was the last thing I remember talking to
Marilyn about. I told her I couldn't help her with her son. I
probably told her she should hire a private investigator or get a
family lawyer. That's what I would have said under those
circumstances. Hell, I've been retired for fourteen years. I still
get calls like that from friends of friends or shirttail relatives.
That's a warning, Wray: when you're out, don't let people try
pulling you back in."

"I'll keep that in mind, Ned," he said.

"So, she's still alive?" Ned asked, directing the question to me.
"Huh. That's rough. She's in a coma?"

"Not a coma. She had a closed head injury. She's awake and
somewhat aware. But she hasn't really said anything coherent.
It's unclear if she even remembers who she was."

"That's hell. If anything like that ever happened to me, you
might as well just put a bullet in my head. 'Course, don't tell
Daisy that, I don't need her getting any ideas." Once again, Ned
Corbett laughed himself into a coughing fit at his own weak
joke.

"I hear ya," Eric said. "That's all you can remember about
Marilyn?"

"Yep. Sorry. She was a needy divorcee. That's what I remember.
A nice lady. But the kind that could be drama if you don't keep
her on a short leash. I remember giving her short, simple

answers and I always ended up telling her to get a lawyer. I don't know if she ever did."

"Thank you," I said as Eric started to rise. He shook hands with Ned once more.

"We can show ourselves out," Eric said. Ned finished the last of his beer and tipped the neck toward Eric in a type of salute.

"Ned!" Daisy called from inside the house. "Your lunch is on the table!"

Ned winked at me. "Better not keep her waiting."

"Thanks," I said as I followed Eric back around the pool toward the gate.

"What do you think?" I asked Eric as we walked back to the car. He didn't answer right away, waiting until he'd pulled away from the curb.

"I don't know," he said. "He felt ..."

"Off," I finished for him.

"Yeah."

"Not like he was lying exactly," I said. "But ... like maybe he wasn't telling the whole truth. Or thinking things up on the fly. Do you think it's because I was there?"

"Maybe," Eric said. "Why don't we give it a day and I'll try reaching out to him by myself. You know, ex-cop to cop. Man to man."

"Right," I said. Something caused me to look over my shoulder. Daisy Corbett stood in the road. She stared after Eric's car, shielding her eyes from the sun with her hand. Odd, I thought. I wondered if Daisy might tell a different story when her husband wasn't around.

It was something I might pursue later. In the meantime, I had a courtroom clash with the rest of Marilyn Paul's family scheduled next week and Marilyn's neighbor coming to the office first thing in the morning.

Chapter 13

"I appreciate you meeting with me."

Frieda Jones, Zoe and Marilyn's neighbor, came in promptly at nine. I'd offered to come to her, but she insisted on coming to me and showed up bright and early. We set up in my office and I asked Jeanie to pop in. It turned out Jeanie knew her. They'd gone to high school together, though Frieda was a couple of classes ahead of her. Jeanie said Frieda had been one of the most popular girls in school. I could still see a little of the teenager she might have been. High cheekbones and a ready smile, Frieda had a positive energy that would have been a welcome presence in young Zoe Paul's life.

"Oh, I'd do anything for Zoe and Marilyn. They're like family."

"Has Zoe clued you in to what's coming down the pike?" Jeanie settled herself on the couch next to me. Frieda took a corner chair and sipped on a giant tumbler of coffee that she'd brought in with her.

"She said her uncle is causing some headaches. He's known to do that from time to time."

"You and Marilyn were close though. Before her accident?"

"I was kind of like a big sister to her. She's a couple of years younger than me. She and her ex moved into that neighborhood for their son. So he could go to St. Cecelia's. As you know, it's one of the best schools in the county. Or was at the time. By then, I'd already gotten divorced myself. A few years into it, when her marriage started to fall apart, we got close. Boy, that caused problems."

"How so?" Jeanie asked.

"Well, her ex. Billy. He blamed me for being a bad influence on Marilyn. Anyway, that kind of resolved itself on account of Billy dying in the middle of their divorce proceedings. Or maybe right after? It's hard to remember that far back. But Marilyn's life was a mess. You'd have thought that would have fixed a few things. It did. But she was having all kinds of trouble with Bradley, her son."

I didn't know how much she knew about the petition Bradley and Roy Lockwood filed. It was better to get Frieda's story unfiltered.

"What can you tell me about that? How was Marilyn and her son's relationship?"

"Oh, he took Billy's side in the divorce. Billy was gonna make Marilyn sell the house. Brad was just ... bad news. Ran with a rough crowd of kids. He ended up getting expelled from St. Cecelia's for threatening the principal. You know, I don't know if he even ever finished and got a diploma or a GED. But Marilyn wouldn't throw him out. She felt guilty because he lost his father. Then Brad got that girl pregnant. He was maybe eighteen, nineteen then. That set off a whole other drama. The girl was on drugs. By the time Zoe was a year old, the mother was long gone. There was talk about maybe putting Zoe up for adoption but by then, Marilyn was attached. She wouldn't hear of it. So, she ended up taking that sweet little girl in. That was the last straw for Marilyn and Billy. Billy didn't want anything to do with raising Zoe. That guy was a grade A sexist pig. Marilyn started worrying Billy would mistreat Zoe like he mistreated Marilyn. So she finally threw him out. Her son, Bradley, took off not long after that. I think he's maybe seen Zoe only two or three times since then."

"Frieda," I said. "To your knowledge, did Marilyn have contact with her son after he abandoned Zoe?"

"He was supposed to pay child support. The state tried to go after him. Marilyn felt bad about that. That's the thing about her. She let people take advantage of her. She was gullible. Always believing the best of people even when they treated her the worst."

"That's awful," I said. "But she was a good friend to you?"

"The very best. I did what I could to return the favor. Zoe was just eighteen when we lost Marilyn. I mean, I know she isn't really dead. But ... she might as well be. I helped Zoe take care of the house. I helped her organize her finances. Made it so she could stay in that house while she was going to college."

"She's lucky she had you," I said. "Not too many adults showed up for Zoe when she was growing up."

"Marilyn would have done anything for her. That's what you need to know. And that's why ... this business with the money. It makes no sense. Two million dollars? She could have done so much with that. She could have paid for Zoe's schooling. She could have fixed up the house. That girl? She worked two and sometimes three jobs after Marilyn's accident. Billy left Marilyn in financial shambles when they divorced. Then he up and died. And she had a fortune hidden in that damn bathroom. I just don't get it."

"Frieda, do you have any idea who might have given that money to Marilyn?"

"I've thought and thought about that. There's only one thing I think it could be. Now, this is something I haven't even talked to Zoe about. It's ... um ... indelicate. But ... Marilyn, she got around. She had boyfriends."

"Zoe has mentioned that," I said. "You think someone she was dating gave the money to her?"

"You think it was more nefarious than that, don't you?" Jeanie chimed in.

Frieda cast a nervous glance toward Jeanie. "I know she's not dead. But saying this ... well ... it feels like speaking ill of the dead. Or at least ill of someone who can't defend herself anymore. But ... I don't know. Maybe she had someone on the side. Somebody with money. Someone willing to pay Marilyn for certain things."

"You think she was a prostitute?" I asked.

Frieda's face went white. She fidgeted with the hem of her blouse. "I don't know. I'd say kept woman. Only ... she sure never acted like she'd come into money. The last conversation I had with her, she was complaining how her air conditioner was on the fritz. She was trying to pick up extra hours at Valentine to try and cover it. She asked me if I could float her a temporary loan. We got into a little argument about it. I've always regretted that. It's the last conversation we had. She just made bad financial decisions. Until Bradley up and left, he always had his hand out and she was always throwing good money after bad where he was concerned. She'd have done the same for Zoe, only she was broke. I just do not understand how she could have kept that kind of secret to herself. About that check."

"Maybe she just didn't have a chance to figure out what to do with it," Jeanie offered. "The check was written just a few months before she had her accident. We'll never know what her plans were."

The desk phone intercom buzzed. "Jeanie? Sorry to interrupt, but your nine-thirty is here."

"I'll be right down," Jeanie said. She hoisted herself out of her chair and headed for the stairs. She was able to get around without her cane now. She said a quick goodbye to Frieda. Frieda rose, attempting to shake her hand. She knocked her knee against the coffee table and spilled her thermos all over her lap.

"Oh. Oh my!" Frieda said. "I'm sorry."

"It's okay," I said. "Let me get some paper towels. Did you burn yourself?"

Frieda Jones started to sob. "I'm sorry. I'm so sorry. I'm just ... this whole thing."

"Get some tissues too," Jeanie said. She and I walked into the hallway together. We made our way downstairs. I went back to the kitchen to grab a roll of paper towels out of the cupboard.

"Is she okay?" Miranda said, peeking around the corner. "Should I go check on her? That woman is sobbing like crazy."

"I'm on it," I said.

"She's always been pretty high-strung," Jeanie said.

"What do you think so far?" I asked her.

"I don't know. Marilyn would have had to be pretty spectacular to get some guy to give her two million bucks for *things*."

"But if they were close, how in the world does Marilyn not tell her best friend about that kind of a windfall?"

"I don't know. None of this makes any sense to me."

I unwrapped the paper towels from their wrapper. "She keeps saying Marilyn would do anything for Zoe. Yet she didn't set her up financially with the money she had."

"That girl was eighteen. You know many eighteen-year-olds that would be able to handle two million dollars in a responsible way?"

"I'm not saying she should have given it to her outright. But Zoe was trying to figure out how to pay for college in that timeframe. Something just doesn't feel right."

"Jeanie," Miranda said. "Your appointment."

"Yeah. Yeah. Keep your pants on. I don't know, Cass. Just because Marilyn loved her granddaughter, maybe she felt like she'd given her enough. Maybe Marilyn just wanted to enjoy her own money. I can't fault her for that."

"You're right," I said.

"Give me fifteen minutes and I'll rejoin you."

"Thanks," I said.

I left Jeanie and Miranda and headed back upstairs. I found Frieda Jones sitting with her hands buried in her face.

"I'm sorry," she said for the umpteenth time. "I don't know why this is making me so emotional. Zoe just doesn't deserve this."

I handed her some towels and sopped the spilled coffee off the floor. Frieda tried to help.

"It's okay," I said. "Would you like a refill?" I hoped she said no. The woman was on edge enough.

"I'm fine. Really. I don't want to put you to any more trouble on my account."

Once I had the mess under control, I threw a wad of paper towels in the waste basket and took my seat across from Frieda. "Are you okay? We can stop for today. But I do have a few more questions."

"I'm fine. I want to help. I love Zoe like my own daughter. She doesn't make friends very easily. She has abandonment issues. She's been alone so much. It worries me. The last thing she needs is drama with her family. They aren't very nice people. I'm afraid Zoe's going to get hurt."

"What about Marilyn's brother?" I said. "What do you know about Marilyn's relationship with Roy Lockwood?"

Frieda's expression went cold. "That one's no good. No good at all. Just a bully. He lived in that house for a few months after Marilyn's accident. Said he was doing it to look after Zoe. I had her come and stay with me. Zoe didn't even know him. I wasn't about to let her stay with some strange man she barely knew when she was in grief like that. Luckily, it didn't last long. Once he realized there wasn't gonna be some big payout from Marilyn's accident, he moved on. That's about the time Zoe got herself appointed Marilyn's guardian."

"Do you know anything about a fundraiser at what would have been Delphi Savings Bank after her accident?"

Frieda looked puzzled. "Maybe. It's been such a long time."

"I have reason to believe Roy might have absconded with whatever funds were raised. Zoe says she never heard about it or saw a dime."

"That snake. That sounds exactly like Roy. My God. That money should have been used for Zoe if there was any. Ugh. And you're saying now he's coming around trying to make even more trouble for that poor kid. He should be in jail."

I pulled out a copy of the will on file with the Probate Court. "Have you ever seen this before?" I asked. Frieda took it from me.

"I haven't. Is this Marilyn's?"

"It is."

"Do you recognize the signature?" I asked. Frieda peered closer.

"I'm no expert. But yeah, I'd say that looks like Marilyn's handwriting. It's been a really long time though."

"Did you have many occasions to see things she'd signed?" I asked.

"It says here she's leaving everything to Zoe. That's what I would expect. So no, like I said, I'm not an expert. But it looks like it could be Marilyn's writing. And I know she would have wanted to provide for Zoe if something happened to her."

"Bradley and Roy Lockwood will likely try to contest this," I said.

"What? They know about the money. Those sons of ..."

"If this will is ruled invalid," I said, "then Marilyn's estate is what's called intestate if she passes. It means state law would determine who gets her assets. Since she was unmarried, it would go to Bradley, her son."

Frieda's lips disappeared into a bloodless line. "He wouldn't dare. That kid has been nothing but heartache to Marilyn. She raised his daughter for him. If he does that, can you sue him for all the child support he never paid? It's gotta be thousands and thousands. It's gotta be her damn brother behind all of this. They have a lawyer, don't they? Bradley wouldn't be able to afford that on his own. Those two … match made in hell."

"That's what Zoe thinks too," I said. "We suspect Bradley made his Uncle Roy some kind of deal. A cut of the proceeds of that check if he agreed to front the cost of the litigation. I think we must be prepared that they'll try to say Zoe unduly influenced Marilyn or maybe even forged this document."

"If she did, I'm glad she did. It's what Marilyn would have wanted. I'm sure of that."

I cringed. Though I appreciated the sentiment, if she said that on the stand, it's exactly the kind of thing that could sink Zoe's case before it even started.

"I'm not saying she did," Frieda quickly covered. "I'm saying I know Marilyn. She would have wanted to make sure Zoe was taken care of. She would have protected her over Bradley. He was a grown man when Marilyn had her accident. I don't think she'd seen or spoken to him in several years. They had a big fight over Zoe. I wanna say she was twelve? There was this Daddy Daughter dance at her school, and she'd been communicating with Bradley. He promised to take her. Zoe got all dressed up. Another neighbor down the street was a beautician. She did

Zoe's hair and makeup. Then Bradley didn't show. I'll never forget that. Zoe was beside herself. Broke that little girl's heart and that was just the last straw for Marilyn. As far as I know, she and Bradley didn't talk after that. He never even showed up after Marilyn's accident. We couldn't find him. Honestly, I don't think Zoe's had any contact with him before this since the lead-up to that dance. So that's what ... twenty-plus years ago now? And now he's doing this?"

Frieda slapped the copy of the will down on the table. I picked it up.

"I really appreciate your candor," I said.

Frieda had tears in her eyes again as she rose. "Anything. I'll do anything I can for Zoe. I always have."

As I walked her downstairs, Jeanie came out of her office. Her client had just left. Jeanie and Frieda embraced before Frieda left. I was still staring at the copy of Marilyn's will as I walked into Jeanie's office.

"She wants to help," Jeanie said, closing her office door behind her. "She really loves that girl."

"I know."

"You know those two snakes are only doing this because of that check."

"I know," I said. "But Jeanie? Don't you find it strange that Roy Lockwood just happened to have moved into Marilyn's house right after her accident? You heard Frieda. He had no relationship with Zoe and barely one with Marilyn. I suppose it's possible he was trying to do the right thing. But has it occurred to anyone that maybe ..."

Jeanie leaned against the door frame. "Maybe," she interjected, "Roy Lockwood wanted a reason to be in the house so he could find that check."

"Right."

"Which means he might have known it existed even back then."

"Right."

"Does it matter?" Jeanie asked.

"I don't know," I said. "But I'm getting that feeling like some other shoe is about to drop in this case."

"Right," Jeanie said. "Me too."

"And I'm afraid it's gonna drop right on my head in the middle of open court."

"When's your next hearing?"

"First thing in the morning," I said.

Jeanie let out a sigh. "Well ... maybe wear a hard hat."

Chapter 14

JUDGE MICHAEL WENTZ had his own way of doing things. He'd presided over the Woodbridge County Probate Court for thirty years and in that time, had made a legend or a nuisance of himself, depending on who you asked. Today, he glared at me over the top of the pleadings I'd just filed in response to Roy Lockwood and Bradley Paul's petition. For inexplicable reasons, the judge seemed to want to make it look like he was reading my documents for the very first time while I stood in open court. We both knew that wasn't true. It was stuff like this that had given Judge Wentz a YouTube following he probably didn't even know he had.

"All right," Judge Wentz said, finally putting the paperwork down. "So, we're here on the petitioners' request to remove Zoe Paul as guardian and conservator for her mother, Marilyn Paul."

"Grandmother," I said. "Zoe is Marilyn Paul's granddaughter."

Wentz waved me off. At the table beside me, Roy Lockwood and his attorney locked heads in a hushed whisper.

"Mr. Einhorn?" the judge said. "Would you care to state your grounds?"

Chad Einhorn came from a high-powered firm out of Southfield. As far as I knew, he'd never stepped foot in Woodbridge County before today. A quick google search revealed he'd spent a good ten years as a CPA before heading to law school. He cleared his throat and approached the lectern. Beside me, Zoe fidgeted in a way I didn't like. Jeanie caught it too. She sat at the table with us. She nudged Zoe and got her to settle.

"Your Honor," Einhorn started. "We believe Ms. Paul has exerted undue influence over her grandmother and has absconded with funds that rightfully belong to Mrs. Paul's estate. We also believe that Ms. Paul has attempted to file a fraudulent will in this case. As the interested parties, we'd like to challenge Ms. Paul's most recent annual accounting and have Mr. Lockwood replace her as his sister's guardian, conservator, and patient advocate. I can detail my legal arguments now if you'd like. Though they're all part of the brief in support of my clients' petition."

"You represent both Roy Lockwood and Bradley Paul? Is Mr. Paul here in the courtroom today?"

"No, Your Honor," Einhorn said. "Bradley Paul resides in Missouri. He couldn't take off work this week to get here. He's filed his affidavit and it's attached to the petition."

"Ms. Leary?" the judge said.

"There's a lot to unpack, Your Honor. Let me start off by stating that the petitioners' requests regarding Marilyn Paul's will aren't ripe for litigation. The woman is still very much alive. Beyond that, they can make no showing that my client, Zoe

Paul, has acted in any other way but in the best interests of her grandmother. Her Uncle Roy has had no involvement in Mrs. Paul's care in the sixteen years she's been hospitalized. He's only now coming forward because he believes there's money to be had. Money that he has absolutely no claim to. We also believe that it is Roy Lockwood who, in fact, has absconded with money belonging to his sister's trust."

Roy Lockwood made a noise and started to rise. Einhorn got a hold of him and forced him back into his seat.

"Your Honor," Einhorn said. "This case involves some rather complex facts and nefarious deeds on the part of Zoe Paul. We've done our best to outline what we know, but Mr. Lockwood is here to give his own statement if he's permitted to do so."

Wentz sat back in his chair. He chewed on the end of his pen as he regarded Roy.

"I'll hear from him," Wentz said.

"What?" Jeanie whispered it to me across the table.

Lockwood came around the table and made his way up to the witness box.

"Bailiff, swear him in," Judge Wentz said.

"Your Honor," I said, rising. "Mr. Einhorn hasn't requested to call witnesses in these proceedings. We aren't ..."

"I'm requesting it," the judge said. "You'll have your chance to cross-examine this man."

"I'm sorry," I said. "This is a motion hearing. Cross-examine? This isn't a trial ..."

"What this is," Judge Wentz said, "is my courtroom. I said I'd like to hear from the petitioner. I'll let you know when it's your turn to talk again, Ms. Leary."

I felt blood rising into my cheeks. Beside me, Zoe Paul started to tremble.

"Mr. Lockwood," the judge said. "Why do you feel your niece isn't acting in your sister's best interests?"

Lockwood puffed out his chest. "It's a long story, Your Honor. But ... I've been worried about Marilyn and her care for a very long time. I've asked for updates. Asked to be let in to see her. Zoe never returns my calls. Then when she does, there's always some excuse why I can't go see my sister. She's kept Marilyn isolated from the rest of the family since her accident. And she's barred us from getting inside Marilyn's house for close to fifteen years."

"Your sister is at Maple Valley Rehab Center here in town, isn't she?" the judge asked.

"Yes, Your Honor."

"It's not a prison. You're family. Are you telling me you've somehow been prevented from seeing your sister during their normal visiting hours?"

"Not exactly. But Zoe has overseen my sister's care. We've tried to respect that. I wanted to believe Zoe knew what was best for Marilyn. I'll admit. I've had my own troubles over the years. I wanted to believe Zoe was taking care of my sister for me. I regret that. I should have been more involved. I am now, though. And some things have come to light. Disturbing things. I felt it was necessary to bring them to the court's attention before it's too late."

"What things?" I said at the same time the judge did.

"Can I go back?" Roy said. "I think it would help you, Judge, if you understood a little about what's happened in our family."

"Your Honor!" I said. "Mr. Lockwood has filed a petition asking for a very specific form of relief. He has the burden of showing that Mrs. Paul's granddaughter has in some way breached her fiduciary responsibility to Mrs. Paul. But before we even get to that, he's got to establish that he's got standing to do so. We haven't ..."

"He's her brother," the judge said. "I'm interested to hear what he has to say. Mr. Lockwood, what's this about? Really?"

Roy Lockwood looked down at his shoes. His face turned gray. His hand began to shake as he reached into his breast pocket and pulled out a crumpled piece of paper.

"It's hard for me to say this. Maybe we could speak in private, Judge?"

"Absolutely not!" I said. I got a look from Jeanie. I knew I was having trouble controlling my temper. This was exactly why I usually sent Tori in to handle hearings in front of Judge Wentz.

"That would be inappropriate, Mr. Lockwood," Judge Wentz said. "The proper way to communicate with the court is by filing a petition. Which you have. Now, if there's something you'd like for me to consider, you can bring it up now."

"She knew, okay? My sister knew this day might come," Roy said. "She wrote me a note. I think you should see it."

"You Honor," I said. "I object. Whatever Mr. Lockwood's got there, it should have been made part of his petition. I've not had a chance to see it. To authenticate it. Is he claiming it's some sort of testamentary document? In which case, once again, Marilyn Paul's not dead."

"She might as well be!" Lockwood shouted. "Marilyn can't speak for herself. I have to do it for her and according to her wishes."

"Her wishes," I said. "Your Honor, this witness wasn't in contact with his sister in a meaningful way for years before her accident."

"That's a lie. And my sister was under duress," Lockwood said. "That's the right word, right? She was under the influence and control of my niece. And it's time for all of this to come out. You don't know how Zoe is. She's conniving. Manipulative. I have reason to believe that she was drugging my sister against her will before her accident. For all I know, she's the reason Marilyn got hurt in the first place."

"You're a liar!" Zoe vaulted out of her seat. "He's lying. The only reason my uncle is here today is because he sees dollar signs. He had no relationship with my grandma before her accident. She hated him. Now I know why."

Judge Wentz banged his gavel.

"Your Honor," Roy said. "I can prove everything I'm saying. I can prove that my niece forged my sister's signature on all the documents you have. Her medical papers. Her will. She's been biding her time. Waiting for a payday. Well, now it's here. Now that my sister probably won't live to see next year."

"Your Honor," I said. "Don't you think this has gone far enough? If Mr. Lockwood is asking for an evidentiary hearing, then let's have one. All we have right now are the self-serving statements of a man who has no standing to challenge his sister's will. Who has not shown the slightest interest in his sister's well-being for over fifteen years. The reason we're standing here today is because Mr. Lockwood has caught wind of the fact that his sister may have substantial assets that were not previously known to us."

"And why is that?" Roy shouted. "You ask that little witch why that is. She's been hiding my sister's money all this time. You think it's some coincidence she just happened to find a two-million-dollar check now? Now that Marilyn's days are numbered? No. No, sir. She's trying to line things up so she can get that money the minute my poor sister dies."

I blew out a hard breath. Chad Einhorn just sat back and let his client spout off his claims. For the moment, so did Judge Wentz. Jeanie managed to wrangle Zoe back into her seat.

As calmly as I could, I faced the judge. "Your Honor, again, I'd like to lodge my objection to the … well … unusual nature of these proceedings. The asset in question hasn't even been liquidated yet. It's still an open legal question whether it will be. We may have to file suit against the bank to get them to honor this check. Assuming they do, Mr. Roy Lockwood has absolutely no standing to say anything about it. Marilyn Paul is alive. Her brother is not a named beneficiary under Marilyn Paul's will on file with the court even if she were deceased. And he does not stand to inherit anything from her in the absence of a will as Mrs. Paul has lineal descendants. He is wasting the court's time with this."

"Your Honor," Einhorn said. "Our petition was filed on behalf of Bradley Paul *and* Roy Lockwood. Ms. Leary's point is well taken as it relates to intestate succession. But Mrs. Paul has a living son. Bradley Paul. Surely, Ms. Leary understands his claim."

"She's not dead yet," I said, exasperated.

"You're giving me a headache," Judge Wentz said. "I'm going to agree with Ms. Leary on a couple of points, Mr. Einhorn. Mr. Lockwood has no legal interest in his sister's monetary estate. He is of course free to challenge his niece's guardianship and conservatorship. But it seems that's not a matter we're going to be able to resolve here today. So yes. Let's set an evidentiary hearing on that portion of the petition for next week. I've got time then. I want specifics on how your clients feel Ms. Paul has breached her duties. And on the matter of the will on file, if you have evidence to present on the claim that it's been forged or is otherwise not valid, I'll take them under advisement."

"Cass!" Zoe started to rise. Jeanie had a vice grip on her shoulder.

"In the meantime, Ms. Leary, what's going on with the bank?"

"I've sent a demand letter," I said. "If I haven't received a response by the end of the week, I'm prepared to file suit for payment on behalf of Mrs. Paul's estate."

"Well, let's hope it doesn't come to that. At this rate, you people are going to eat up this woman's assets in legal fees. Please keep that in mind, counsel. We'll adjourn until next week. Let's everyone have their ducks in a row by then. And Mr. Einhorn, if you're representing both the petitioners make sure you have them here. Got it?"

Wentz didn't wait for an answer. He banged his gavel and got up from the bench.

Jeanie had to physically restrain Zoe from going after her uncle. It was a side of her I hadn't yet seen and hoped she could control.

"Chad?" I said. "If you have ..."

"I just got a copy of this myself," he said, producing another paper from his briefcase. I glanced down. I could only assume it was a copy of the mysterious letter Roy Lockwood claimed Marilyn had written. I snatched the paper from him and stuffed it into my bag.

Judge Wentz's headache seemed contagious.

Chapter 15

"WHAT DOES IT SAY?" Zoe asked. She'd refused a chair when we got back to the office. Instead, she tore a path through the carpet in front of the conference room table.

Jeanie sat next to me, rereading the grainy copy of the letter for the third time.

"Is it bad?"

"Only if it's real," Jeanie said. "Which it can't be."

Finally, Zoe took a seat. She blinked back tears. "I should have burned that check. Torn it up. It's worth millions to me not to have to deal with my dad and my uncle and all this drama."

I smoothed the paper out and slid it next to Zoe so she could read it.

Roy,

I hope I don't regret writing to you. We've had our differences, but I don't know who else to turn to. I know you think I took everyone's side but yours over the years. I'm sorry things ended up how they did for you. Please know I tried to help in my own way, but I've had my own stuff to deal with too. We're coming up on our sixties now though. I for one don't want to be carrying these bad feelings to the grave. You're my older brother. We're all that's left.

At any rate, the purpose of my letter is about my granddaughter. For the last sixteen years, I've devoted my life to her. It cost me my marriage. It cost me my relationship with my son. When she was little, I knew it was the right thing to do. Now? I'm at my wits' end.

I do not feel safe in my own house anymore. I wanted to believe this was all just typical teenage girl drama. But it's gone beyond that now. Zoe has made threats. I believe she's been going through my mail. I know for a fact she has stolen from me.

I know what I'm asking. I expect you'll say no. Please do talk to Cora. Zoe likes her. I think they have a connection. I know it's not a permanent solution, but please think about it. Whatever ground rules you set, Zoe will have to abide by them. If she understands this is the last straw, I don't think they'll be a problem.

I am hoping you and Cora can find it in your heart to let Zoe stay with you this summer like Cora offered. It will be good for Zoe. She loves Cora. I know Cora loves her too.

I'll try calling you in a couple of days. Please answer this time. I love you, Roy. Even if things have gone sideways with us. You're still my brother. Again ... I miss you. M.

Zoe's face had gone purple. Trembling, she let the letter drop to the table.

"The judge is going to read this? This is a lie. My grandmother couldn't have written this."

"It's typed," Jeanie said. "There's just the signature at the bottom."

"The second page," I said. "Those three paragraphs in the middle where he talks about the threats you allegedly made and how she doesn't feel safe, they're on a separate page from everything else. Someone could have easily slipped them in. If you take those out, she's just asking if you could stay in Florida with them for the summer. Do you remember that ever being discussed?"

"Not really," Zoe said. "I mean, she might have asked me if I wanted to go down and visit my Uncle Ray and Aunt Cora. But nothing ever came of it. We went through a phase where things were tense in the house for a little while. The summer I turned sixteen we argued a lot. She didn't like the guy I was dating. I didn't like the curfew she set."

"That doesn't sound too terrible," Jeanie said.

"He forged it," Zoe said.

"This?" I said, picking up the letter. "It's meaningless. Even if your grandmother did write it, it's completely irrelevant to any of the issues your uncle and father are trying to raise. You were sixteen years old. So what if you and your grandmother weren't getting along."

"We were though!" Zoe said. "We had arguments sometimes. But they were normal. Minor. I wasn't some monster. My God. She wasn't afraid of me. And if my uncle was so worried about how my grandma was being taken care of, he said nothing. For sixteen years. He never tried to be made her guardian. Or mine.

He never stepped up. He just moved himself into the house without anyone asking him to. Because my Aunt Cora threw him out. That's what was going on. He just figured with Grandma in the hospital he could just live in her house for free. He is making all of this up."

"I told you, it doesn't matter. The issue is whether you've looked out for your grandmother's best interests. You have. She's getting the very best medical care. You've drawn reasonable fees from her estate. You've filed annual accountings and not once until today has your uncle taken issue with anything. This is nothing, okay? This is about the money he thinks he can get his hands on."

"Judge Wentz will see through all this, won't he?" Zoe asked.

"That's my hope."

"Is there anything to this? Could they win? Please. Tell me the truth."

"They have an uphill battle," I said. "The fact that you've been the only one caring for your grandmother and her affairs all these years will hold a lot of weight, Zoe. What's not in your favor is the timing. It looks bad that you produced this check on the heels of your grandmother's terminal diagnosis."

"Do you think I'm lying? Do you think I've been holding on to this thing all these years? That's insane. How would I know if the bank would cash it after all this time?"

"And that's the counterargument," I said. "It's a strong one. I'm just trying to prepare you for what I think your family is going to try and hammer home."

"Zoe," Jeanie said. "There's no point in letting yourself get worked up. Cass is going to make sure Judge Wentz focuses on the law. It's on your side. Now go home and let us do what you're paying us for. It's gonna be okay, honey."

Zoe Paul moved like a zombie as she made her way out to the lobby. I didn't see Miranda at her desk. Zoe let Jeanie hug her, then said her goodbyes.

When Jeanie came back to the conference room, she was fuming.

"This is bad," she said.

"Well, everything you just said to Zoe was true. This is self-serving nonsense. I'd like to let Frieda Jones look at it. See if it tracks with anything she remembers about that summer."

"It's not a testamentary document," Jeanie said. "It's not a will. It's got no bearing on any of the issues in Zoe's case. It's just ... well, it's mean. At worst, it's a complete forgery. At best, if Marilyn really did write this, all it does is cause Zoe pain. For no reason."

I plopped down into the nearest chair. "Tell me I'm wrong, Jeanie. Tell me Judge Wentz isn't running his courtroom like the wild west. Because I don't trust the man to not do something stupid and let this ridiculous letter become something it's legally not."

I waved the copy of the letter in the air. I wanted to throw it into the wastebasket.

"Oh, come on," Jeanie said. "Wentz is a rogue judge. I won't deny that. But this is so far-fetched. I just cannot imagine that old fart would let Roy Lockwood or Bradley Paul go down this road."

"Imagine it," I said. "That son of a bitch is about to allow what amounts to a will contest before the woman is actually dead."

"If he does ... and if he's crazy enough to rule against Zoe, he'll be overturned on appeal. You know that."

"I know you're talking about two or three years' worth of costly litigation."

"So does Chad Einhorn," she said. "That weasel. That's why he even agreed to take this case. He's betting you'll talk Zoe into settling. Give those bozos half that check or something."

"That's a pretty big gamble."

Miranda appeared. She had a smile on her face that seemed completely incongruent to the topic of conversation. One I knew she'd been listening in on from the very beginning.

Miranda walked into ... no ... she practically floated into the room, humming some Disney song I couldn't place. She had a folded piece of paper in her hands.

"You okay?" Jeanie asked.

"Oh, I'm more than okay," she said. "And the two of you will be too."

"You have good news?" I asked. "Please share it with the rest of the class. We could use it."

"You," she said, "just got a registered letter from one Elroy Banks. Comptroller for Knight Bank."

"His name is Banks?" I said. "From the bank?"

"Ironic, I know," Miranda said. "Anyway, Cass ... it does appear that one of your superpowers is letter writing. You most certainly garnered Mr. Banks's attention."

"Okay … I give up. What did I do that's so incredible it's got you singing?"

Miranda put the piece of paper in front of me.

"Just tell me," I said. "I've had enough of letters today."

"Oh, you'll like this one. Read it. I promise. You're about to start singing show tunes. You too, Jeanie."

I took the paper and read it. As Miranda claimed, it was written on Knight Bank letterhead and signed by one Elroy Banks.

It took me two passes. I blinked hard, making sure I'd read the thing correctly.

"Miranda?" I said.

"I know. It's too good!"

"What's going on!" Jeanie shouted.

Heart racing, I handed her the letter. "They're gonna pay it," I said. "Knight Bank has assumed the debts and accounts of Delphi Savings Bank and they are gonna pay the face value of the check written to Marilyn Paul. They're cutting a new check for the full amount payable to Marilyn's trust!"

"You bet your ass they are." Miranda laughed. "They know they're facing ridiculous fines for their own screw-up in not reporting those funds as unclaimed to the state. This is a bargain in their eyes."

"Holy crap!" Jeanie said. "You did it."

"Did you doubt me?" I asked, though my bravado was just that. I was just as shocked as Jeanie was.

"Two million bucks," Jeanie said. "That ought to brighten Zoe's mood. Is she still out there? Can we catch her?"

"Sorry," Miranda said. "She had already pulled away by the time I opened that. I can try getting her on the phone."

I picked up the bank's letter again. I laid it right beside the copy of the letter Roy Lockwood had produced.

"This is all but over, Cass," Jeanie said. "Marilyn's gonna get paid. Down the road, this money will do good. For Zoe. She deserves it. I don't believe whatever lies her uncle and father are trying to spin. Nobody who knows Zoe or knew Marilyn will believe it either."

"I hope not," I said. "I'd feel better if we could solve the mystery of where this money came from. And why didn't Marilyn cash it herself? Who was she trying to hide it from?"

"Her brother, clearly," Jeanie said. "And her good-for-nothing son."

She was right. Probably. And yet, I had that nagging feeling that someone else out there knew the truth. If I was going to put this case to bed for good, I knew I'd have to find them first.

Chapter 16

MONDAY MORNING, two things happened. Knight Bank deposited two million dollars into Marilyn Paul's estate account, and Chad Einhorn served me with a witness list with four names on it.

"I've entered bizarro world," I said to Jeanie. "Judge Wentz is actually going to conduct a mini trial on a will contest for a woman who isn't dead yet."

Jeanie picked the list up from me. "Zoe. Frieda Jones. Bradley Paul. Roy Lockwood. Well, it seems to me, Roy and Bradley versus Zoe and Frieda Jones cancel each other out, don't they? You can make an argument that they're all gonna say self-serving crap. What else do we have?"

"I'm going to pay a visit to someone Marilyn worked with. See if she can provide any insight into what was going on when she last knew her. One of the numbers Eric pulled up on Marilyn's phone belonged to an Eileen Maguire. She worked with Marilyn at Valentine Pizza. I think she was their bookkeeper. She agreed to talk to me. I'm heading over there in an hour. Her number was one of the most frequently called ones on Marilyn's cell phone. You wanna tag along when I go talk to her? I could use an extra set of ears."

Jeanie looked uncomfortable. "What?" I asked. "What is it?"

"You're gonna find out anyway. Now, don't get excited."

"Jeanie ... you're not doing a great job of stopping that. What's going on?"

"Joe's got a hearing in family court later this afternoon. Katie filed for divorce. She's asking for temporary spousal support and she wants Joe barred from entering the marital home."

My head started to pound. "He never said a word. When did all this go down?"

"Late last week. He called me. He asked me not to say anything to you. I told him I'd honor that through the weekend, but that I'd fill you in this morning. And so, I have."

"I need to talk to him," I said. "I need to talk to Katie. This is ridiculous."

"This ... for the moment ... is none of your business, Cass."

"He's my brother! Jeanie, this is Joe we're talking about. Katie and Joe."

"Yes. And he's handling it. What were you gonna do, represent him? You don't do divorces, I do. And it's what you said. You're his sister. You gotta let him deal with this in his own way."

"He's shutting me out," I said.

"Give him time. And trust me. I'll get him through this afternoon. And I'll work on him to talk to you more. He's just ... he's embarrassed."

"Over what?"

"He just is. This feels like a failure to him. He doesn't want to disappoint you."

"Jeanie ..." My throat felt thick.

"Cass, go. Go talk to Eileen Maguire. Focus on Zoe's case. Let me do what I do for Joe. We'll meet back here this afternoon. It's all going to be okay."

I wanted to strangle someone. Katie, maybe. Joe. I also hated that Jeanie was right. I grabbed my bag and tried to clear my head. As I passed by Miranda's desk, I found it empty. I turned back to Jeanie, holding my arms up in a questioning gesture. Miranda hadn't missed a day of work in three years.

"She texted me on my way in," Jeanie said. "Car trouble or something."

"I need something to go our way," I muttered as I headed out the back.

I sent a text to my brother.

"Jeanie told me. Please let me help."

I stared at three blinking dots for a full minute.

"Talk later," he said.

Shaking my head, I knew it was as good a response as I would get from him.

"I love you," I texted back.

"Love you too," he immediately responded. I clutched the phone to my chest, then slipped it into my bag.

Eileen Maguire met me at a coffee shop off the Ann Arbor-Saline exit. A bit of a hike for both of us and I soon realized, she might not want anyone to know she was talking to me.

She was soft-spoken, with thick, white hair she wore in a flattering bob. We sat on the outdoor patio, and she asked me if I minded if she vaped.

"Not at all," I said. There was a strong breeze blowing in the opposite direction.

"I chain-smoked for thirty years," she said. "My doctor says I'm a medical miracle. Quit cold turkey eight years ago. But then my husband took a turn. I nursed him through Alzheimer's. I wanted to pick up a cigarette. I went for these."

"It's understandable," I said. "Thank you for agreeing to talk to me."

"Not my preference," she said. "Not that I've got anything against you. I just feel like this is a not my circus, not my monkeys' situation."

"Well, I appreciate your time."

"I haven't seen Marilyn Paul since the day she got in that car accident. It's been sixteen years." She blew out a puff of air. "We were close, Marilyn and me. I considered her my best work friend. I'm the one who recommended her to Tim Valentine. Helped her get that job."

"She was a receptionist?"

"Started out that way. Then they moved her back to Tim's staff. I did payroll for the company. Marilyn ended up as Tim's personal secretary. For a while, she was his right-hand woman."

"Tim was the CEO of Valentine Pizza?"

"Valentine Foods was the official name," Eileen said. "But yes. Tim and his brother Tony founded the company. Started out making pizzas out of their mother's kitchen. Secret family sauce recipe. That was the gimmick anyway."

"That and the heart-shaped pizzas," I said.

"Yeah. Anyway, there were five of us in Tim's office. By the time Marilyn moved back, Tony had already retired."

"Can you tell me who else worked in that same office?"

"Me. Marilyn. Tim, of course. Jean Francis. Holly Billings."

"Who did what, if you recall?"

"Jean worked with supply chain. Tim did the books. Holly was the office administrator. I told you, I did payroll and employee management. I oversaw new hires. Marilyn did whatever Tim asked her to."

"Tim did the books and Marilyn kept track of Tim?"

"Yeah. That's exactly how I'd describe her job. She set all his appointments. Made sure he was prepared for every meeting he took. Wrote all his correspondence. She'd run personal errands for him too. Get his dry cleaning, take his dog to the groomer. All kinds of crazy stuff you and I wouldn't have been caught dead doing. But the Valentines paid well. And Tim was a decent boss. Tony, not so much."

Her expression turned dark.

"But Tony had retired by the time Marilyn became Tim's secretary?"

"It was around that time, yes. Look. This has nothing to do with me. I'm sorry about what happened to poor Marilyn, but I don't want to be involved in this."

"Hopefully, your involvement won't go further than this conversation," I said. "I'm just trying to get a sense of what was going on with Marilyn. You said you were close. Zoe Paul's uncle and father are claiming Zoe should be removed as Marilyn's guardian and conservator. Do you have any reason to think she should be?"

Eileen flapped her hands. "What difference does it make at this point?"

"To the Pauls, it makes about two million dollars' worth of difference. That's what this is about. Are you aware of that?"

Her eyes got big. "You're saying Marilyn had two million bucks? I don't believe it."

I wasn't sure how much I should tell her. Technically, the bank deposit would be public record as soon as Zoe filed her next accounting.

"Where the hell did she get that kind of money?" Eileen asked.

"I was hoping you might know. You said you were work besties. Did Marilyn talk about money with you?"

"I knew how much Marilyn was making. Just over forty grand. And she had medical and dental care. But no, we didn't talk about money. Certainly not that kind of money."

"What about her relationship with Zoe? Did she talk to you about that?"

"Zoe was what, seventeen, eighteen when Marilyn had that accident? Yeah. We talked about her a bit. Things were kind of tense. Marilyn was looking forward to being an empty-nester. Zoe wasn't an easy kid. And look. I can understand. She was testing boundaries and Marilyn's patience. They had some fights."

"Did you ever get the sense they were physical?" I asked.

Eileen shook her head. "I never saw bruises on either one of them if that's what you mean. But they broke stuff. Marilyn said Zoe smashed her phone once. Threw it against the wall."

"Marilyn's phone?"

"No. Zoe broke her own phone. Then when Marilyn wouldn't pay for a new one, Zoe took off for a little while. She'd stay with a neighbor, I think. I don't know why Marilyn put up with it. But that was when Zoe was younger. Fifteen. Sixteen. She calmed down. They were close, those two."

"So, as far as you know, things were good between them by the time Marilyn had her accident?"

"As far as I know." Eileen waved a cloud of smoke away from her face, then put her vape pen away. "I do think Marilyn was ready to finally be an empty-nester. She'd earned the right to a peaceful house. Her ex? Billy? He was a mean son of a bitch. And Marilyn? She was having what I'd call a renaissance."

"How so?"

"Oh ... she started taking care of herself. She lost a bunch of weight. Started going to the gym. But she looked like a million bucks."

The moment she said it, Eileen's face went hard again. "Or maybe two million." Her tone was bitter. This woman would be a wild card if I ever had to call her to the stand. One moment, she seemed to miss her friendship with Marilyn, the next, she almost sounded resentful.

"Eileen, the main issue in this estate is this check Marilyn had for two million dollars. It was a mystery to Zoe. It's a mystery to me. You spent every day with Marilyn in those months before her accident. Do you at least have a theory as to where that money might have come from?"

Eileen looked up and down the sidewalk then back at me. "I don't know. I really don't."

"Could you take a guess? Did Tim Valentine have that kind of money?"

She let out a haughty laugh. "Uh ... no. Tim was terrible with money. That was a big beef between him and his brother. Tony was really the brains of the operation. When he retired we figured it would only be a matter of time before things took a turn. Tim liked playing the part of the boss. He didn't actually like to do any of the work. Tim was a great guy. Easy to get along with. But Tony was the better business manager. He was just a garbage human."

"I see. So no theories on where Marilyn got that money?"

Her nostrils flared. "I don't know. This is speculation. But ... well ... Marilyn? She was getting around in that last year, year and a half. She looked like dynamite. In the first few years I knew her, she dressed real frumpy. Then she fixed herself up. Started coming to work dressed to the nines. Mr. Valentine noticed. He ... well ... he pulled her from the front reception and set her up as his personal secretary, okay?"

"Were they having an affair, do you think?"

"Not that she ever told me. Not that I ever saw. I just know Valentine liked looking at her and flirting with her. She used it to her advantage. That doesn't mean he would have written her a check for two million bucks. We weren't doing that kind of business. God no. It's just ... she started seeing a bunch of other guys too. She went to this divorcee support club that was nothing more than a meat market."

"Can you remember the names of any of the men she was dating?"

"I only met one. Hal Dolenz. She met him at the support group. She was already seeing him by the time I met her. He was nuts about her. I don't think it was mutual. Then later, I know for a fact she started seeing this guy who was married. She wouldn't tell me his name. She just showed me a picture of him once. I warned her. I'm no prude. But I just don't condone adultery, you know?"

"Of course." I pulled out my phone and followed a hunch. It took me a second, but I found a photo of Ned Corbett online from his retirement announcement. I turned it so Eileen could see it.

"Was this the man in the picture?"

Eileen squinted. She put on her readers.

"No. That's Ned. I mean, she could have been sleeping with him too for all I know. But no. That's not the guy she showed me. She was playing with fire. And I just wonder ..."

"Eileen," I said. "How did you know Ned Corbett?"

"He was a cop. The Valentines hired him to do security after hours."

I was dumbfounded. That was a completely different story than Corbett had told Eric or me. He insisted Marilyn had been a friend of his ex-wife's. A clumsy lie if that's what it was. I made a mental note to check in with Eric on it as soon as I got back to the office.

Her voice trailed off. Again, Eileen started looking up and down the street. Her paranoia started to rub off on me and I found myself wishing we were somewhere more private.

"Mrs. Maguire, something's bothering you. It has been since the second I mentioned the money. I can tell you right now, the source of it probably won't be an issue in this court case. The only real issue is whether Zoe has fulfilled her duties as Marilyn's guardian. I firmly believe she has. But ultimately, that will be for the judge to decide. It *is* important to me to try and figure out the source of that money. Zoe wants to do what's right and I'm trying to help her."

"She was seeing men she shouldn't," Eileen said. "That married one. And ... he wasn't the only one. I didn't like how she strung Hal along. He seemed like a nice guy and he was definitely more into her than she was in him. As far as Tim? I told you. I never witnessed Tim and Marilyn being unprofessional with each other. But he was married too. I don't know. I just wonder ... if a man wanted to keep something like that quiet. His affair. Wouldn't he be willing to pay money to do it?"

"You think Marilyn was capable of blackmailing a man she was seeing?"

"I just don't know," she said. "I just know ... she was maybe doing a few things she shouldn't have. I don't want to judge. But

I believe in karma. I know what happened to Marilyn was tragic and an accident. But ... maybe it was a little bit of karma too. That's all I'm saying. And I've said too much. So, I'm going to leave now."

She did just that. Abruptly. I sat for a moment and watched her go. Then I took out my phone and texted Eric.

"Can we meet? I have more questions about Detective Corbett. You free for dinner?"

A moment later, Eric texted back. "Can I call?"

I quickly punched in his number. He answered immediately.

"What's up?"

"Have you talked to Miranda?"

"No. She didn't come in this morning. Jeanie said something about her having car trouble. But hey ... I just finished a meeting with this woman who worked with Marilyn. There's this ..."

"Cass," he interrupted me. "Where are you?"

"What?"

"Right now. Where are you?"

"I'm sitting on an outdoor patio at this coffee shop in Saline. I told you. I just ..."

"Honey ... something's up. Miranda's run into some trouble. I just left her house."

I felt bile rise in my throat. "What's going on?"

"She's trying to downplay it. But someone slashed her tires and knocked out the windows of her car last night."

My mind reeled. This was Tori's accident all over again. No. No. No.

"Is she okay?"

"She's pretty shook up. But physically she's fine. I'm sending a crew to sit outside her house. Cass. I need to ask you something and I don't want you to freak out."

"Too late."

"I want you to come home. Now. And I want you to be very careful. Take only main roads, okay? Do you know how to tell if someone is or has been following you?"

My skin crawled. My blood turned to ice. Eileen Maguire was long gone. There were two other couples sitting at bistro tables near me. Nothing suspicious. No one paying any attention to me.

"Yes," I said. "I think I'm alone."

"Good. Just come home, baby. It's going to be okay."

He said the words, but they brought me no comfort. Shaking, I left a twenty on the table and went to my car. I looked over my shoulder the entire way.

Chapter 17

MIRANDA'S CAR hadn't just been vandalized. It looked ... violated. Smashed safety glass covered every seat. Her headlights had been kicked in as well. She didn't feel safe at home, so I drove her into the office with me. Now, she sat in the conference room, white as a sheet, as Eric tried to calm her down.

Jeanie was worried. She hovered near Miranda, patting her on the back. Eric followed me into the kitchen, leaving the two of them alone.

"She's okay," he said. "Terrified, but okay."

"This wasn't random, was it?"

"I don't know," he said, his tone grim.

"Eric ... I can't go through this again. We can't go through this again. I need to know she's safe. That my staff is safe."

"There's no reason to think this had anything to do with what happened to Tori last spring. Let's not jump to conclusions."

"It feels like a message," I said.

"Yeah. It does to me too. I told you. I'll have some extra patrols around Miranda's house. Here too. And your place. Just ... keep your eyes and ears open, but don't panic, okay?"

I wanted to cry. I wanted to smash something. Miranda didn't deserve this. No one did.

"She'll be okay," Eric said. "Miranda's a tough old bird."

"Thank you for taking extra care of her. She loves you. She trusts you."

"She's family." I pushed past my own tears and threw my arms around Eric. He hugged me. Tight.

"When are things ever going to be normal again?"

He laughed. "Have they ever been where you're concerned?"

"Thank you. Just ... thank you."

"Things are as under control here as they can be for now. I've got to leave," he said. "I'm going to oversee this report and see if I can get a look at the doorbell cameras her neighbors have. So far, nobody says they saw anything or heard anything."

"How is that even possible?"

Jeanie came into the kitchen. She looked haggard. Worried. "I'm gonna have Miranda stay with me for a while."

"Good." Eric and I said it in unison.

"She's too rattled to be of much use here today. You mind if she calls it a day?"

"Of course," I said. "You know you don't even have to ask. Will you stay with her this afternoon?"

Jeanie got a strange look on her face. It was then I realized what else Jeanie had going on today. "Joe's hearing?" I said. She had been headed there when I went to meet Eileen Maguire.

Eric kissed me quickly, then excused himself. He promised to come over to my place when his shift ended.

"It went okay," Jeanie said. "Judge is going to turn everything over to the Friend of the Court. There'll be an evidentiary hearing in a couple of weeks."

"How's Joe?"

Jeanie gave me a weak smile. "He went home. Took the rest of the day off. Look, he might not be great company. He might not want to talk. But maybe you should take the rest of the afternoon and check in with him. I'll handle things with Miranda."

"Divide and conquer," I said, feeling bone-weary.

"See you tomorrow, okay, kid? Try not to worry too much."

Easier said than done. But it was clear none of us would get any more work done today. I said a quick goodbye to Miranda and left her in Jeanie's care.

When I got home, I found my brother.

"How'd it go?" I asked.

"It went."

"What does that mean?" I stood in the doorway to my guesthouse. Joe was in the kitchenette, adjusting his belt and collecting his keys, wallet, and phone.

"Joe, it's been a really shitty day for me too. Don't make me beg. Please tell me what's going on or I'll make Jeanie do it."

"Attorney–client privilege," he said.

"She's my law partner. Which means my firm is representing you. If you were planning on invoking that, you might have considered asking someone else for help."

"I did ask someone else for help. I asked Jeanie. Isn't there some sort of ethical wall or something? I haven't given her permission to talk about my case with you."

"Joe, please. You don't have to go through this alone. If you don't want to talk to me, talk to someone. You've cut me, Matty, Vangie, all of us off."

"Matty has his own stuff to deal with," Joe said. "What exactly do you expect Vangie to do? And you? Cass, I love you. But I don't need you to try and fix this for me. I trust Jeanie. You do too. I'm fine."

"You're not fine," I said. He brushed past me and headed down the exterior stairs. Shutting the door behind me, I followed close at his heels.

"You're not fine," I said again. "You've let her put you out of your house. You know I've heard the rumors. She's cheating on you, Joe. Everyone in town knows it."

He whirled on me. "I don't want to talk about this. If it bothers you having me here, I'll go. I probably should anyway."

"It doesn't bother me. I built that guest house for exactly this reason."

He froze. Then rolled his eyes. "Say what you really mean. You built it because you expected the rest of us were going to fall on our faces and you'd get to swoop in and save everyone."

"Stop it. You know that's not what I meant."

He turned again and headed to his car, waving a dismissive hand at me behind his head.

Eric pulled in just as Joe climbed into his truck. They gave each other a wave, then my brother pulled out, leaving a cloud of dusty gravel in his wake. Though I wanted to chase after my brother, I knew it would do no good. From the expression on Eric's face, I knew he had something to tell me I might not like. I let Joe go and turned to Eric. I had something to tell him too.

Chapter 18

"You gotta let him go, Cass," Eric said, putting an arm around me. He led me back up to the house. "He knows you're here if he needs you. Trust me. Right now, that's all he needs."

"He doesn't even know what he needs. How is it that you do?" I said. I stayed arm in arm with Eric as we walked into the house.

"Because," Eric said, "you're forgetting. I've been exactly where he is."

I felt like an ass. The men in my life had been bringing that out in me lately.

"I'm sorry," I said. "I know things were rough between you and Wendy before she ..."

I couldn't even bring myself to say it. When I came back to Delphi, Eric's marriage to his first wife had collapsed. He found out she'd been cheating on him. Before he had a chance to confront her about it, she'd suffered catastrophic injuries that put her in a coma.

"Tell me what to do," I said. "How can I help Joe?"

We stood in the kitchen, my butcher block island between us. Eric reached across it and took my hands in his.

"You already are. This place. The lake. It's a sanctuary for Joe as much as it is for you. He knows he could stay at a friend's house. Hell, he could stay with Matty, that house is big enough. But he's staying here because it does his soul good to be able to come home and watch that sunset. It's enough for now. I swear."

I smiled. I didn't want to. But I smiled.

"How'd you get to be so smart?" I said.

"Beats me."

"Let's talk about something else." I went through the list of topics and realized I had no mental respite anywhere. I was worried about Joe. I was worried about Miranda. About Tori and Matty.

Eric frowned. He went to the fridge, grabbed himself a beer and poured me a glass of wine. We walked out to the porch. In about forty-five minutes, we'd be able to watch that stunning sunset over the lake.

"You want to go out on the pontoon?" he asked.

"Here's fine," I said. "It's just the two of us. I have no idea where Joe was even going. Add it to the long list of things he's keeping from me."

"Stop," Eric said. "Every fire that can be put out has been put out for the day. Miranda's okay. Joe's okay. It's just us now. Tell me what you found out at your meeting with Eileen Maguire?"

"Ah," I said, sipping my wine. "Eileen Maguire. She was Marilyn Paul's closest coworker. Based on your crackerjack cell phone mojo and Eileen's confirmation, she was the last person to talk to Marilyn before her accident."

"Any insight?"

"I don't know. She was hard to read. She liked Marilyn. That was clear. But I don't think she was a big fan of Marilyn's lifestyle the last few months of her life ... ugh ... now I'm doing it. She's not dead yet. I mean before the accident."

"How so?"

"Well, it seems that Eileen Maguire is of the opinion that after Billy Paul died, our Marilyn turned into somewhat of a floozy."

Eric smiled. "Yeah. That's kind of the impression I got too."

"I asked her about Detective Corbett. Whether she knew if their relationship was romantic. This is where it got strange and what I wanted to talk to you about. She knew Ned Corbett. She said he was doing side work as security for Valentine Pizza. Eric, Corbett never mentioned that. I think he lied about how he knew Marilyn. Why would he do that?"

Again, that frown came back. He drank his beer and looked out at the water.

"Eric? Now you're reminding me of Joe. What aren't you telling me?"

Another sip. "I don't know. It's just a feeling. A vibe. I knew Corbett wasn't being completely forthright when we met. I had a hunch it was because you were there. His mistrust of defense attorneys. Or women in general. So, I went back and talked to him alone."

"When?"

"It was a few days ago. I told you I thought it might help. You know. Man to man. Cop to cop."

"Did it?"

"It did not. Corbett more or less threw me off his property."

"Huh."

Eric turned to me. "What? You're getting that look you get. What are you thinking? Or plotting? And why am I sure I'm not going to like it?"

"It's just something Eileen said. I asked her if she had any theory as to how Marilyn came into that windfall. She seemed just as shocked about it as Zoe was. Eileen did payroll for Valentine Foods. She knew exactly how much money Marilyn was bringing home. Anyway, she kind of hinted that Marilyn had a habit of hooking up with married men in the last year and a half."

"Men? As in plural?"

"That's pretty much what Eileen said. She gave me one name. Hal Dolenz. I'm going to track him down. But Eileen also thinks Marilyn was seeing a married man. Then she talked about karma."

"Sheesh. Dark. And you mean a married man in *addition* to possibly Ned Corbett?"

"I think so. Anyway ... she danced around a lot of the topics. But Eileen's clearly wondering if one of Marilyn's married men might have either made a kept woman out of her. Or ... um ... maybe Marilyn got herself some hush money."

"Blackmail," Eric said. "She thinks Marilyn might have been blackmailing one of these men."

"It seems pretty far-fetched to me."

"Well, we talked about this before. Ned Corbett, for one, would not have had two million bucks on a detective's salary. Unless he was ..."

Eric's voice trailed off. He covered by taking another sip of beer.

"Eric, what? You said on the phone you had something to tell me about Corbett."

"Just that I'd gone to talk to him myself."

That wasn't it. I knew Eric too well. He was keeping something back.

"Fine. But do you think Eileen Maguire might be on to something? You've tracked down her frequent call list. There's no mystery man there unless she had a different phone. There's no evidence to suggest that. We've been through everything."

"I don't know," Eric said. "Blackmail? She'd have to be shagging someone a lot richer than Ned Corbett. Yeah. He was married. Never mind the fact he wouldn't have had the capital; I just don't see him giving in to something like that. Besides, I don't know too many blackmailees who pay in cashier's checks. Do you?"

I set my wine glass down on the ground. "No. I guess not."

"Is any of this going to matter? The bank paid the money you said. It's in Marilyn's estate account. Nobody seems to be disputing that it's rightfully hers. This whole court case is about Zoe's conduct, not Marilyn's, right?"

"It is. At the same time, I just can't shake the feeling that there's another bomb about to go off out there. I'm trying to protect my client. If this money is tainted somehow, she needs to know."

"But it wasn't paid to her. It was paid to Marilyn. And Marilyn's not in a position to spill any secrets."

"I just don't like it. It's that whole thing about things that are too good to be true, you know?"

"I get it. It *is* disturbing. There's something else that's been bugging me about this one. Look. Of course, Marilyn's deadbeat family came out of the woodwork as soon as that money was found. It's to be expected. But what if the reason Marilyn hid that check is because she didn't want Zoe to know about it? They were living in the house together at the time it was written."

I considered the scenario. If Zoe weren't my client. If I were only hearing about this case second-hand, I would have the same questions.

"You mentioned vibes," I said. "I just don't get that kind of vibe from Zoe. In sixteen years, she's done all the right things in terms of making sure her grandmother got the best care. She's lived modestly. Hell, she's barely scraped by."

"But she produced the check after her grandmother got a terminal diagnosis."

"Whose side are you on?" I teased.

"I'm just playing devil's advocate. And I'm trying to look at the motives here."

"If Zoe were trying to steal money from her grandmother, she's taken an awfully convoluted path to get it."

"Yeah. So, what's next?"

"Evidentiary hearing on Thursday. It's going to go nowhere. Lockwood and Zoe's dad, if he shows up, will say one thing. Zoe and her neighbor will say another. So that leaves Roy Lockwood and Bradley Paul with the burden of proving Zoe violated her duties to her grandmother by a preponderance of the evidence. They don't have it. They just don't. If they want to file a legitimate will contest after Marilyn dies, that's another story. But even then, you're talking potentially years of litigation."

"They want to force a settlement, that's what this is."

I agreed. We sat in comfortable silence for a few minutes. Finally, Eric looked at me. "What?"

"I want to know more about what Marilyn was up to. I just do. I can't stop picking at that particular scab."

"Sure." Eric laughed softly.

"I want to know more about Corbett. He's hiding something. You suspect it too. I know you. You've already come to the same conclusion. So, dig."

He didn't say yes. He didn't say no. Plausible deniability. I knew I was asking a complicated favor. Eric still worked for the Delphi P.D. I was asking him to look for dirt on a former cop.

Before he could commit one way or another, his phone rang. He pulled it out and frowned at the caller ID.

"Wray," he answered. His shoulders dropped as he listened to the call. He rose and walked off the porch and down the dock.

"Where is she now?" I heard him say. "It was the two of them? Jesus. Yeah. No. I'm glad you called me."

I stood up. My spidey senses started to tingle. Eric heard me step onto the dock. He held up a finger.

"Okay," he said. "Yes. If you can drop them both off here … er … at Cass's place. You know where that is? Gotcha. Okay. Thank you. I owe you."

Still frowning, he clicked off the call.

"What?" I asked, though a part of me didn't want to know.

"That was Deputy Steuben. There was a bit of a disturbance at Joe's place."

I looked back toward the driveway. "Again? What did he do now?"

"Not him. Joe wasn't there. It's Emma. She, uh … got into it with Katie. Steuben got called out there on a domestic disturbance. He just called to give me a heads-up as a favor."

"Oh God," I said. "Was she arrested?"

"Katie isn't pressing charges. But she's hopping mad. Emma threw Katie's things out on the lawn. And that would have been the end of it, but Vangie showed up. Emma called her."

"Oh … shit," I said. "She might have just poured gasoline on a bonfire."

"Pretty much. Anyway, Steuben was the one who got the radio call. He got there before things escalated any worse. Katie, to her credit, said she wouldn't press charges against either one of them. For now. But Emma and Vangie are still running pretty hot. Steuben's got 'em both in the back of his cruiser. He's bringing them here now."

My stomach twisted into knots.

"Joe's going to kill both of them. I'm going to kill both of them."

"Yeah," Eric said. He walked up the dock just as the deputy's cruiser pulled up my drive. Eric gave him a wave. "Let's just work on keeping them out of jail for the night. You can kill them in the morning."

Taking a deep breath, I walked up the dock behind him, wishing I were an only child.

Chapter 19

"Thelma? Louise?"

My wayward sister and delinquent niece sat in the back of Deputy Jeff Steuben's cruiser. They stared straight ahead, refusing to look at me.

"Were the cuffs really necessary?" Eric asked Steuben.

"The little one's a scrapper," Steuben said. "I'm sorry, Vangie. I told you it was just until I got you here."

Vangie finally turned her head. Her eyes blazed hot.

"I'm sorry," Steuben said to me. "Katie said she won't press charges, but they did it right in front of me. Smashed Katie's window with a brick."

"Leave the cuffs on," I said through gritted teeth.

"They drew a crowd," Deputy Steuben said. "Now, I'm willing to look the other way. If Katie's okay, I'm okay. But this can't keep happening."

"Keep ... happening?" I said.

"It's my dad's house!" Emma shouted from the back seat of the cruiser. "It's not her house!"

"Emma, zip it," I said to her through a clenched jaw.

"I'm real sorry about everything that's happened. Joe doesn't deserve it. Only ... I guess you never know what goes on behind closed doors. It's just a shame," Steuben said.

Deputy Steuben opened the backseat door. "All right. You two can come on out. If you promise to cool off and stay away from Katie's place."

"I told you. It's not her place. And I technically still live there," Emma spat. She looked so much like her mother. Josie Banfield had been one of Joe's youthful bad decisions. Getting Emma away from her when she was a baby had been one of his best. But now, as steam poured from Emma's eyes, I saw Josie again. Volatile. Ready to fight. Vangie wasn't much better. At the moment, Emma's DNA was a powder keg.

"She can stay with me," Vangie said. "Jessa'd love it."

"Where is Jessa?" I said. The last thing I figured my other niece needed was to see Vangie and Emma like this.

"She's at a sleepover," Vangie said. "End-of-season swim team party. She won't be back until noon tomorrow."

"Thank God for small favors."

"Steuben?" Eric gestured toward Vangie's wrists.

"Oh. Right." Steuben stepped forward and unlocked Vangie's cuffs. He gave Emma a dubious glance. When Eric nodded, Steuben reluctantly took Emma's cuffs off. She made a big show out of rubbing her wrists, then stormed past us all, headed for the guest house.

"Joe's gonna kill her," I said.

"She's angry," Vangie said. "She feels just as betrayed by Katie as Joe does."

"That doesn't give her the right to break the law," I said.

"Vangie, please don't hold all this against me," Jeff Steuben said. "You know I had to do what I did. It's like I said. We can forget it ever happened if Katie doesn't change her mind. I don't suppose she's gonna."

Steuben's moony-eyed gaze at Vangie told me this particular situation would resolve itself. This time.

I walked away from Vangie and Steuben. Eric wisely followed.

"Thank you," I said. "No matter what Steuben said, he didn't just do this because of Katie."

"You think you can handle things from here?" he asked.

"You're leaving? To go where?"

More often than not, Eric stayed at my place. He kept a condo in town but rarely used it. Someday soon, we might have to talk about that. We'd meant to. But things kept getting in the way.

Eric let out a hard breath and gave off that same look I'd seen him share with Steuben.

"What aren't you telling me?"

"Nothing," he said, kissing the top of my head. "I just think … somebody ought to track Joe down. If he doesn't know about this yet, he will soon. I'd like to talk to him. I'd like to be the one he hears it from."

"You're right," I said. Eric's eyes went wide.

"See?" I teased. "I can say it. I can also say thank you. If it's possible ... um ... maybe you can convince him to crash at your condo tonight. I feel like all of them could use some time in neutral corners."

Eric looked over my shoulder. "That could be trouble."

I turned to follow his gaze. My sister was straight up batting her eyelashes at Steuben.

"Terrific," I said.

"I'm gonna need to have a talk with Jeff too."

"Yeah. Warn him off."

Eric laughed. "You think there's any man in town who can resist the charms of a Leary woman once she's set her sights on him?"

I punched Eric lightly in the arm.

"I'll call you when I know anything," he said. "Try and keep those two at a simmer. I'll keep Joe from here."

"I love you," I said.

"Back at ya," he said.

Before Eric got in his truck, he peeled Deputy Steuben from my sister's side. Steuben might as well have had cartoon hearts swirling above his head.

I waited until the men drove off. Steuben gave a quick chirp of his siren as my sister waved goodbye.

"Vangie," I said. "You better not be toying with that boy. You've been down this road with him before. I don't remember it ending all that well."

"He's cute," she said. "Annoying, but cute."

"What were you thinking?" I put a hand on her arm.

"I was thinking nobody gets away with hurting my brother or my niece like that. And I was thinking it was a good thing I showed up when I did or else things between Katie and Emma might have escalated."

"Worse than her smashing her window?"

"Um ... that was me. I got a little carried away," Vangie said. "Emma just used spray paint."

I put my hand up. "You know what? Stop. I don't want to know anymore. This is a fine mess you've made."

Vangie gave me a wide smile. Then she threw her arm around me as we walked back up to the house. I was just glad this awful day was finally over.

Chapter 20

By morning, Vangie and Emma's crime spree was all over town. The clerks were talking about it at the gas station where I picked up my coffee. I got some sympathetic looks from Ernie, the parking attendant at the courthouse when I pulled in to handle a handful of pre-trial conferences. On the way back, I decided to ignore the multiple calls and texts from Jeanie and Miranda. Unless the building was on fire, I wasn't coming in.

Instead, I made my way out to Hyde Street to meet Zoe Paul. She'd been stunned by the news that Knight Bank had honored her grandmother's check. Early yesterday, before all the chaos, Jeanie had gone with her to deposit it in Marilyn's trust account. Today would be my final chance to let Zoe know what to expect once her hearing started in full tomorrow. It might have helped if I'd known what to expect. Judge Wentz seemed to be operating under his own playbook rather than the court rules.

I found Zoe in the living room, surrounded by more of Marilyn's boxes.

"There was more in the attic," she said. Zoe held a remote control and pointed it at the large screen television in the corner of the room. She pressed play. On screen, a cute, round-tummied blonde toddler danced across the screen holding a sparkler.

"Oh wow," Zoe said. "I haven't seen these in probably twenty years or more."

I peered into the nearest box. Inside were four black cartons filled with DVDs in jewel cases. I pulled one out. It was labeled, "Zoe Age 2 + Cedar Point."

"There was a huge box of VHS tapes up there," Zoe said. "Home movies going back to when my dad was little. It looks like she had everything transferred to DVD. I rarely go up in the attic. This stuff has just been sitting there. I've been meaning to go through it for ages. It was just easier to ignore. Now? I don't know. I suppose the good thing about all of this is it's forcing me to get organized with Grandma's things."

"What a treasure," I said. "You know, I don't have a single home movie from when I was a kid."

Zoe clicked off the television. "Really? How is that possible?"

"You'd have to know my dad," I said.

"But your mom?"

"She passed away when I was young. We've got lots of pictures up until then. She was a pretty good amateur photographer. But no videos as far as I know."

"Grandma was a menace with her camcorder." Zoe smiled. "The thing was so outdated and clunky. She used it up until …

well ... she always used it. She wouldn't let anyone get her a new one."

"Have you been out to see her?" I asked.

"Every Tuesday and Thursday."

"You haven't run into your uncle or anyone?"

"Nope. The nurse told me Uncle Roy came out that one time when he picked a fight. Then once more a couple of days later, but not since."

"Did they mention whether his visit seemed to help your grandmother?"

"They said she got agitated. I wouldn't doubt it. I've told you a hundred times, she hated my Uncle Roy at the end. He's the last person she'd want to see."

I sat on the coffee table. "Tomorrow things are going to start getting hard. Your uncle, if he's allowed, is going to keep saying crappy things about you. To get anywhere with his petition, he must prove you've been mistreating your grandmother and her assets. Hard as it might be not to react, I need you cool as a cucumber in court. No outbursts. You're going to want to ..."

"It's okay. I get it. My grandma would say don't let anyone get my goat. That's what you're saying."

"That's it exactly."

"Are you worried?"

Her question threw me. It's one I should have been asking her.

"No. I'm not worried. Anyone with half a brain is going to see this is just a play for money."

"What about my dad?" she said. "Cass, what if he shows up? I haven't seen him since I was a kid. He never even came around after my grandma's accident."

"Which is a point you'll get a chance to make. And I'll be there the whole time. We're gonna get you through this."

"I almost don't care," she said. "I don't want the money. I just wish I had my grandma back. The only thing I care about is making sure she's comfortable and gets the best treatment. Cass ... she's getting worse. I can see it. She's skin and bones. The cancer is eating through her. She used to smile. She used to like the sound of my voice. Now ... she just seems so vacant. Like she's already gone, and I can't get through to her."

"That has to be so hard," I said.

"I got these out," Zoe said, pointing to the box of DVDs. "I dragged them down here because I was thinking maybe she'd like to see some of them. I know she can hear me. She knows who I am. I thought maybe watching some of these with her would cheer her up."

"I think that's a great idea."

"She likes you too," Zoe said. "She gave you her biggest smile when you were there. Would you like to come with me the next time I go visit?"

"I'd like that," I said. "I'm going to be there the day after tomorrow. My sister-in-law is coming home." It felt good to say. Sister-in-law. It wasn't technically true yet. But soon enough that was one more milestone Tori and Matty would cross.

"Tori," Vangie said. "I knew her in high school. She's one of the reasons I gave you a call. I knew she'd gone to work for you."

"She's very interested in your case too. I'll tell you what, after the hearing, we'll both go to Maple Valley to tell her how it went. Then we can spend some time with Marilyn."

"I appreciate it," Zoe said as she walked me to the door. "I've been handling all this alone for so long, it's nice to have a partner."

This girl had been through so much in her life. I had my siblings. Zoe had been all alone. I told her I'd pick her up tomorrow morning at nine, then got back in the car.

I had two unread texts. One from Eric reassuring me that Joe was fine. The two of them were going to stay at Eric's condo another night.

I thanked Eric then read my second text. It was a number I didn't recognize. The text read simply:

Have info regarding Paul check if you want it ...

I pulled out of Zoe's driveway. A few minutes later, as I made the turn toward town, I pressed the number on my phone. My Bluetooth speaker blared as the phone rang. I turned it down.

"Ms. Leary?" the caller said immediately. A woman's voice. A smoker.

"With whom am I speaking?" I asked.

"Don't worry about that. But you have something. Two million somethings."

"What do you know about that?" I asked.

"I'll call you again. Tomorrow night. Now's not a good time."

"Then why did you answer the phone?" I said. "Why did you text me in the first place?"

I heard a heavy sigh. "I could get in a lot of trouble for talking to you. For even knowing what I know. But someone has to speak up. Can I trust you?"

"I don't even know you," I said.

"Tomorrow night," she said. "I'll call you again."

"Do you know something about the check Marilyn Paul has? Look, I'm about to go to court on this. If you know something, I'd like to hear it. Do you?"

Silence. Then. "I might. I really think I might."

Then the caller clicked off. When I tried to call back, no one answered. I called a second time and got an automated message from my cell carrier that the number was not in service.

Chapter 21

THE NEXT MORNING, for the first time in twenty years, Zoe Paul sat in the same room as her father. She went rigid beside me as Chad Einhorn called the man to the stand.

Bradley Paul wore a brand-new suit. So new, he hadn't cut off the white, X-shaped stitching on the vents. Freshly shaved, his long hair was greased back and combed behind his ears. He was awkward, extending a hand to Judge Wentz to shake. The bailiff instructed him into the witness box and swore him in.

"Mr. Paul," Einhorn started. "Can you explain your relationship to the decea ... I'm sorry, the protected individual in this matter?"

"You mean my mom? Oh. Yeah. Yes. Marilyn Paul is my mother. I'm her only son. Her only child."

"Mr. Paul, do you understand why we're here today?"

"Well, sure. I want to make sure everything is being done properly where my mother is concerned."

"Do you have concerns that it isn't?"

Bradley Paul sat straighter in his seat. The entire time he'd taken the stand, he hadn't once looked at Zoe. It mattered. She was strong. Calm. Staring straight at him. But I knew she felt shattered inside.

"I have concerns," Bradley said. "I don't think things are being handled in a way that reflects what my mom would want. I think my daughter is trying to steal things that don't belong to her."

Zoe balled her fists on the table. "Can you object?" she whispered to me.

"Not yet."

"What is the basis for your fears, Mr. Paul? Why do you think that?"

"Can I talk about this paper my daughter filed? The one saying my mom left everything to her?"

"Your Honor, if I may approach. I'd like to refer to the purported will filed by Zoe Paul."

"We're not on trial, Mr. Einhorn. We're not formally entering evidence. Yet."

"All right. Mr. Paul. What is it you'd like to bring to the court's attention about this document?"

Bradley held a copy of Marilyn's will. "She didn't write this. This isn't my mother's signature. And it's not what she wanted."

"What do you base that claim on?"

Bradley put the paper down. "Can I just tell it? Will you let me just explain?"

"By all means," Einhorn said.

"Okay. Look. I'm not gonna sit here and pretend Ma and me were close. We had our differences. Our issues. That's normal for any mother and son. I was wild when I was a kid. My dad was a drunk and a gambler. She was the one paying the bills for a lot of it. When I got old enough, we just kind of went our separate ways. I'll never not be grateful for what she did for me."

"Your Honor," I said. "I'm sorry. I've been patient. But this hearing is about a very narrow issue, not a relitigation of this man's childhood."

"I tend to agree, Mr. Einhorn. Let's stick to the issue at hand. Your client has raised a challenge to the validity of a testamentary document filed in this case. What evidence do you have, Mr. Paul, to support your claim that your mother either didn't write this will, or did so under duress?"

"Your Honor," I said. "Once again, we're not here about a will contest specifically. We're here on Mr. Paul and Mr. Lockwood's petition to modify Marilyn Paul's guardianship."

"Mr. Einhorn?"

"Your Honor," Einhorn said. "The basis for my clients' petition is a pattern of deceit and falsehoods perpetrated by Zoe Paul regarding her grandmother. The validity of this will is part of that. I believe it therefore has direct bearing on our claim."

"All right, I'll allow it. Mr. Paul, you may answer. What is your concern about the validity of this purported will?"

"I'm getting to that," Bradley said. "I just ... I know what she's gonna say." For the first time since he walked into the courtroom, Bradley Paul acknowledged his daughter's presence.

"She's spent her whole life poisoning my mother against me. For a long time, my mom was blind to it. But the point I'm trying to make. She wasn't blind to it before her accident. She told me."

"Told you what?" Einhorn said.

"Before her accident, my mother and me were starting to talk again. She was having trouble with Zoe. Zoe was being disrespectful, not listening, hanging around with people my mother didn't like. Smoking pot. My mom was fed up. She called me and asked me if Zoe could come live with me. She was worried ... she said she knew Zoe was stealing from her. Ten bucks, twenty bucks here and there at first. Then more. My mom kept mad money in her jewelry box. There was like five hundred dollars cash in there. She told me Zoe stole it and bought pot with it. They got in a big fight and my mom said if I didn't come get her, she was gonna kick her out."

"When was this?" Einhorn asked.

"Two weeks before her accident. She called me from work. She was real upset. Crying. So, I'm telling you, there is no way my mother would have signed any document leaving all of her money to Zoe. She was making arrangements to get her out of the house. My mother told me she was afraid of Zoe. That she had to hide valuables in her own house so Zoe wouldn't take them."

"Objection," I said. "Your Honor, at best this is self-serving hearsay. Also, the will filed in this case was executed two years before Mrs. Paul's accident, not two weeks. There's no relevancy whatsoever to this testimony."

"My client is testifying about his mother's state of mind."

"I want to hear what he has to say," the judge said. I was livid. Beside me, Zoe had gone gray.

"Proceed," Judge Wentz said.

"All right," Einhorn said. "But if I can direct your attention to the document itself. Is there anything about it that you'd like to raise as a concern?"

"This isn't my mom's handwriting," Bradley said. "She didn't dot her i's like that. Hers always had a slash instead of an actual dot. And she never spelled out her whole first name. She'd just write the M with a trailing line after it. Then she'd write out Paul. I have documents she signed. You can see the difference."

"Your Honor," Einhorn said. "We have Mrs. Paul's most current driver's license. A copy of her signature card at Delphi Savings Bank when she opened a joint account with her son. Copies of the documents she signed when she was made guardian of Zoe Paul, who was then a minor. And we've also attached several personal notes she left her son including several birthday cards for comparison."

"I'm sorry," I said. "Is Mr. Einhorn claiming that Bradley Paul is now a handwriting expert? He is unqualified to testify as such."

"I'll take all of that under advisement. Ms. Leary? You may question the witness."

"Thank you." I moved to the lectern.

"Mr. Paul," I said. "When was the last time you spoke to your mother?"

"Like I said. Just a couple of weeks before she had her accident."

"How did you communicate with her?"

"What?"

"In person? On the phone?"

"We spoke on the phone."

"Her cell phone?"

"Um ... maybe."

"You're aware Ms. Paul is in possession of your mother's cell phone. So then we would expect to see a record of these calls, wouldn't we?"

"Uh ... I have no idea."

"Sure. I just want to make sure you're aware that it's going to be pretty easy to check whether your mother either received a call or made one to you. You understand that, right? Your lawyer has explained that to you."

"Objection," Einhorn said. "To the extent Ms. Leary is asking for privileged information."

"Sustained."

"You're absolutely certain you spoke to your mother on her cell phone in the two weeks prior to her accident?" I asked.

"Uh. I might have called her at work. Or she called me from work."

"Right," I said. "But you didn't see fit to come back to Delphi after her accident, did you? Even though you claim you were in communication with her as recently as two weeks prior?"

"Well, I mean, I'm here now. This is after her accident."

He thought he was being smart. "I'm talking about the immediate aftermath of your mother's car accident in which she suffered catastrophic, life-threatening injuries. You didn't come to visit her then, did you?"

"No. What would have been the point?"

"The point? You just claimed your mother called you out of the blue with concerns about your daughter. But now you want this court to believe you didn't think it necessary to come back to town after she nearly died in a car accident?"

"My uncle advised me of her condition. We both agreed my mother wouldn't even have known I was here. Plus, I'd just started a new job and I couldn't take the time off."

"You want this court to believe that you are concerned about her care and the handling of her affairs. You weren't concerned sixteen years ago, were you?"

"I didn't think there was anything I could do."

"You didn't call your daughter then, did you?"

"I don't recall."

"You didn't inquire with other family members where your teenage daughter would live after your mother's accident, did you?"

"I don't recall. Plus, she was eighteen. I wasn't legally responsible for her."

"You didn't call the hospital or the nursing care facility to find out the extent of your mother's injuries, did you?"

"I talked to other family members. I talked to my uncle. He's the one who called and told me my mom was hurt. He told me how badly."

"And in the intervening sixteen years, you haven't once visited your mother in the hospital, have you?"

"What's the point? That's not my mom anymore. She's gone. She wouldn't even recognize me."

"How do you know that if you've never bothered to pay her a visit?"

"I told you. I've been in communication with my uncle."

"Your uncle, who also hasn't seen her in at least a decade. Got it. Did you speak to the nurses caring for your mother?" I asked.

"No. I talked to my uncle."

"Did he tell you about the care she was receiving? Her specific treatment? Her prognosis?"

"She's a vegetable," he said. "And she's now dying of cancer."

"Mr. Paul, the will you're questioning, you're aware it was filed with the Probate Court fifteen years ago?"

He shrugged. "My lawyer said ..."

"Objection," Einhorn said. "I just don't want to get into an area where my client is being asked to waive privilege."

"Mr. Paul, you don't have to answer questions about what your lawyer and you discussed," the judge said.

"I'll rephrase," I said. "Mr. Paul, you're holding a copy of the will that was filed in this matter. There's a stamp in the upper right corner from the clerk's office. Can you read the date on it?"

He did.

"That's a file stamp," I said. "It's fifteen years old, isn't it?"

"I guess so. But I'd never seen this before."

"Mr. Paul," I said. "There's no dispute that you're an interested party in this case. I'd like to hand you another document that was filed along with a copy of that will. May I approach?"

Judge Wentz waved me forward. I handed Bradley a document.

"Would you like to read what that says?" I asked.

"It says proof of service," he said. "Then there is a list of documents under it."

"Proof of service upon whom?" I asked.

"Me," he said. "It's got my name on it. But it's listing an address I don't live at anymore."

"What else does it list?" I asked.

"There's a copy of a newspaper clipping."

"Right," I said. "Do you understand that the law only required Ms. Paul to send copies of her filings to your last known address by certified mail? And she was allowed to post a notice of her filings in the newspaper if you couldn't be personally served."

"Well, I didn't see any of this. You asked me why I didn't come forward. That's why."

"You never bothered to reach out to your daughter, your eighteen-year-old daughter, who was being cared for by your mother. You didn't tell your daughter how to get a hold of you after your mother's accident, did you?"

"No."

"You were ordered to pay child support to your mother on behalf of Zoe, weren't you?"

"My mom never wanted that. The court made her do it. That wasn't our agreement."

"But you understand you were under a legal duty to update the Friend of the Court with your current address if you'd moved, isn't that right?"

"I don't know."

"But you didn't."

"I never talked to the court, no."

"No," I said. "You never notified the court or your daughter about where to find you. Not until you became aware that your dying mother might actually have substantial assets herself. Then, you were all too willing to come forward and try to claim it. Isn't that right?"

"I'm not lying," he said. "I didn't want drama. I don't like court. I don't want to be here. But I know my mom wouldn't want Zoe to steal from her again. Since she can't speak for herself, I gotta speak for her."

"Mr. Paul, what was the nature of your mother's injuries stemming from her accident?"

He looked helplessly at Chad Einhorn.

"I don't know. Her head got scrambled."

"What is the name of her primary care doctor?" I asked.

"I don't know."

"What specialists has she seen while she's been at Maple Valley?"

"I don't know."

"What's the annual cost of her medical care? How much does insurance pay?"

"I don't know."

"I see," I said. "And what's the amount that was deposited into her estate account this week?"

"Two million dollars!" he shouted.

"Got it," I said.

"Mr. Paul, the will Ms. Paul filed was written two years prior to your mother's accident, was it not?"

"That's what it says. But I'm saying it wasn't signed by Mom."

"But you're claiming your mother had misgivings about Zoe in the weeks before her accident. You're not claiming there's another will out there reflecting those claimed misgivings, are you?"

"No. I don't know of another will."

"You claim your mother asked you for help with Zoe, your daughter. But you didn't give her any, did you?"

"What?"

"You didn't come to Delphi and pick Zoe up."

"No, ma'am, It wasn't a good time for me."

"You didn't send your mother money for Zoe's support."

"She didn't want that."

"Sure," I said. "You didn't even contact Zoe yourself to get her side of things, did you?"

"No. I believed my mom."

"And until this very day, in this court, you haven't laid eyes on your daughter Zoe in twenty years, isn't that right?"

"I don't know. It's been a long time."

"Thank you," I said. "I have nothing further."

When I walked back to the table, Zoe Paul had finally broken. Silent tears streamed down her face. Her father didn't even look at her as he left the witness box and stormed out of the courtroom.

Chapter 22

JUDGE WENTZ ADJOURNED us until the day after tomorrow. I gathered my things. Zoe hadn't moved. She hadn't spoken. She seemed frozen in place.

"It's going to be all right," I said. "It's just words, Zoe. Your family hasn't produced any real proof of what they're claiming."

"Family? I don't have a family. I have vultures and thieves."

I gave her the most encouraging smile I could. "You have time to grab lunch? Off the clock."

"Sure. I'd like that."

I felt protective of her. In a way, Zoe reminded me of myself. She was doing the best she could under horrible circumstances. Her father wasn't that different from my own. He came around when he thought he could get something from me. As hard a shell as I'd grown over the years, it still hurt. It still triggered all my insecurities when he showed up.

We made it halfway down the hall before all hell broke loose. Bradley Paul stood alone in front of the stairwell we were about to enter. Zoe turned to stone.

"I see you," Bradley said, his voice dripping with contempt. "I know what you're doing and I'm not gonna let you."

"Mr. Paul," I said. "This isn't appropriate. You have an attorney. You speak through him. Zoe's got nothing to say to you right now."

"Well, I've got plenty to say. She's got you snowed too. She poisoned my own mother against me. It's just like I said. That money? You hid it. You waited until Ma's got one foot in the grave to cash it in. You thought you were going to do it without any of us knowing. If I can figure out a way, I'll make sure you end up in jail for it."

Zoe's entire body trembled. Tears she'd been holding back sprang from her eyes. "Why do you hate me so much? I've never done anything to you. You haven't bothered to visit me since I was twelve years old! And before that? You never showed up to a single thing for me. Not a birthday. Not my graduation."

"Zoe," I said. "Let's go. Not here. Don't give him the energy."

It took some doing, but Zoe finally let me drag her into the stairwell. "You have to ignore him," I said. "You cannot let that man have a piece of you. Do you hear me? It's what he wants. Your power is in not showing him he bothers you at all."

"She should have let them put me up for adoption," she said. "I might have had a chance at a normal family."

"It wasn't always like that," I said. "You have to hold on to the good times you had with your grandmother before her accident.

She loved you. She showed up for you. She's your family. The judge is going to see that."

I stopped short of promising her. I wanted to. The truth was, I had no idea what Judge Wentz would do. He was indulging Chad Einhorn far more than I felt proper. I just hoped in the end it would work in our favor if he sided with Zoe. It would cut the legs off any argument for appeal if we won.

"I'm sorry," Zoe said. "I'm going to take a rain check on lunch. I've lost my appetite."

"Okay," I said. "Can I give you a ride home?"

She shook her head. "I'm fine. Really. I can shake it off. I just wanna be alone. Maybe I'll go sit with Grandma later this evening."

"That's a good idea," I said. "You can call me if you need anything."

"How long is the judge going to let this go on?" she asked. I wish I had an answer for her.

"Just hang in there, okay?"

"I wish I'd never found that check. You know, I'd almost rather give it to them to make them go away."

"You know that's what they want," I said. "It's what they're counting on. That you don't have the stamina for this fight."

She nodded. "And they'd make me admit to something that isn't true. Everyone would think I did the things they're accusing me of."

"Maybe. But you can't worry what other people think, Zoe."

She smiled. "That's exactly what my grandma used to tell me."

"It's good advice."

Zoe rushed forward. She hugged me. It caught me off guard for a moment. It occurred to me then, there might not be that many people in her life she felt comfortable hugging.

"Just take care," I said. "We're gonna get through this."

"I know," she said. "And thank you."

I waited as Zoe headed out of the courthouse. I looked both ways to make sure no other Paul family member was trying to follow her. A strong feeling came over me that this might get much worse for Zoe before it got better.

As I headed for the parking lot, my temples began to throb. I pulled out my key fob. I'd almost made it to my car when my phone started to ring. The caller ID was a number and area code I didn't recognize. I would have ignored it. But I had a suspicion who it might be.

I slipped behind the wheel and answered. "This is Cass Leary."

For a moment, I heard nothing but static silence. Then, "Don't hang up."

"I'm not hanging up. To whom am I speaking?"

I realized then, I recognized the voice. This was the caller from earlier. The one with the cryptic warnings about Marilyn Paul.

"They're going to come after you," she said.

"Who?"

Nothing. Dead silence.

"Listen. If you know something relevant about the case I'm working on, please enlighten me. At the moment, I'm assuming this is a prank. I don't have time for it."

"I warned her, okay?"

"Warned who?"

"Marilyn. I told her this wasn't going to end well for her. She wouldn't listen. So, you have to. I don't want anything bad to happen to Zoe. I couldn't live with myself."

"Is she in danger? Where are you? Let's meet. You can come to my office; I'm headed there now if you're close by."

"No! No. I can't do that. I can never do that. I can't be seen with you."

This conversation was doing nothing for my headache.

"Listen, if you know something about what happened to Marilyn, or her court case, now's the time to come forward."

"I can't." The caller started crying. "I wish I could. I wish I'd done more to stop her sixteen years ago. She wouldn't listen. She thought she had it all figured out."

"Zoe?"

"Marilyn," she said.

I sat back. "She was your friend. Or ... you tried to be a friend to her, is that it?"

"Yes. Oh. Yes. I'm so sorry for what happened."

"Ma'am, was there something about Marilyn's accident I should know about? Is that what this is about?"

"No. God. I don't know. I wasn't there."

"You obviously want to tell me something very badly. So, say it. I can't help you. I can't help Zoe if I don't know the whole truth. Do you know where Marilyn got those two million dollars?"

Silence. Heavy breathing.

"Ma'am?"

Her next words came out in a burst. "You have to ask yourself, where would Zoe's dad get the money to pay for a lawyer like that? That new suit. Fresh haircut."

She rambled. Then something dawned on me. New suit. She was here. Close by. Close enough to have seen Bradley Paul in his suit so new he hadn't cut the stitching on it.

"Marilyn never talked to her son before her accident, did she?" I asked.

"He's a liar. She never would have called him like that. She never would have gone to Bradley if she were having trouble with Zoe."

Never would have called him. My God. This woman was very close. She'd been in the courtroom during Bradley's testimony. I wished I could remember the faces of who had been sitting in the gallery behind me. It had been a fairly packed courtroom with two hearings coming in right after ours.

"Where are you?" I asked. I looked around the parking lot. Tried to see inside the other vehicles.

No answer.

"You said I should ask myself how Marilyn's family could afford to hire Chad Einhorn. Is that your advice? Are you actually telling me I should follow the money? This isn't some spy novel.

These are real lives. Zoe's life. Marilyn's. If you were a friend to her. If you still care about Zoe ..."

"I do care. That's why you're hearing from me in the first place. Look. I've heard about you. I know you're good. I was glad when I heard Zoe hired you. You can help her better than I can now."

"Listen to me," I said. "You know what's happening in that courtroom. You know I'm dealing with a rogue judge who seems determined to let Chad Einhorn and Zoe's family do and say whatever they want in there. I'll be honest, this case isn't exactly a slam dunk for me. If they throw out Marilyn's will, Zoe will get nothing. Not if her father is still alive."

"Maybe that's for the best," she said, her voice trailing off. "I don't even know anymore. Zoe shouldn't have touched that money. It's cursed. That's all I can say."

"What's your name? How do you know all these things? Give me something. Anything. You obviously want me to figure out where those funds came from. You've hinted at blackmail. Am I on the right track?"

"I can't do this. It was a mistake ..."

"It's not a mistake. That girl is all alone. She has nobody. She's been on her own trying to hold things together since she was a kid. Now people are saying she's a liar and a thief. They're trying to destroy her. Marilyn might as well be gone. Whatever secret she was trying to hide, it doesn't matter anymore. She can't hurt anyone. She can't tell her story."

"There's just ... they're out there, okay? You have no idea what kind of hornets' nest Zoe has kicked over."

"So, tell me ..."

Three beeps told me she'd ended the call. I stared at my phone.

It could be a prank. It probably was. She was just some kook who'd followed the case in the newspaper and showed up in court today. It made more sense. Only ... I knew in my gut that wasn't it.

I pulled out of the parking lot and headed to my office. I was flying blind here. And I had the nagging feeling that money would come back to haunt Zoe Paul. Even if we won, she would lose.

Chapter 23

"On paper, nothing's raising any red flags." Jeanie sat across from me, rifling through the file I'd just placed on my desk.

"Graduated from Notre Dame Law School. He's got a wife who's a psychologist specializing in PTSD. She was a soldier. Looks like he inherited his practice from his daddy after spending some time as a CPA."

She flipped to a picture of Chad Einhorn from the Oakland County Bar Directory.

"But what's he doing in Woodbridge County Probate Court then?" I asked.

Jeanie shrugged and sat back.

"My mystery caller was adamant that Einhorn's bill was being footed by somebody else."

"But nothing more concrete than that?"

"Nope. She wouldn't even give me her theory on where Marilyn's millions came from."

"I still think she was screwing somebody that could afford to pay to keep her quiet."

I stared at Einhorn's picture. He smiled up at me with big, white, teeth.

"Maybe," I said absently. "But why a cashier's check? Why not cash? Why leave a paper trail at all?"

"I think that's not your problem," Jeanie said. Just then, Miranda poked her head in.

"Your eleven o'clock is here. Want me to send him up?"

"My eleven o'clock?" I said. "Since when did I have an eleven o'clock?"

"Whoops. That's on me," Jeanie said. "I finally tracked down Hal Dolenz, Marilyn's ex-boyfriend. He dodged my calls for three weeks then finally agreed to come in. I thought that name sounded familiar. Turns out he went to high school with me too."

"Good," I said. "Then you're sitting in."

She rose and took a chair in my sitting area in the corner of the office. A moment later, Miranda walked in with Dolenz.

He had a kind, unassuming face and held a Tigers baseball cap in his hands. The man was in his late seventies with wispy white hair, dented at the sides most likely on account of the hat he held. He wore a tan windbreaker and shuffled a bit when he walked. What he did not look like was a man with two million dollars to give away.

"Thanks for coming in," Jeanie said. "This is my partner, Cass Leary. She's handling Marilyn's estate."

"Good to meet you," Dolenz said. "And good to see you again, Jeanie. Boy, you sure held up good."

Flirting. The man was flirting with her. Jeanie plastered on a smile, but I could tell by her eyes she wasn't amused. Dolenz helped himself to a wing-backed chair in the corner.

"You mind?" he said, pulling a cigar out of his pocket. Before I could answer, he put it in his mouth. "I don't light 'em anymore."

"By all means," I said, taking a seat next to Jeanie.

"So how is she?" Dolenz asked. "You're taking care of Marilyn?"

"Well, more her granddaughter, Zoe. I represent her in an estate matter. She's had some trouble with Marilyn's son and brother."

Dolenz took the cigar out of his mouth and pointed it at me. "They're scum. Both of 'em. Never did anything for Marilyn but cause trouble."

"That's the general gist, yes. I'm actually trying to get a clearer picture of what was going on in Marilyn's life in the weeks or months before her accident. Would you mind telling me how you met her? What was your relationship like in those final weeks?"

Dolenz looked at the chewed end of his cigar, then pocketed it.

"We were on and off. Mostly off that summer."

"How did you meet?" I asked.

"It was a social group. For the recently divorced. There was this outing we had at the American Legion. Karaoke night. She had some pipes. Zoe ever tell you that?"

"No." I smiled.

"Oh, she did 'Proud Mary' like nobody's business. My buddy Ron used to DJ. She dated him for a while. He was half a drunk though. But me and her ... we hit it off. Ron didn't seem to mind so one night I asked her out. That was more than twenty years ago now. Man. I hadn't thought about that until just now. Anyway, we were pretty serious for a while. I wanted her to move in with me. But she had Zoe. She was funny about that. Never invited me over to her place cuz the kid was there. Which ... I mean ... I get it. She was protective."

"Were you exclusive?" Jeanie asked.

Dolenz fingered the lettering on his baseball cap. "For a while we were. Maybe a year. But then ... no. Back then, I thought maybe I wanted to get married again. Marilyn wasn't interested. So, we'd go our separate ways. Then we'd end up back together again. That went on for three or four years."

"Were you aware whether she was seeing anyone else?" I asked.

Dolenz took a deep, nostril-flaring breath. "Yeah. Marilyn was getting around. That's what I heard anyway."

"From whom?" I asked.

"It's not that big a town. And in our age group, well, it's not like there was a huge dating pool. I heard Marilyn was seeing some guy at work. Her boss maybe."

"Tim Valentine?" Jeanie said. "Or could it have been his brother Tony?"

"I think Tim," he said. "And I don't know it for a fact. It was just something I heard second-hand. Hearsay. You know. I warned her that was gonna lead to trouble. You don't shit where you eat, you know?"

I winced at the reference but took his point.

"Tim Valentine was married," Jeanie said. "So was Tony, for that matter."

Dolenz stopped maintaining eye contact. He looked out the window.

"Did she do that often?" I asked. "Get entangled with married men?"

"I don't know. One or two maybe. Marilyn was a catch, you know? Most women her age, they don't keep themselves up like she did. She wore nice clothes. Got herself a gym membership and worked out. She had a lot of guys buzzing after her. Plus … for most of them, it was a selling point that she wasn't interested in tying the knot anymore. That's where I screwed up. I put some pressure on her. I was stupid. Wanting to get married again. Dodged a bullet there."

"Mr. Dolenz," I said. "What about the last few weeks before Marilyn's accident? How did she seem to you? Were things okay at home, with work, with Zoe?"

"She never really talked about that stuff. Never complained about the kid as far as I remember. Though I know she felt guilty for spending money on herself. She tried to get me to join that gym. But the money, she was always, you know, beating herself up for not using it for the kid's education or something. But I told her … Mar, you gotta do something for yourself. You raised your kid. You're putting a roof over Zoe's head. And it's not like twenty-five bucks a month was gonna be enough to put that kid through college. Not in those days. Not today. Only … I don't know. It didn't seem to make her happy."

"In what way? What makes you say that?" I asked.

"She was always thinking something bad was gonna happen. Woe is me. You know. Everything in her mind was always worse for her than anybody else. Know what I mean?"

"What was worse?"

"Her old man was a bastard. But she got rid of him. She got free of it. She loved Zoe, but raising another kid at her age, well, it wasn't what she had mapped out for herself. And she was always comparing herself to other people. Always thinking the grass was greener, you know? So ... she was a looker. A catch in that way. But ... Marilyn was a lot. She had her baggage. And she was paranoid."

"Was there anything specific she was afraid of?" I asked.

"She just second-guessed everything. We could barely make it on time to anything because of how much she fussed with what she looked like. And I swear, she started dating married guys because her old man cheated on her. Like she never wanted to be the one being cheated on again. She was always on me about that. Who was I friends with? Was I talking to my ex-wife? Just ... paranoid. I couldn't take it after a while. Maybe a month or two before her accident, it came to a head. I told her I needed a break. By that point, I'd asked her to marry me maybe three different times. I gave her an ultimatum with the last one. I wanted her to choose. I knew she was seeing somebody else. She wouldn't say who, but people were kind of talking. Giving me looks, you know?"

"Did you ever ask her who she was seeing?" I asked.

Dolenz shook his head. "I didn't wanna know. I mean, I did ... but I didn't. Marilyn was at least honest with me. We weren't exclusive. I wanted to be. But we weren't."

"This paranoia, was it confined to men?"

"No. That's the thing. The last few times we went out, she wouldn't leave the house. She just wanted to stay at my place. Watch movies. That wasn't like her at all. Marilyn was a party girl. Liked to be the center of attention. She wasn't a homebody. But that last summer, I couldn't get her to go anywhere. It was like she was turning agoraphobic or something. It was really kind of the last straw for me. I couldn't get her to snap out of it. So ... I suggested we take a break. I thought absence would make her heart grow fonder, you know? Maybe it would have. But then ... I got a call from her neighbor, Frieda Jones. About Marilyn's accident."

Dolenz hung his head. Tears fell silently down his cheeks. "That was it," he said. "It was over. She was just ... gone. Worse than gone. I went to visit her a couple of times at the hospital. But when they said she was probably never gonna be Marilyn again ... I just couldn't ... there was nothing I could do for her."

"That must have been very difficult for you," Jeanie said, but there was an edge to her tone I don't think Dolenz picked up on.

"What about Zoe?" I asked.

"She was being cared for," Dolenz said. "I knew Frieda was looking out for her. Making sure she could stay in the house. All that. We weren't married. We weren't even together at the time this all went down. It broke me up pretty bad though, just the same. It was all just a waste. A damn waste. I know it's awful to say, but I've always thought it might have been better if Marilyn had just passed away when it happened. To live like she is. God. She'd hate it. You gotta understand. This woman was vain. She cared what she looked like. What she dressed like. To see her how she is now. It just tears me up."

"Mr. Dolenz," I said. "This is public record now. But you're aware that her granddaughter found a large sum of money in the house recently. Do you have any idea where Marilyn might have got it?"

"I don't know. That's the truth. I just know that it doesn't surprise me that Marilyn hid money like that. I told you; she was acting kooky in those last few months. Scared to death of what, I don't know. Whatever it was ... it's to do with that. Maybe she wasn't in her right mind even before she hit that tree. I don't know. But this? I can't talk about it anymore. I'm sorry. It's all just too sad."

"Well, I appreciate your candor. But you're sure Marilyn never spoke to you about this money?"

"No, ma'am. Nothing. Not a word. It makes me think maybe I didn't know her as well as I thought I did if she was keeping something like that from me. I'm sorry I can't be more help. I really do hope things work out for her grandkid. I know Marilyn was crazy about her."

"Thank you," I said. "You've been helpful."

He got up, slid his cigar back in his mouth. Then before I could even give him my card, Hal Dolenz showed himself out and hurried down the stairs, practically knocking Miranda over as he passed her.

"Well, that was ... interesting," Jeanie said. "A real prince, that one."

"I don't know," I said. "He just seems ... sad."

Miranda came into the room. Tears spilled down her face.

"Are you okay?" I said, rising. "Did he hit you harder than I realized? Did something else happen?" In the week since Miranda's car was vandalized, she'd been jumpier than usual and hadn't yet left Jeanie's place.

Miranda shook her head. "No. Oh no. It's good, Cass. It's wonderful. I just got off the phone with Matty. He didn't want me to interrupt your meeting. But he just got word. Tori's being discharged tomorrow morning. Guys ... our girl is coming home!"

Miranda threw herself at me. I got my arms up just in time to fold her into an embrace.

Chapter 24

IT WAS HARD NOT to step in. Not to take control. Not to try and fix it. To breathe. But I stood in the corridor, watching my baby brother wait patiently while the mother of his child accomplished the simple task of closing her own suitcase and sliding it off the bed.

A nurse waited beside me, her hands firmly planted on the handles of the wheelchair that would take Tori to the lobby and out the door. The first time she'd left this place and got into a car in four months.

Four months. Since that awful night when the car I was supposed to be driving ended up in a ditch and changed all our lives forever.

"I've got it," Tori said. And she did. Her movements were slow, deliberate. She would forget a word here and there. Or replace one where it didn't belong. Little by little though, she came back to us. And now she was coming home for good.

My phone buzzed with a text from Vangie. She'd stayed behind at Matty and Tori's place, watching baby Sean. Matty had dutifully brought him to see his mother every day for the last six weeks since he'd been discharged from the hospital too.

"We're almost out," I texted her.

"Seanie's asleep," she texted back. "He'll be hungry by the time they get here."

Perfect, I thought. Simple. Tori could sit in the fancy recliner I'd bought for her and feed her son. Hold him. Be the mother that he needed.

Matty held an arm out for Tori. She smiled but waved him off. "I've got this," she said. "I've been practicing for weeks."

She'd been so frail. Thin to begin with, Tori had dropped below ninety pounds at one point. She'd put some weight back on, but her legs looked like two sticks to me. The spandex leggings she wore hung off her.

Little by little, I thought. But today she was coming home.

"It's going to be a little bit yet," the nurse said. "We're just waiting on your final discharge paperwork. But if you'd like to hang out in the lounge off the lobby, you'll have the room to yourselves. It's a nice day. The geese are out."

"That sounds perfect," Tori said. "Cass, you don't have to wait. I feel bad this is taking so long."

"There's no place I'd rather be. Let me just text Joe. He and Emma are bringing dinner over to the house. I've managed to keep it just family. Jeanie and Miranda want to swing by tomorrow if you feel up to it."

"Jeanie and Miranda are family too," she said. "But that's nice. I miss them."

"Jeanie's assigned herself the role of surrogate Nana," Matty said. "Did she tell you she's trying to knit Sean a hat?"

"She didn't," I said. "Jeanie? Knitting? She's more likely to stab someone with her needles."

"Don't make me laugh," Tori said. "Oh. It's perfect. I can't wait to see her creation."

Tori gave the nurse a hard look. She clearly didn't want to bother with the wheelchair. Until she was off Maple Valley grounds, it was a nonstarter. So, she took her seat in the chair.

"I've got this," Matty said, taking the wheelchair handles from her.

"All right," the nurse said. "But no wheelies. And just to the lounge. I'll see if I can speed your paperwork along."

I waited, falling into step behind Matty as he wheeled Tori down the hall. I picked up her suitcase.

"You sure this is okay?" Matty asked. "Tori's right. I didn't think this was going to take this long."

"This kind of stuff always takes forever," I said. "And yes. It's more than okay."

As we made our way down the hall, something pulled my attention to the stairwell down the hall. Marilyn Paul was one floor up. As I looked that way, I saw Zoe headed for the stairs, holding a cup of coffee.

"Actually," I said. "Is it okay if I just meet you down there? Text me when you've got the green light to escape. I'll pull the car around."

"Yes!" Tori answered for Matty. "Go! Talk to Zoe."

With everything she was dealing with, Tori didn't miss a trick. As much as she was ready to be a full-time mother to Sean, I knew she was eager to get back to work too. Whatever it took, I intended to let her.

I hooked Tori's bag over Matty's shoulder and headed for the stairwell. Zoe was just entering her room as I got up there.

"Cass!" she said, surprised to see me. Marilyn was sitting up in bed, staring out the window. It had only been a couple of weeks since I last saw her, but they had taken a toll. She was hooked up to an IV and her eyes looked sunken in, her cheeks hollow. I thought of everything Hal Dolenz had said. Marilyn had been vain. She had been beautiful. Now, her body had finally betrayed her.

"She just finished a round of chemo," Zoe explained. "It left her pretty dehydrated. They're trying to push fluids. She was vomiting all last night."

"God. I'm so sorry."

Zoe put her coffee down. It was then I noticed a small black box on the bedside table. Zoe went to it and pulled out a jeweled DVD case. Using the remote, she turned on the television bolted to the wall. "I thought maybe some of these would cheer her up," she said. "I brought them from the house."

"Your home movies," I said, going to the box. "Zoe, that's a great idea."

"I feel bad for not thinking of it sooner."

Zoe popped the DVD into the player at the bottom of the set. It played automatically, showing first grainy static. Then the picture stabilized. The date on the bottom was twenty-five years ago. A young Zoe with buck teeth and long hair waved at the screen.

Zoe. She would have been nine years old. She wore a pink-and-green bathing suit and held a melting ice cream cone in one hand, a small toad in the other.

"Don't mix those up," a female voice said off screen.

Young Zoe stuck out her tongue. "If I kiss the frog, maybe he'll turn into a prince."

The woman holding the camera laughed. "If that works, find me some more of those toads, kiddo. I could use a prince. All I seem to find are frogs."

"Gram, you're so weird," nine-year-old Zoe shot back.

"She's funny," I said, taking a seat in the corner of the room.

"She had a dry sense of humor," Zoe agreed. "She never talked to me like I was a kid. I was never around other kids much."

"I can relate to that," I said.

Zoe got quiet. Then, she turned to me. "They said we're getting close to the point where I'll have to decide how much more treatment she can take."

"What do you mean?" I asked.

"The chemo hasn't been working. And it's making her so sick. Just look at her. The doctor didn't come out and say it, but it may be time to stop."

"Oh Zoe, I'm so sorry."

"I know what they're going to say," Zoe said. "My uncle. My dad. They're going to tell that judge I want her to die."

"Zoe, you can't think that way. You have to think about what you feel is in your grandmother's best interests. And what she'd want if she could decide for herself."

"I just don't think I can watch her suffer like this anymore. She doesn't understand. She fights the needles. The nurse told me when they took her down for her treatments this last time, she just started sobbing."

"You've been put in an impossible position. But you need to know ... whatever you decide is best for Marilyn, I've got your back. You let me worry about the judge."

We watched as Zoe's younger version mugged for the camera, held her toad out, and wiggled her butt. She squealed as the little toad finally relieved himself down her arm.

"Told ya," Video-Marilyn said. "Now go wash your hands."

The video switched to a different event. A birthday party. Young Zoe ran around with a bubble wand, chased by three other little kids about her age. Marilyn wasn't the one filming this time. She sat in a plastic chair, smoking a cigarette. She was tanned, toned, her blonde hair pulled back in a neat ponytail, the front sky-high in a bump popular during the era.

"Who's that standing behind her?" I asked. There was a man rubbing Marilyn's shoulders. I tried to do the timeline math. This would have predated her off-and-on-again phase with Hal Dolenz.

"You know, I'm not sure," Zoe said, moving closer to the screen. "That wasn't my party. We were over at Frieda's. Her granddaughter was a year or two older than me. She lived in Phoenix and Frieda would have a second birthday party for her sometimes if she was in town. I remember her being a real bully. Stuck-up. She used to make fun of my clothes."

"The man though," I said. "Is that someone your grandmother was dating?"

Marilyn reached up and touched his arm. She said something to him and jerked her chin in the direction of the camera. The man looked that way then quickly moved away from Marilyn's chair as if he hadn't wanted to be recorded.

"Huh," Zoe said. She turned to her grandmother in the bed. Marilyn's eyes were open. She seemed transfixed by the images on the screen.

"Do you remember that day, Gram?" Zoe asked. "Gracie had a SpongeBob cake. Frieda made it. She was always good with cakes. She made me a ballerina one when I turned seven. Buttercream frosting. She put a full-size Barbie Doll on it. At the time I thought it was the most glorious thing."

Marilyn tilted her head to the side. Whoever was holding the camera had zoomed in on her face. Video-Marilyn stuck her tongue out and laughed. The man in question had moved off into the shadows.

"Was he your boyfriend?" Zoe asked. "I don't remember that one."

The scene changed. It was Christmastime. Marilyn recorded Zoe opening her presents in front of a tall, skinny tree in the living room.

"What do you want to watch, Gram?" Zoe asked. She sat on the edge of Marilyn's bed and flipped through the DVD collection. "This one's from our trip to Florida. We stayed on the Gulf side with some friends of Grandma's. The Littletons. I remember thinking it was boring except for the beach. I wanted to go to Disney thinking it had to be close by because it was in Florida too. Oh. Or here's you with some of your friends. Let's try that."

Zoe switched the discs. After a moment, a new scene popped up. It looked like a New Year's Eve party. All adults. Someone shot Marilyn in profile as she stood in front of the roulette wheel.

"She was stunning," I commented. Marilyn wore a green, sequined dress that hugged her curves. Her hair was piled high, revealing elaborate rhinestone earrings. She was laughing, holding a cocktail.

"Remember that, Gram?" Zoe asked. "I think this was the New Year's before her accident. It was one of the only vacations I remember her taking by herself."

Five months before someone had written Marilyn Paul a check for two million dollars. I found myself trying to find clues in the footage. I recognized none of the people she was with.

"That's Holly Billings," Zoe explained. A woman wearing a long black dress came into view. "She worked with Gram at Valentine. And that's Jean Francis. She worked there too. This was in Atlantic City. She went for this three-day weekend with work people. Oh, she was so excited to go. I remember that. But she was worried. Afraid to leave me home by myself."

"You were eighteen," I said. "This was your senior year in high school."

"Yeah. I think so. She was worried I was going to throw a rave at the house or something. I gotta be honest. I probably thought about it."

Marilyn sat up straighter in her bed. Her eyes darted across the screen. She opened and closed her mouth.

"Do you remember that, Gram?" Zoe asked. "Holly still asks about you. She called me a few weeks ago. She wanted to come and see you. Would you like that?"

Marilyn grabbed the sheet covering her legs and balled it in her fists.

"She seems upset," I said.

"Oh geez," Zoe said. "Gram?"

Marilyn made a noise, a strangled cry. I watched the screen. Her younger self stood beside Holly Billings and another woman. I recognized her as Eileen Maguire, the payroll clerk from Valentine Pizza who I'd met in Saline. The three of them stuck their legs out for the camera. Marilyn laughed.

"No!" Marilyn yelled from the bed. "No. No. No!"

"What is it?" Zoe said. "Grandma. Do you want me to turn it off?"

Marilyn threw her head back and howled. The sound cut through me. It was so loud, one of the nurses came running. Marilyn thrashed on the bed, pulling at the IV in her arm.

"What the devil?" the nurse said.

"Maybe turn it off," I said. Zoe fumbled with the remote control.

"What happened?" the nurse asked. She tried to hold Marilyn down. Another nurse rushed in. He ran to Marilyn's side and held her while the first nurse fiddled with Marilyn's IV and shut the alarms off her monitor.

Zoe shut off the player.

"We're going to have to give her something to calm her down," the nurse said.

"I'm sorry," Zoe said, tears beginning to fall. "I'm so sorry. I thought she might like to watch. I didn't mean ..."

Zoe backed away. She knocked over the case of DVDs from the table. Marilyn's eyes went wide. Then she fell back against the bed as the nurse got her sedative on board.

My phone went off. A text from Matty. Tori's discharge paperwork went through.

I gathered the DVD cases that had fallen to the ground and hastily stuffed them back into the black box.

"Just take them," Zoe said. "Get them out of here. I'm so sorry. I didn't mean to upset her."

"It's not your fault, hon," the nurse said. "These things just happen sometimes. It's okay."

Zoe and I walked out into the hall together. I stuffed the DVD holder into my purse.

"Are you okay?" I asked. "Can I call someone for you?"

Zoe shook her head, and I realized my mistake. There was no one to call. There was never anyone to call for her. My brother and Tori were down in the lobby waiting for me. I would take them home to a houseful of people. Family would surround them for as long as they needed. And we would wait at the ready if they told us they wanted to be alone.

But for Zoe Paul, all she had was Marilyn. She would go home to an empty house. And soon enough, she wouldn't even have her grandmother at all.

"It's okay," Zoe said, as if she could read my mind. "Really. I'm used to this. I'll be all right."

Guilt washed over me as I left her there. "I'll call you tomorrow," I said.

Zoe nodded. She straightened her back as she waved goodbye. She was so young. She had always been so young. But I knew that woman had a spine made of steel.

Chapter 25

"You sure this is a good idea?"

"No," I said. Jeanie stood next to me on the narrow porch. We'd knocked three times, heard movement inside the house, but as yet, no one had come to the door. I couldn't shake the things Hal Dolenz said about Marilyn Paul's paranoia in her last few months before the accident. So, I decided it was time to talk to someone who'd been there.

"Mr. Wallace," Jeanie yelled. "We're not from the utility company, okay?"

"You're lawyers," a crackled male voice yelled from inside. "You wanna deny it?"

Jeanie and I looked at each other. I'd dressed casually in a pair of black pants and a sleeveless blouse. Jeanie had her standard summer uniform on. White linen pants and a blue fitted tee shirt. We looked about as non-lawyery as we knew how to.

"How can you tell?" Jeanie asked, smiling.

"I know the look," the man said.

"Well, we're not here for any reason that'll get you in trouble or cost you money," I said.

He cracked the screen door open. A pair of beady, dark eyes stared up at me.

"I'm Cass Leary," I said. "I just want to ask you some questions about an accident you witnessed sixteen years ago. Marilyn Paul. Her granddaughter is a client of mine?"

He swung the door open with such force, it startled me.

"She's got money," he said. "I read about it. Found a pot of gold under the floorboards or something?"

"Or something," I said. "Do you have fifteen minutes for me?"

"Depends," he said. "I want a witness fee."

"I don't think I'm gonna need you in court, Mr. Wallace. This is more to satisfy my own curiosity on something."

"Hmm," he said. "I'll take five hundred dollars."

"Yeah. Not gonna happen. I can subpoena you for a deposition if I want. That's a court order."

"You saying my time isn't as valuable as yours? Cuz I already told the cops whatever they wanted to know about that accident sixteen years ago. You can read my report for free."

"True," I said. "But the cops were trying to rule out any criminal behavior."

"Talked to an insurance adjuster too. A couple of them. Suppose there's a report somewhere for that," he said.

"Also true. But the adjuster was interested in establishing liability. I'm not interested in either of those things. I just want to ask you some follow-up questions to what you said to the cops and the adjuster."

"Fine, then my follow-up fee is five hundred."

"I'll give you fifty bucks," I said.

Gus Wallace squinted at me.

"A hundred," he said.

I reached into my bag. "Seventy-five. Final offer." I held the cash out.

Wallace grumbled, came out onto the porch and snatched the money from my hand. He took a seat on a rickety folding chair in the corner of the porch and pointed Jeanie and me to two wooden Adirondack chairs with chipped, blue paint.

"Fifteen minutes," he said.

"Thank you," I said. I pulled out a copy of Gus's statement to the police. There wasn't much to it. I handed it to him.

"I read what you told them," I said. "Can you just, in your own words, tell me what you remember about that accident?"

He spent a moment looking at the report, then folded it.

"Wasn't much to tell. I was driving home from work. Stopped at Lowell and Coventry roads. There's a light there now but at the time it was a four-way stop. Anyway, this lady driving a red Accord turned left at the stop sign so she was in front of me after I went through. I remember reading her license plate. It was GRAMS7. I remember that. Anyhoo. I wanted to pass her cuz she was driving kinda slow at first. A lot of people do. It's fifty there. People drive like it's thirty-five. But it's a no passing zone there until after you get past the curve near Salisbury Road. Well, she started speeding up. So, then it was okay."

"How fast were you going?" Jeanie asked.

"Fifty-five, fifty-six. I mean, I'll push it a little. But not so much so I risk a ticket. That's a speed trap over there. Anyway, right after the curve there's that house with that mailbox that looks like a Detroit Lions helmet. This stupid fat squirrel darted out into the road."

"How could you see the squirrel if Mrs. Paul was driving in front of you?"

"She was at the curve ahead of me. So, she wasn't directly in front of me at that point. The damn squirrel came out into the road and did that thing they do. You know, dart left then right, like they can't decide. She hit her brakes, but she took that curve a little too fast. You really shouldn't be going more than twenty-five there. She hit her brakes so hard she skidded. Lost control and hit that big oak tree right past the mailboxes. Shocked the hell outta me. That stupid squirrel just sat there. She didn't hit it. She hit a damn tree and wrecked her own life instead. Can you believe that?"

"What did you do?" I asked.

"Well, I pulled over. I saw her airbags go. I mean, she wasn't going that fast. Forty doesn't seem like that fast. But she hit that tree head-on at that speed. And that little car of hers. If she'd have been driving something more substantial, maybe it would have made a difference. Anyway, I put my hazards on and went running to her. The sound of the crash was loud. Guy who owns the Lions mailbox came running out of his house too."

"How long had you been following Mrs. Paul before the crash?" I asked.

"Like I said. Just from the Lowell and Coventry intersection to the curve past Salisbury. What is that? Two miles? Three?"

"Do you remember seeing any other cars? Any that passed you in either direction?"

"Not that I recall. That's not a super busy road. It's kinda my secret back way from the plant. I like to avoid the highway. Especially if we've got weather. Not that there was any that afternoon. It was still sunny. Seventy degrees and sunny. We hadn't even had any rain in a few days. The woman just slammed on her brakes coming out of that curve going faster than she should. If that squirrel hadn't stopped in the road like that. If she'd gone just a few feet further, she'd have avoided that tree altogether and just wound up in the ditch. I don't think she would have gotten hurt so badly."

"Dumb luck," Jeanie said.

"Dumb luck and bad driving. These crazy animal people. Putting your own life at risk. My life at risk if I hadn't kept enough of a distance between her and me. Or hell, if that guy had been out in front of his mailbox. Just ... dumb luck and bad decisions."

"Was Mrs. Paul conscious when you got to her vehicle?"

"She was moaning something awful. She had a huge gash on her forehead. Blood everywhere. I gotta be honest, I couldn't believe she was still alive the way her front end got smashed. Folded up just like an accordion. I told her to just stay calm. Try not to move. That help was coming. I called 911 on my cell. The guy from that house. Found out later his name was Joel. We're acquaintances now. I see him every once in a while, at the grocery store or wherever. We'll stop and say hello. It's a weird thing to know somebody over though."

"I'll bet," I said. "You said Marilyn was moaning. Did she ever say anything?"

"Nope. Not anything we could understand. I had Joel stay with her while I got the dispatcher on the phone. They got there pretty quick. I wanna say within five minutes. It just seemed like it took forever to get her out of that car. They had to use the jaws of life. I stayed for a while. Gave my statement to the cops. For the longest time, I avoided that stretch of road. Joel ended up cutting that tree down. It was a beautiful, two-hundred-year-old oak. But people came out there and put one of those crosses and flowers on it. And look, that's nice and all. But it wasn't their property. Joel told me once it wasn't even Mrs. Paul's family or friends that did it. Just some random do-gooder. Anyway, Joel cut the tree down because he said it felt like it was haunted or cursed after that."

"I can see how that would be tough to keep looking at," Jeanie said.

"Mr. Wallace," I said. "You're sure you never saw anyone else on that stretch of road before the accident?"

"No, ma'am. It was just me and that poor lady. I mean, some cars passed after the fact. Coming and going. They did what people do. Rubber-necked. That was at first. But the cops closed off that stretch of road pretty quick. Man, I've never been so shook up in my life. I thought she was dead when they finally pulled her out. She looked it. All white and waxen. They asked me all kinds of questions. Whether I smelled booze on her breath or anything."

"She hadn't been drinking," I said. "They determined that at the hospital."

"Yeah. It was just one of those fluke things. And a dose of stupidity. I'm sorry. I suppose it's not nice to say that. But honestly. To put your own life at risk over a damn squirrel? I could see a deer because they could screw up your car. Or even a dog maybe. But that woman just slammed on her brakes hard. Like a dead stop. And that was all she wrote."

I pulled out my business card and handed it to him. "I appreciate your time. I know it's been so long. But if there's anything else you can think of about that day and Mrs. Paul."

"Like what?"

"I don't know. Has anyone else ever asked you about it like I am? I mean, besides the cops and that insurance adjuster?"

"There were two of 'em," Wallace said. "Two insurance adjusters."

"That's odd," Jeanie said just as I was thinking it.

"I filled out paperwork for the first one. The second one showed up asking all sorts of stuff about her car and the condition of her body. That made me really mad. It was morbid."

"What about the condition of her body?" I asked. "That does seem odd."

"Yeah. Anyway, that's all I remember. And that's all seventy-five bucks is gonna get you of my time. I've got things to do."

"Mr. Wallace," Jeanie said. "If we paid you another hundred, would it improve your memory for details?"

Wallace frowned. "I don't exactly like your tone. I told you what I remember. And I'm getting real sick of you people coming out here and asking. I told that adjuster last week the same thing."

Jeanie and I looked at each other. "I'm sorry. Last week?"

"Yes. Big guy. Dark glasses. He's asking me all kinds of sick questions about how much blood there was. If I remember if anything got thrown out of her car. Guy came short of accusing me of stealing something off her like some vulture."

"Let me get this straight," I said. "You're telling me the second adjuster you spoke to called you last week?"

"That's what I said, yeah."

Jeanie and I exchanged a look.

"Did this man leave a card or a number?" I asked. The description Wallace gave didn't sound like Chad Einhorn. Plus, I couldn't fathom what purpose Einhorn would have in bothering Gus Wallace.

"No," Wallace said. He rose and went to his front door.

"Can you be more specific about what he looked like?" I asked.

"A meathead," Wallace said. "Bald. Maybe late sixties. Cheap suit. Ugly black shoes. Smelled awful too. That skunky pot-smoke smell. Made my eyes water."

"Did he leave his name?"

"No," Wallace said.

"How much cash did *he* give you?" Jeanie said, her tone flat.

Wallace's eyes darted back and forth. "None of your business."

"Was it more than seventy-five?" I asked.

Wallace scowled at me. Then he went inside and slammed the door in our faces.

Chapter 26

THE FOLLOWING MORNING, I stood in front of Judge Wentz for what I thought would be our final hearing on Bradley Paul and Roy Lockwood's petition against Zoe. Chad Einhorn had other plans.

"Your Honor," he said. "The petitioners call Jason Mackin to the stand."

"Your Honor," I said. "I've been given no notice of this witness. No chance to depose him. No motions were filed on behalf of the petitioners to allow his testimony and for what purpose."

"I'm asking now, Your Honor," Einhorn said. "MCR 2.119 permits me to file a motion in open court."

I stared at him. "We're in Probate Court, Chad. Not Circuit Court."

"Um ... forgive me ... um ... I meant MCR *three* point ..."

"Save it," Judge Wentz said. "What is this witness here to talk about? This is an evidentiary hearing, Ms. Leary. So, I'm inclined to give some latitude."

"Your Honor," Einhorn said. "Mr. Mackin is a respected attorney in Monroe County. A member in good standing with the state bar. He represented Marilyn Paul."

"He what?" Zoe and I said it together.

"Again, this man wasn't on any witness list I was provided with," I said. "I'm getting this information in real time, Your Honor."

"And you'll have a chance to cross-examine Mr. Mackin and produce your own witnesses if you feel the need," Wentz said. "Mr. Mackin is here now. Let's get his testimony on the record and go from there."

I threw my hands up.

"I've never heard of this guy," Zoe whispered.

"I'd like to call Jason Mackin, attorney at law, to the stand," Einhorn said.

The bailiff opened the courtroom door and an elderly man made his way to the witness box.

"Can you identify yourself for the court?" Einhorn started.

Mackin leaned forward. He had on a freshly pressed gray suit and yellow tie. Thick glasses perched at the end of his nose.

"I'm Jason Mackin. M-A-C-K-I-N."

"Mr. Mackin, are you familiar with Marilyn Paul?"

"I know ... or ... rather ... I knew Marilyn Paul. Yes."

"How did you know her?"

"She was a friend of a friend. I think. It's been a long time. I can't recall now where the referral came from. But she came to me on some estate planning matters in the summer of 2006."

"Can you explain the nature of the advice she came to you for?"

"I'm sorry," I said. "If … and I cannot stress the word if enough … Mr. Mackin was engaged to provide legal counsel to Marilyn Paul, these communications would be protected under attorney–client privilege. Ms. Paul is the only individual with the power to waive that privilege and allow Mr. Mackin to testify. Obviously, that's not going to happen."

"Mr. Einhorn?" the judge said.

"Your Honor, these proceedings in part involve a will contest. Mr. Mackin's communications with Mrs. Paul relate directly to her testamentary intent. As such, the law recognizes an exception to the privilege."

"Once again, Your Honor," I said. "Marilyn Paul is still very much alive. Incapacitated. But alive. The exception Mr. Einhorn raises doesn't apply."

"I don't agree," Judge Wentz said. "Proceed, Mr. Einhorn."

I fumed but took my seat.

"Mr. Mackin, did Marilyn Paul hire you as her lawyer?"

"She did. She came to my office in Monroe and we spoke about drafting a will and a trust."

"When was this?" Einhorn asked.

"This was in June of 2006."

"Do you recall what Mrs. Paul's desires were regarding her estate plan?"

"I do indeed. She wished to provide for her son in the event of her death. We discussed preparing a standard will. She filled out an estate planning questionnaire while she was right there in my office."

"What types of things were on your questionnaire?"

"Oh. The usual. She provided me with information about the nature of her assets. Who her living relatives were. I recall she had a unique situation in that she had raised her granddaughter. But the granddaughter was over eighteen at the time we met."

"Were you aware where her granddaughter was living?"

"My understanding was that the granddaughter, now that she'd turned eighteen, was preparing to leave Mrs. Paul's home."

"You're certain that it was Mrs. Paul's intention to provide only for her son?"

"Yes. It was a point of discussion. She specifically told me she didn't want to leave anything directly for her granddaughter. She told me she felt she'd provided for her enough during her childhood. She was attempting to reestablish a relationship with her son, Bradley Paul."

"Mr. Mackin, as an estate planning attorney, is it customary for you to inquire about any prior wills executed by your clients?"

"Oh, of course. That's always one of the first questions I ask."

"So, you asked it of Mrs. Paul?"

"Absolutely. She indicated she had never prepared a will prior to coming to meet with me. She said it was something she'd been putting off for a very long time."

"I see," Einhorn said. "You're sure about that?"

"I'm positive. As I said, it's one of the first questions I ask of estate planning clients. You have to. I also ask my clients to bring in copies of whatever existing wills or estate planning documents they have. In the case of wills, I always want the originals. It is my preference to physically destroy them as well as revoking them in the language of the wills I prepare for my clients."

"I see. And did you ever prepare a will or other estate planning documents for Mrs. Paul?"

"I did. I've brought them with me today."

Einhorn walked over to my table and set a stack of papers in front of me. It was an unsigned draft of a will. There was only one name under the beneficiary clause. Bradley Paul.

"Was this document ever executed?" Einhorn asked.

"It was not," Mackin said. "Mrs. Paul had an appointment in late August of that year to sign everything. She didn't make that appointment. It's my understanding that she suffered catastrophic injuries in a car accident. Such a shame."

"Thank you, Mr. Mackin. I have nothing further."

"Your witness, Ms. Leary," Wentz said. I was thunderstruck. I stepped up to the lectern.

"Mr. Mackin," I said. "You claim you were engaged to prepare estate documents for Marilyn Paul. And you claim you were aware of her accident in the summer of 2006, is that correct?"

"That's correct, yes."

"But you've never met Zoe Paul before, have you?"

"No, ma'am."

"Did you reach out to her family at all after hearing the news?"

"No, ma'am."

"Why not?"

"What could I have done? As you stated at the top of the hour, my communications were privileged at the time."

"I'm sorry, Your Honor," I said. "This is untenable. You are asking me to conduct discovery in open court. I have no idea how this man came to be involved in this case. How the petitioners found out about what he's claiming."

"Well, you can ask him," Judge Wentz said, completely missing my point.

I had about a dozen four-letter words to mutter under my breath.

"How much are you being paid to be here, Mr. Mackin?" I asked.

"What? Nothing. I'm here because I read an article in the news about this case. I hadn't heard the name Marilyn Paul in sixteen years. I took it upon myself to check the docket entries for this matter, which are public record. I reached out to the attorney of record for the petitioners."

"You reached out," I said. "To them. My name also appears in the court file as an attorney of record. I represent the estate. If what you're claiming is true, you represented Marilyn Paul. Yet you never reached out to me."

"As I said, Mrs. Paul discussed leaving her estate to Bradley Paul. As such, I reached out to his attorney."

"How much did Mrs. Paul pay you for your alleged services?" I asked.

"I'm sorry?"

"How much did you charge for the work you claim Mrs. Paul engaged you for? What was your bill?"

"Um ... at that time. A simple estate plan like she wanted would have been five hundred dollars."

"You claim you did the work, yes?"

"Did I prepare her documents? Yes, I did. You have copies of them."

"Did you bring a copy of the bill you prepared for her with you today?"

"What? No, ma'am."

"Do you bill your clients in advance or after you complete the work?"

"Generally, I ask for half of the bill to be paid upfront as a retainer. The balance after they sign their estate planning documents."

"I see. You should know, Marilyn Paul kept meticulous records. Her conservator, Zoe Paul, has provided me with all of her check registers and her bank statements up until her unfortunate accident. So, you're saying there should be a check written to you for two hundred and fifty dollars that summer?"

"I wouldn't know. She might have paid cash."

"You'd have a record of that somewhere, wouldn't you? Did you provide her with a receipt?"

"I'm not sure. I can't remember that."

"Right. But you would normally keep that information with her file, wouldn't you?"

"Yes."

"And you *have* a file on her, right? Because you showed up here today with these?" I waved the documents he brought in the air.

"Of course. I have a file. I'm happy to provide it."

"But not your billing receipts."

"Um..."

"Or a copy of this property questionnaire you said she filled out."

"Um ... I'll have to check and see if I still have those. I can get back to you."

"Please do."

I went back to my table. Blood roared in my ears.

"Ms. Leary?" Judge Wentz said.

"Your Honor, I have nothing further for this witness, but would like to reserve the right to recall him later."

"If you need to," Judge Wentz said. "Mr. Mackin, you're excused for the day."

He waited for Jason Mackin to leave the courtroom before turning to Einhorn and me.

"All right. How much more do you have to present, Mr. Einhorn?"

"Your Honor, I believe this is my last witness."

"You believe?"

"Yes, sir."

"Ms. Leary?"

"Zoe Paul would like the chance to address the court herself."

"All right. We'll get her on the stand Monday ... then I'll prepare a ruling on the validity of the filed will and Mr. Paul's underlying petition for the removal of Ms. Paul as guardian."

"Thank you," Einhorn said, gathering his papers. He scuttled out of the courtroom.

"This is insane," Zoe said. "I've never seen that man before. Never heard of him."

"It's too convenient," I said.

"Do you think my uncle or my father paid him to do this?"

"I don't know," I said. "But I'm not done looking into Jason Mackin. For now, though, his testimony has nothing to do with your conduct as your grandmother's guardian. I'm not even worried about that."

We walked out of the courthouse together. I did what I could to reassure Zoe that her family's tactics shouldn't matter. There was still zero proof that she'd failed to act in her grandmother's best interests. She sat silently staring out the window as I drove her back to my office where she'd parked her car. As I pulled into my parking spot, Zoe finally turned to me.

"Are they going to win? After all of this, are they going to convince the judge that I was some kind of teenage monster? Or that my grandma wanted to give everything to my asshole father?"

"No," I said. "What matters is how you've cared for your grandmother over the last sixteen years."

"They're willing to tell all these lies about me. Two men who have had nothing to do with either me or my grandma my whole life. Why doesn't the judge care that they've only just come forward when they knew there might be money at stake?"

"He will see," I said and prayed it was true.

She followed me out of the car. I opened the back door to the office just in time to hear Miranda's blood-curdling scream. I dropped my keys on the counter and ran to the front lobby.

Miranda stood in front of the reception desk, her hands on her cheeks. Trembling, she pointed to a package on the floor. A stack of mail fell in a pile beside it.

"What on earth?" Jeanie came out of her office.

I stepped forward to get a better look at what had Miranda so upset.

"Is that ...?" Zoe stepped forward.

I kicked over the upturned package. There, duct taped to the bottom of it, was a dead squirrel.

Chapter 27

ERIC POKED the dead thing with a stick and slid it into a plastic baggie. He sealed it and handed it to the rookie officer who had been dispatched to my office.

"Unlikely we're gonna get anything off any of this," Eric said. "There's no postmark."

"Which means somebody dropped it off," I said.

"Did you check your security cameras?" Eric asked. He'd supervised their installation at both my office and the ones at my house.

"It was on the side of the building," Miranda said. "We don't have a camera out there. Only at the front and back. I only saw it because I'd gone around to throw the trash in the dumpster."

Eric put a comforting hand on Miranda's shoulder. The thing had shaken her up the worst. She was fond of the squirrels that hung around downtown. She even had a tiny squirrel picnic table set up outside her office window in a flower box. She fed them peanuts.

"Why would somebody do this?" she asked. "There's no note. There's nothing. It's just … sick."

"Thanks, Bentley," Eric said to the female officer.

"I'll file my report before the end of my shift," she said.

"Can we talk?" Eric said to me quietly, so Miranda couldn't hear. Jeanie stepped forward and took over comforting Miranda.

"Let's go upstairs to my office," I said.

Eric followed me up. He shut the door behind him and made his way over to the couches. I joined him.

"This was probably random," he said. "You're a defense attorney. There's any number of …"

"Stop," I said. "You know the possible significance of that particular dead animal, Eric."

The worry lines didn't soften in his face.

"I'm not Miranda," I said. "I'm not scared of stuff like this."

"All right. So tell me what you think."

"Marilyn Paul swerved to avoid a squirrel. Jeanie and I just went out and interviewed the eyewitness to her accident. A guy by the name of Gus Wallace. Then today, a dead squirrel got delivered to my office. It can't be a coincidence."

"I'll admit," he said. "I don't like it."

"Today, Chad Einhorn shows up in court, miraculously finding a lawyer who claims Marilyn Paul came to him about writing a will disinheriting Zoe in favor of her son who she hadn't seen or spoken to in years. What he says just *happens* to line up with Bradley Paul's testimony. Things are just too convenient. My source, if that's what she is, is implying that someone's bankrolling Einhorn other than Paul and Lockwood. This guy. This lawyer. Do you think you could look into him for me?"

I wrote down Jason Mackin's name and handed the paper to Eric. "I feel it in my gut. This is all connected. And you've been acting funny."

"What are you talking about?"

"You were going to look further into Ned Corbett. I know you have. But every time I ask you about it, you're cagey. What gives?"

Eric's scowl deepened. I knew I'd hit on it.

"You're not supposed to be this good at it," he said.

"Good at what?"

"Reading me."

I smiled and moved closer to him. "You're easy. At least for someone who's paying attention. Something's bothering you. Tell me what it is."

"Corbett," he said. "I did some things I probably shouldn't have done. Things it's better you don't know."

I sat up straighter. "Eric, this is us. This is me. And there's a dollar bill taped to my fridge. Remember that?"

His eyes flashed darkly. He did remember. Neither of us would ever forget. Years ago, I had demanded Eric pay me with that bill. A token retainer. But it was enough. I was his lawyer. He'd shared his darkest secret. I was duty bound never to share it. Now, he had to know it was more than just that dollar bill tying me to him.

"I did some digging," he said. "There're some things about Corbett that just don't track. In the last few years, he's spent some money he shouldn't have."

"What do you mean?"

"He drives around in a tricked-out Mercedes. Three years ago, he bought a vintage Chris-Craft boat worth about a hundred thousand dollars. He and his current trophy wife, he treats her well. Took her on a European vacation that probably set him back twenty grand."

"Eric, how do you know Corbett's living beyond his means?"

"I checked his personnel file."

I took a sharp breath. "Eric ... they can fire you for that."

"Corbett paid his last ex-wife a lump sum. Fifty grand to keep her away from his pension. And it's not that much. The guy is netting only about thirty-five hundred a month from the pension board."

"So maybe he cashed in a 401k or something, bought stuff on credit."

Eric's face changed. "He didn't buy it on credit."

"Do I want to know how you found that out?"

"I haven't done anything outright illegal."

"Yet. Eric, I didn't ask you to do any of that."

"I know. It's just the guy gives me a vibe. I'm not wrong about this stuff, usually. So, I started asking around a little. I never worked with the guy. He retired before I moved over into the Bureau. I only knew him by reputation. And that isn't a bad one. People say he was no-nonsense but kind of a blowhard."

"All right," I said. "But none of that explains the look you've got in your eye, Eric."

"Look, the guy has two ex-wives and a current one that looks like she's on her way to be an ex. I'm not saying it's right. But that alone might be why he'd try hiding how much he was really worth. Not keeping a ton of money in the bank."

"Only it didn't take you very long to figure out he's been spending beyond his means. Why wouldn't one of his exes come to the same conclusions?"

"I don't know. And none of this has to mean anything. Only, he's in Marilyn Paul's phone. She came into a huge amount of money. And we know his story wasn't that tight on how they knew each other. He withheld his connection to Marilyn's employer. It doesn't *feel* like a coincidence. It feels sloppy. From everything I'd heard about Corbett up until now, he was a decent cop. Straight shooter of a detective. It's just ..."

Eric's voice trailed off.

"Eric ... what?"

He closed his eyes, resigned to the fact I think he knew I wasn't going to quit until he told me what he was thinking.

When he opened his eyes again, he leveled a cold stare at me. "I got some pushback I wasn't expecting."

I got comfortable on my end of the couch. I think Eric knew I wasn't about to let him leave this room without hearing every detail.

"I talked to a lieutenant who's been around forever. I know Corbett worked directly under the guy. Anyway, when I asked about Corbett, he clammed up quick enough to arouse my suspicions."

"What exactly did you ask?"

"I told him I heard Corbett was a master of side projects. That he was making great cash over the counter doing security. Which is true, by the way. We already know he was working for Valentine Pizza. But I wanted to know if his lieutenant could tell me who Corbett's hook-up was. I said I was in a position where I needed to make a side hustle."

"You think Corbett was dirty?" I asked.

"I don't know. Sometimes ... you hear things about a guy. Rumors. I never did about Corbett. The lieutenant, like I said, clammed up real quick. Kinda stormed off on me. Well, fine. That alone wouldn't be that big of a deal. Only, yesterday ..."

Eric started rubbing his thumb into the opposite palm.

"You know Larry Kaminski?" Eric asked.

"He's one of the deputy chiefs, isn't he?"

"Yeah. Well, yesterday, he paid me a visit to my office. He said he'd heard I'd been asking questions about Ned Corbett. His tone wasn't exactly friendly."

"What exactly was it?"

"It was guy shit, Cass."

"So, translate."

"Kaminski basically told me I needed to quit digging into stuff that didn't concern me. Said if word got around that I had, people might get the wrong idea."

"He threatened you?"

"More or less. The thing is, if it had just been my conversation with Corbett's lieutenant, fine. He and Corbett were buddies. If someone came sniffing around about someone I was close to, maybe I'd react about the same. We're all suspicious by nature. But for Kaminski to take it upon himself ... to go out of his way to ..."

"Somebody doesn't want you asking too many questions about Corbett."

"Yeah."

"Eric ..."

"I've got a terrible feeling about all of this, Cass. Now you add in this crap with your little package. Miranda's car. You feeling like you were being followed. I think you're right. This isn't random. It's all connected to whatever Marilyn Paul was hiding."

"We have to find out what that was."

"Why?" Eric rose. His eyes flashed fire. "Seriously. Why? That isn't what you were hired to do."

"Excuse me?"

"Zoe Paul hired you to get the bank to cash that check and represent her in court. You did that."

"She also hired me to make sure she can continue being the one to take care of Marilyn. My job isn't over. And I don't have to tell you ... whatever this is, whoever doesn't want me on this case, I'm not afraid of them."

"Maybe I am," he said. "For you."

"Eric ..."

"Cass. Maybe this is a hornets' nest that doesn't have to be kicked."

I watched him pace. I knew Eric didn't really believe what he was saying. This had become about far more than Marilyn Paul's mystery check.

"You want answers just as badly as I do," I said. "We're more alike than you like to admit."

He stopped pacing.

"You want me to let Zoe's case go?"

"Yes."

"Are you going to let things drop with Ned Corbett?"

He didn't answer. He didn't have to. It was in the set of his jaw. The narrowing of his gaze.

"That's what I thought," I said. "Deputy Chief Kaminski overplayed his hand. You're more determined than ever to figure out how Corbett fits into all of this. You just want me safely uninvolved when you do."

He let out a low growl.

"I'd say we're in this one together, Detective. Again."

"Cass ..."

I got to my feet and went to him.

"Cass," he said again, his body going rigid. I put my hands on his shoulders. He felt carved in granite.

"Come on. You know I love a caper."

"I don't."

"Liar. Besides, you're already up to your elbows in it. You going to try telling me you haven't pulled more from Corbett's personnel files than just his pension information?"

His silence was all the answer I needed.

"Perfect," I said. "After you go through it, let me know what you found."

He dropped his shoulders in resignation. I went up on my tiptoes and kissed his cheek.

"Come on. This will be fun. What could possibly go wrong?" I teased.

Chapter 28

"You sure you're up for this?"

I pressed my cheek to baby Sean's soft, downy head. His hair had gotten darker. The bones of his face seemed to reshape day by day. The tiny, wrinkled scowl of a newborn was gone now, replaced by a round-cheeked baby.

"Up for it," Tori said. "I'm going crazy, Cass. I need this. I've been staring at the same four walls for months. I've been killing myself in physical therapy. Getting strong. I need my mind to get stronger, too. Just give me a job. Tell me what we're looking for."

"Let me get my little man out of your way," Matty said. He came in from the garage, sawdust covering his hands. He'd been working on refinishing the kitchen cabinets. He washed his hands in the sink then came to me, stealing his son away. Sean went rigid, sticking his arms straight out, arching his back, then promptly farting on his father.

"Good boy," Tori said. "I've been calling him Poop Dad. Something about Matty just gets things flowing for the boy."

My brother drew baby Sean to his chest, cooing at him as he took him into the nursery.

"He's really so great with him," Tori said. "He's been amazing."

"Yeah," I said. "That's a special guy you've got there. Both of them."

Tori looked good. In the week since she'd come home, I could tell she was starting to put weight back on. Her cheeks looked less hollow. The dark circles under her eyes had faded. It helped that Sean had sailed past the fussy early weeks of sleepless nights and now seemed settled into a good rhythm.

Tori picked up the sleeve of DVDs I'd set on the coffee table between us and thumbed through them.

"So, what are we looking for again?"

"Probably a needle in a haystack," I said. "Those are all the home movies Marilyn had from January '06 until the end ... August. Just before her accident. I'm just trying to get a clear picture of who was around her. What she was doing."

Tori also had a copy of Einhorn's amended petition, attaching Mackin's purported will draft.

I popped the first DVD into Matty's player. I'd seen this before with Zoe. Marilyn's trip to Atlantic City with the few women she worked with. Eileen Maguire, Jean Francis, and Holly Billings.

"How'd she pay for this trip?" Tori asked. She had a fresh legal pad in her lap. It took her a moment to grasp her pen. Her hand kept shaking. Then, she steadied her wrist and began writing.

"Credit card," I said. "It was one of the first bills Zoe submitted when she filed the conservatorship."

"It was shrewd of her to do that," Tori said. "She was what, eighteen, nineteen?"

"Just."

"How many girls that age would have the wherewithal to handle that?"

"She had help. She was a student at Great Lakes U. at the time. They had a student legal clinic since they're connected to a law school. Their interns helped her prepare all the initial paperwork. It was all straightforward back then. It's *been* straightforward up until she found that check."

I had my own notepad in front of me. I wrote down the timestamp of the video playing, plus the names of everyone I recognized and made notes of whom I didn't.

"The will is problematic," Tori said. "I gotta be honest. Especially if the judge believes Mackin."

"Except Zoe filed it fifteen years ago. It's not like she found the check and *then* tried to claim Marilyn had disowned her son."

"Yeah. I see that."

I put the video at 4x speed. We watched as Marilyn and company sped through a limbo contest, a day at the beach, then a grand buffet. There were men in the scenes, ones Zoe had no knowledge of. People Marilyn and her group had met on the strip.

The next DVD was from Marilyn's last birthday party. She had turned fifty-eight. A few friends gathered in her backyard. I recognized Frieda and her same friends from work. They had all paired up. Only Marilyn seemed to be solo, but happy. She toasted the camera with a glass of champagne.

"Geez," Tori said. "This was just two weeks before her accident."

"Does this bother you?" I asked. "Tori. I didn't even think. What happened to Marilyn. And you ..."

"No," she said. "It doesn't bother me. It's okay. I'm serious. It's good for me to be able to focus on work again. I needed it."

"Me and Little Man are gonna head out to the park," Matty called out. He'd changed Sean into a fresh onesie with a giraffe on the front. "I might head over to see Joe. Stay out of your hair for a few hours."

"Pack sunscreen," Tori said.

Matty held up the diaper bag. He had things under control.

I popped in another DVD; this one was out of sequence.

"I've seen this one," I said. "Frieda had a birthday party for her niece or something."

I sat back down and held my pen poised on my notepad.

"How's that going?" Tori asked. "Having Joe live over your garage."

I put my pen down. "I barely see him. I swear he leaves when I'm home on purpose. He's mad at me and I haven't done anything wrong."

"He's mad at everyone," Tori said. "Trust me. If Matty weren't bringing the baby as bait, Joe would probably come up with some excuse not to be around Matty too."

"It's not like him," I said. "Well ... it's exactly like him. I'm just worried this time."

"Joe's strong. This thing blindsided him."

"I know, right?" I picked up the remote and froze the playback. "I had no idea things had gotten bad between him and Katie. They seemed solid. She seemed solid."

"She came to see me," Tori said. "A few weeks ago, at Maple Valley."

"How'd that go? What did she say?"

"We talked about the baby a lot. She told me I could call her if she needed anything. Then it got a bit awkward. She made a comment that she didn't have much to offer in terms of how to care for a newborn. Emma was three years old when she became a stepmom."

"Emma has never thought of her like that," I said. "At least, not until now. Katie was the only real mom she's ever known. That's why this is so awful."

"I heard what she and Vangie did. Have they cooled off?"

"For now. I think Emma realizes it's not worth getting herself into trouble I can't get her out of."

Tori nodded. She stared out the window for a moment. She was getting tired. Matty warned me about that. She would be fine one second, then about to pass out the next.

"She just seemed so sad," Tori said. "Katie. But not ... I don't know ... remorseful. I probably shouldn't tell you this. She didn't ask me to keep our conversation private. But she said she and Joe just don't want the same things anymore. She said I was indirectly responsible for what she did."

"What?" My blood heated. "She blamed you?"

"Not blamed. I probably didn't say that right. She wants a baby, Cass. She feels like she missed out. Then seeing Matty with Sean. And now me. She said it finally dawned on her that she's running out of time. She's thirty-nine years old."

"Joe doesn't want a baby," I said.

"No. And I don't blame him for that. He had Emma so young. She's a grown woman now."

"So, she cheats on him? That's how Katie deals with this?"

"Look, I don't know. I'm certainly not justifying her actions. I just feel bad for all of them and think maybe we should all just give everyone involved some grace."

"Except for Tom Loomis, Eye on Sports. Screw that guy."

Tori laughed. "Obviously."

I looked back at the TV screen. I'd paused it just as Frieda's niece was about to blow out her candles. I popped the DVD out. There was one more disc left in the sleeve. This one wasn't labeled like the others.

"I finished looking through Marilyn's bank statements and check register," Tori said. "There are no payments to that attorney, Jason Mackin. So, either he never got around to billing her, or he's lying about all of it."

"My gut says he's lying."

"Cass, two million bucks is a lot of money. But it's not *that* much money. If Mackin is lying, he's risking a heck of a lot. He could be disbarred for giving false testimony if you prove it."

"I think he's banking on the fact there's nobody to contradict him if that's what's going on."

"And Einhorn. He can't come cheap."

"Eric's trying to figure out what he can about him," I said. I hit the play button. There was nothing but static. I tried again. Nothing. I hit eject and waited for the disc to pop back out.

I looked at it closer. "That's not a DVD," Tori said. "That's a CD."

"You're right," I said. I blew on the disc then put it back in the player. "It should play anyway."

I could hear the disc spinning, then the screen went black. A second later, the file menu popped up. I selected it with the remote.

"Pictures?" Tori said.

"Spreadsheets," I answered, tilting my head. I hit fast forward on the remote. There were dozens of photographs of various spreadsheets. Ledger entries.

"What are we looking at?" Tori asked.

"I'm not sure. It's ... an account ledger of some sort."

"Valentine," Tori said. She stood next to me in front of the television. She pointed to a column at the very top.

"What on earth?" I said. Then my blood chilled. I kept advancing the photographs. There were hundreds of entries. Thousands and thousands of dollars.

"Cass," Tori said, her voice dropping an octave. "Is this what I think it is?"

I took a step back and grabbed my phone off the table. I punched in a number. He answered on the first ring.

"Eric," I said. "I think I need you."

"Everything okay?"

I stared at the television screen, the numbers on the spreadsheets dancing in front of my eyes.

"Maybe," I said. "Maybe not. Meet me at the office. And Eric? Hurry."

Chapter 29

I COULDN'T STOP PACING. I chewed my thumbnail, paced in front of my desk, stopping every other pass as Eric scrolled through the spreadsheets on Marilyn Paul's CD. We'd been at it for two hours. I had one laptop that still had a disc player in it. It was old, clunky, but still worked.

"It's what I think it is, isn't it?"

Deep lines carved through Eric's brow as he stared at the screen through a pair of readers. Those were new. I had to drag him kicking and screaming to the optometrist last month.

Eric sat back, scratching his chin. I took the seat beside him, perching on it sideways so I could face him.

"They were cooking the books at Valentine," I said. "What else could it mean?"

"This goes back years," he said. "Hundreds of thousands of dollars' worth of transactions. Millions."

"It starts out small," I said. I reached over him and scrolled back to the first dated entries.

"Duplicate entries. Double billing suppliers. Little bits at a time. And here ... she's taking screenshots of billing discrepancies later on."

"I see it."

"And here." I slid the laptop closer to me. "Look at this. She's got pictures of bank statements. Dozens of them. The money going into the corporate account, if that's what this is, doesn't match up with their accounts receivable. Somebody's skimming. Could it have been Marilyn?"

"I don't know," he said. "Maybe. But this is way more than two million dollars' worth of skimming."

"Right. And why would she hold on to evidence of her own crime? It makes more sense she was building it for something else. For someone else."

Eric sat back. "Right. What we're looking at. If you're right? This is multiple felonies."

"Hal Dolenz, the guy she was dating off and on, said Marilyn was acting paranoid in the last few months before her accident. Eric, what if she *was* blackmailing someone. I'd assumed all this time it had to do with some married man she was seeing. But what if it was this? She knew someone was cooking the books. Skimming off the top. Maybe she was in on it. Maybe that two million was her getting a cut."

"Again, though, why a cashier's check?"

"I don't know. That's the one thing that's bothered me about all of this. It's too messy. But this money? These discrepancies? It adds up to a lot more than two million bucks, Eric."

"It's definitely enough where someone might have killed to keep it silent."

"There's just nothing there. No evidence that Marilyn's accident was anything but that. An accident. You saw the report yourself. I told you I talked to Gus Wallace, the man driving behind her. There's no reason to call his story into question. And if someone wanted Marilyn dead, they've had sixteen years to get to her."

"There was no need," Eric said. "Marilyn's own dumb luck would have solved a problem for someone. She hasn't said anything cogent for sixteen years."

"Wallace did say something though," I said, my brain spinning. "He said there were two adjusters that came out to talk to him. He said the second one was asking a lot of questions about what he found when he came up on Marilyn's vehicle. He said they specifically asked him if he saw any packages or bags in her back seat or thrown out of the car. That's odd. Don't you think that's odd?"

"Not necessarily," Eric said. "You know as well as I do there could have been a claim for the replacement cost of valuables in the car."

"There weren't though. I've looked at all Marilyn's insurance records. There was no claim other than for the loss of the vehicle itself and for her medical bills under her first party claim. Wallace said this second adjuster contacted him *recently,* Eric. And another thing...he said the guy reeked of pot. That night, when I was in the Dead Law room at the library. When I told you I thought someone was following me. I smelled that too. It could have been the same person."

"It's odd. I'll admit it. Though a lot of people smoke pot. But Cass, this looks like more than skimming. You realize that. What this looks like is money laundering."

I nodded furiously. "Yes. Yes. I think so too."

"Shit." Eric pushed himself away from the table and got up. Now it was his turn to pace.

"What do we do?"

He stood at the end of the table, curling his fists. "Someone knows something. Someone knows you're looking into all of this. All these little odd occurrences. Zoe talked. She never made a secret out of the existence of that check. It's been hidden for sixteen years. You may not have been able to track the account that money came from ..."

"Maybe I can with these," I said, pointing to the laptop screen.

"Someone knows where it came from. Someone in Marilyn's life. They could have followed you to the library that night. Smashed up Miranda's car. Sent that dead squirrel. I don't like it, Cass."

"Einhorn," I said. "My informant told me I needed to figure out who was really paying his fee. What if it's the same person or people who Valentine was laundering money for?"

"Which makes me like all of this even less."

He smacked a palm against the table, hard enough to make it vibrate.

"So, what do you expect me to do?"

"Get out of it. Withdraw from the case. Walk away."

"It's too late for that. And what about Zoe? She's innocent in all of this. If her grandmother was involved in criminal activity, it has nothing to do with her. She didn't know."

"You're sure about that?"

"I'm sure."

"This just isn't worth it," he said. "Haven't you had enough excitement with cases that go sideways?"

"I can't do anything anyway," I said.

"What?"

"I mean … maybe I can't do anything. I have to talk to Zoe. She has to know what we found. But … if she invokes privilege … you know you're bound by it too. You can't tell anyone about this."

"Marilyn Paul isn't your client. Zoe is. And if you're so convinced Zoe wasn't involved in this, this isn't privileged. You have a duty to report it."

"I only have a duty to report if my client is about to commit a crime. Zoe isn't culpable in any of this. And this is potential evidence of a past crime."

"We need to figure out who Valentine was fronting for. I've got some ideas. But I need to verify some things first."

"Eric … be careful. If this is going where I think it is, this could come back and hurt you more than it could me."

"I can take care of myself."

"I know you can. But let's think about this for a second. We know Marilyn was talking to Ned Corbett, maybe sleeping with him. He's been cagey about what all those calls from her were about. What if it was this? What if she told him she had proof of whatever was going on at Valentine Pizza?"

"This thing has laid dormant since that damn squirrel ran out in the road in front of her," Eric said.

"Right. And now? Do you think Corbett tried to help her?"

He leaned against the table, both palms flat against the top. He reminded me of a war general planning out some battle strategy in a map room.

"Eric."

Nothing. His only response was the flare of his nostrils.

"He's a cop. I get it. There's a code. But something isn't right. You said it yourself. He's spending money that on paper, he shouldn't have. What if ..."

Eric straightened. "What if what?"

"What if she cut him in on whatever this is? What if the source of Marilyn's windfall is the same as Ned Corbett's?"

The set of his shoulders changed. I knew he didn't want to admit I could be right.

"You owe no loyalty to Ned Corbett. If he's dirty ..."

"I'm not willing to ruin the guy on guesses, Cass."

"Of course not. I wouldn't ask you to. I'm not willing to do that either. It's just ... he's not trustworthy."

"I need to know what mess we've just stepped into. There's someone I need to talk to."

"Who?"

"I can't tell you that."

"A CI? Do you have somebody in mind?"

"Maybe the less you know the better."

"Zoe's my client. Whoever you're going to talk to, do you trust they won't make things worse?"

I didn't like the expression on his face. Eric looked worried.

"I want to talk to Eileen Maguire, Marilyn's co-worker again," I said.

"And say what? Say ... did you know your employer might have been in the money laundering business?"

"Well ... maybe."

"I think the less people who know what you have, the better," Eric said. "And I want to make a copy of that disc."

"What if it's the tip of the iceberg?" I said. "Eric, I need to go back over to Marilyn's. I need to see what else Marilyn might have hidden in those boxes. These discs were just the ones that were the most recent. She had more. She brought these to ..."

My heart raced.

"What is it?" Eric asked.

"She knew," I said. I popped the CD out of the drive and held it. It caught the light and flashed across Eric's face.

"Who knew?"

"Marilyn," I said. "The other day, when I visited her with Zoe. Zoe brought these discs. She played them for her grandmother, thinking they might cheer her up. Home movies. Familiar voices and faces. They didn't cheer her up. She got really agitated.

They had to sedate her. We thought it was something to do with someone she saw on the home movies. But maybe that wasn't it at all. Maybe she remembered she'd hidden this evidence in *with* her home movies."

"She can't communicate. She hasn't uttered a coherent sentence in sixteen years."

"I know. But still ... I'm worried. I don't want anyone else putting two and two together and thinking Marilyn's talking. In the meantime, I need to call Zoe. I want to go back over there."

"I think I should go with you."

I found my phone in the kitchen and punched Zoe's cell number. It was well after five. She should be on her way home from work by now. She'd just started a new job at a dentist's office.

It rang five times. I expected it would go to voicemail. Then Zoe answered.

"Cass," she said, breathless. "I was just about to call you. I don't ... I can't ... I don't know what to do."

"What's going on? What happened?" Eric got closer to me and mouthed "What's wrong?"

"Are you okay? Zoe, what's going on?"

"No. Yes," she said. "I just got back home from work. The garage door was open. I'm sure I didn't leave it like that. And all the lights were on in the back of the house. When I walked up to the back door, I could see through the window. All the cupboards were open. Plates, bowls, everything from the pantry. It was just scattered and thrown all over the place."

"Zoe, where are you now?" I asked, clicking the button to put her on speaker.

"I'm in my car," she said. "In the garage."

"Did you go inside?"

"No. I was just about to call the police when you rang."

"Good. Don't go into the house. Zoe, I need you to leave. Drive a few blocks away. I've got Detective Wray with me right now. We'll meet you at the gas station at Hyde and Turner. You wait there for us. Okay?"

Eric already had his own cell phone out. He was calling in to dispatch. I heard the words "possible B&E out at 312 Hyde."

I nodded. "We'll be right there, Zoe. You did the right thing. Just get to the gas station and wait for us."

I hung up the phone and Eric and I were on the move. I almost made it to the door before turning back.

"Eric," I said. I went back to the conference table and picked up the disc. "If someone went to Zoe's looking for this, they might come here next."

"Good point," he said. He pulled his phone out again and called dispatch. I slipped the disc into my bag and followed him out the door.

Chapter 30

I WAITED WITH ZOE. She sat in the passenger seat of my car parked across the street from her house. Eric wouldn't let us go in yet. A field ops crew had just finished processing the scene.

"You did the right thing," I told Zoe for about the tenth time. When we arrived, she was so shaken up Eric thought about calling for medical assistance.

"Why is this happening?" she said.

Later, I would figure out a way to tell her what Eric and I suspected about her grandmother's dealings. Now, I didn't think she could handle it.

"I was supposed to be home earlier, but I stopped at Maple Valley," she said, reiterating what I'd heard her tell the officer who'd taken her statement. "Grandma had a really bad day. She's in a lot of pain now, Cass. The doctors asked me if I wanted to sign the DNR now."

"Zoe, it's been a lot. And you've handled it. All of it. By yourself."

"She had a seizure," she said. "We're waiting on the results of her latest scans, but the doctors are certain the cancer has spread to her brain. She doesn't have long. But if I sign the DNR, my father will use it against me."

"You can't worry about your father. Your responsibility is to your grandmother. We'll be in court tomorrow. One last day. You can tell Judge Wentz your story. He'll listen."

"But my father's lawyer is going to try to twist my words."

"That's why I'll be there, Zoe. We'll get through it together. Nothing's changed."

Eric walked across the street toward us. Behind him, two officers came out of the house.

"Come on," I said to Zoe. We exited my car.

"They're finished now," Eric said. "We can go inside."

Zoe grabbed her purse and the three of us walked up to the house together. The place was a mess. Just like Zoe described, the contents of her kitchen cupboards were strewn all over the counter and floors. I stepped over raw macaroni and made my way to the living room.

"Nothing's broken that we could tell," Eric said. "Your televisions are fine. Your jewelry box is still in the bedroom. Still locked. But we think they took your laptop. Your desk in the home office got hit the worst along with the third bedroom upstairs."

"Marilyn's room," I said to him. Zoe had already bounded up the stairs ahead of us.

"They weren't looking for valuables," I said. "They were looking for information."

Eric gave me a sober look as we headed upstairs to join Zoe. She stood at the entrance to her third bedroom. All of her carefully labeled boxes of Marilyn's belongings were torn open. Clothing, shoes, and papers littered the floor.

Zoe cried. I put my arm around her. "Do you think my dad did this?"

"I've got a crew on the way to his motel," Eric said. "None of your neighbors saw anything. Though it's getting dark. We think the perpetrator came on foot. No forced entry. Zoe, are you sure your doors were locked?"

"Yes."

"Does your father or uncle still have a key?" I asked.

She shook her head. "I changed the locks a long time ago."

"We'll get statements from both your uncle and your father. They better have an alibi for this evening."

"Can I clean up? Is there anything else you need?"

"You don't have to tackle this right now, Zoe."

"Yes, I do. I can't stand to have it like this."

She stepped into the room and started picking up her grandmother's clothes. I found an intact box. I picked up another pile of clothing and started folding as neatly as I could.

Eric and I exchanged glances. I knew he was thinking the same thing as I was. Zoe had kept the box of home movies in the attic above the closet in this room. The original VHS tapes. I went over to it and pulled down the stairs.

"Nothing was disturbed up there," Eric said. "I checked myself."

"The boxes of tapes? They're all there?"

He held up another small empty box. That one had originally contained DVD cases.

"Zoe," I said. "The DVDs I took; I still have them in my bag in the car. Where are the rest of them?"

Zoe straightened and wiped her eyes. "They're still in my trunk. I never brought them back inside after we watched them with Grandma. Why?"

"Look," I said. "There's a lot I still have to figure out. But I think there's a good chance whoever did this might have been looking for those discs. I found something on one of them. Bank statements. Ledgers of financial transactions. I'll need you to bear with me a little bit. But I think I'm circling in on where that two-million-dollar check may have come from."

"She was messed up in something she shouldn't have been, wasn't she?"

"Maybe," I said.

"Am I ..." She looked at Eric. "Is it safe for me to stay here?"

Eric took a breath. "To be honest, I'd rather you didn't. Can you crash with a friend for a couple of days?"

"Yeah."

"Zoe, I can talk to the judge and try to get him to postpone your final hearing tomorrow. In light of ..."

"No!" she said. "No way. If my uncle and father did this, I'm not going to give them the satisfaction of seeing me rattled. I want this over. This information you think you found. Does it have anything to do with Grandma's probate case?"

I thought for a moment. "Well ... no. Not directly. Not yet. It doesn't have anything to do with their petition to remove you as conservator."

"All right. Then let's finish what they started. I'll be ready tomorrow, Cass. I'm tired of being on the defensive."

I went to her and put my hands on her shoulders. "Good. So am I. Text me the address where you'll be staying. I'll pick you up first thing in the morning, okay? And we'll finish this. Once and for all."

Zoe hugged me. No. It was more that she clung to me. I hugged her back. At that moment, she reminded me of my own little sister. Strong. Tough. But when Vangie fell she fell hard. I would do everything in my power to see that Zoe Paul stayed on her feet.

Chapter 31

THE NEXT MORNING, Zoe Paul showed up ready for battle. She was a different person than the one I'd left the night before. She wore her hair slicked back into a low ponytail. Her three-inch black heels made her tower over me. She wore stark, white makeup that set off her eyes and the severe arch to her brow. When Judge Wentz called her to the stand, she refused to even cast a glance toward her father and uncle sitting at Einhorn's table.

"All right," Judge Wentz said. "Let's get down to brass tacks, Ms. Leary. I want this wrapped up by this afternoon."

For the next hour, I led Zoe through the accounting she'd filed on her grandmother's behalf. She had every receipt. Every penny spoken for. For sixteen years, this woman had kept meticulous, detailed records of everything she'd spent on behalf of her grandmother. Her books balanced to perfection. I made a point of showing the judge no bills had ever been submitted or paid to Jason Mackin for drafting a new will.

"All right," I said. "How old were you when your grandmother had her car accident?"

"It was a few weeks after my eighteenth birthday. The summer after I graduated from high school."

"You lived with her."

"Yes. I'd been living with Grandma since I was one year old. She was the only mom … the only dad I ever really had."

"Why is that?"

Zoe straightened her back. She looked right at her father. "Because my real dad, Grandma's only son, he just wasn't around. She tried to get him to pay child support, but he'd never show up to court. The only time Bradley Paul would visit was when he wanted money from Grandma."

"Objection," Einhorn said. "This witness has no firsthand knowledge of that. She's speculating."

"Ms. Leary?"

"Zoe, are you speculating?" I asked.

"No, Your Honor. I heard the fights my grandmother had with my dad. And she went to court to try to collect support from him when we struggled with money. She also showed me paperwork my so-called father filed to try and get his parental rights terminated. My grandma wouldn't agree to it. She always felt my father should try and live up to his responsibilities."

"Zoe," I said. "After your grandmother's accident, did you have any family members supporting you? Either financially or emotionally?"

"No. In those first few weeks, I was the only one of Grandma's family going to see her in the hospital. I was the one listening to everything the doctors had to say. They tried to find my dad. But he'd moved so many times and never left a forwarding address or phone number. So finally, after about a month, they had me bring in my birth certificate and a social worker at the hospital helped me fill out forms to be made my grandma's patient advocate. So, I would be the one with the power to make her medical decisions."

"And you were eighteen," I said.

"Yes."

"What else did you do for your grandmother?"

"There was a lady at the billing office for the hospital. She helped me get in touch with Grandma's car insurance company. She coordinated it all so Grandma's bills would get paid. That was a big help. And she suggested I talk to a lawyer and be made Grandma's guardian and conservator. That was so hard. It was after the doctors explained to me that Grandma might not ever wake up. And when she did, her brain had been so badly injured, they didn't know if she'd be able to walk or talk or even know who I was."

"So, who helped you file the petition to open your grandmother's estate?"

"I was going to Great Lakes University by then. There was a legal clinic in the paralegal program. The students there and their supervisor who was a lawyer ... they helped me file everything. And that let me get into my grandma's bank accounts so I could keep paying her bills. The non-medical ones. The mortgage. The utilities at the house."

"Where was your uncle, Roy Lockwood, during all of this?"

"He lived in Palm Beach, Florida, they told me. I called him. I had Grandma's address book and I called everybody I could think of to tell them she'd gotten hurt. It was maybe four or five months later, yes. At Christmas, that first one. That's when he went to visit her in the hospital."

"Did he offer to help you with her care or with her affairs?"

"He came to the house and started trying to go through her things. We got into an argument. I told him to leave."

"What was he looking for?"

"I don't know. Money maybe. Before my grandma died, she always told me my uncle wasn't someone to trust. She said he always had a hand out."

"Objection," Einhorn said. "Hearsay."

"Sustained," the judge said.

"Zoe, to your knowledge, was your grandmother, Marilyn, on speaking terms with her brother before her accident?"

"They weren't talking, no. Not for years before that. My understanding was that Uncle Roy had money problems."

"Objection!"

"Your Honor," I said. "The statement isn't being offered as fact. It's being offered to show what my client's belief and understanding of the family dynamics were at the time of Marilyn Paul's incapacitation."

"Let's not go too far down in the mud, shall we?" Judge Wentz said.

"Of course not," I said. "Let me ask you this, Zoe: did your Uncle Roy offer to help you pay any of your grandmother's bills?"

"No."

"Did he offer to be there when you spoke to her doctors at any point?"

"No."

"Before these proceedings, when was the last time you saw or spoke to your Uncle Roy?"

"Gosh. It's been probably fifteen years. The last time we spoke before all of this. I'd gone to stay with some friends that first year. I just ... it was hard for me to be in Grandma's house without her. Well, Uncle Roy moved in. He didn't ask. He just moved in. I went to that legal clinic to see what I could do about it. They said he had to pay rent if he wanted to stay. I told him that. I thought it was going to be a big fight. That I'd have to sue to evict him. Well, one day, he was just gone. Left the house in shambles. That was the last I saw or spoke to him until now."

"And what about your father? When did you last see or speak to him before all this?"

"Even longer. He called the house once, maybe a year after my grandma's accident. So, fifteen years ago. He wanted to talk to her. He didn't even know what happened to her. So, I know he hadn't been in communication with her in over a year. When I told him Grandma was in a hospital and not expected to get better, he hung up. And that was it. Not until he filed this court paperwork did I even know if he was still alive."

"Thank you," I said. "I have nothing further."

Einhorn charged up to the lectern. "Ms. Paul. You live in the home owned by your grandmother, don't you?"

"Yes."

"You don't pay rent, do you?"

"Um ... the mortgage is paid off. I made sure it got paid off. My grandma got some disability insurance money. An annuity. I used it to keep her mortgage current. I made the last payment on her behalf two years ago."

"But you're living in the house, correct?"

"That's correct."

"You've helped yourself to your grandmother's money so that you could live in it rent free."

"I didn't help myself to anything. If I hadn't paid off the mortgage, the bank would have foreclosed on the house. And beyond that, over the last ten years, I've used my own money to make improvements to the house. I put in a new air conditioner. A new roof. Fixed water damage in the basement. Put in new windows. Nobody helped me with that. I've worked two, sometimes three jobs, put myself through school to get my hygienist's license, and kept up Grandma's house. All by myself."

"And all *for* yourself," Einhorn said. "Your Honor, we've previously submitted an appraisal of the property in question. Ms. Paul, you received a copy of that appraisal?"

"Yes."

"Home values have gone up quite a bit in that area since your grandmother's accident, haven't they?"

"I suppose so."

"In fact, Marilyn Paul's home has appreciated in value by over one hundred thousand dollars in the last sixteen years, hasn't it?"

"I'm not an expert on that," Zoe said.

"But it's your job ... your duty ... as your grandmother's fiduciary to marshal and protect her financial assets, isn't it? You're telling me you haven't even bothered to consider the value of her home?"

"Asked and answered, Your Honor," I said.

"Move on, Mr. Einhorn."

"Ms. Paul, isn't it true that you were the one who told your uncle he wasn't permitted to see his own sister in the hospital? You sent him a text to that effect, did you not?"

"She didn't like seeing him. The one time my uncle came to the hospital, my grandmother got very upset. So much so she had to be sedated. Since I have her medical power of attorney, I'm allowed to decide what's in her best interests. Seeing Uncle Roy was too upsetting for her. You can ask the nurses what happened the last time he came a few weeks ago."

"And you banned him from her home."

"I asked him to leave. He had no business there. He didn't pay rent. And it's my home now."

"Your home."

"I've lived there since I was one year old, Mr. Einhorn."

"And you're telling me you'd vacate if your grandmother asked you, right?"

"She can't ask me."

"Right. And let me get this straight. You also produced a so-called will written by your grandmother when you filed all your probate paperwork sixteen years ago, correct?"

"It was in her papers. The clinic supervisor I talked to at the college, I told her about it. She suggested I file it when I opened Grandma's guardianship proceedings. For safekeeping. And so that any interested parties would be on notice of it. I did that. And I served … or tried to serve copies on my dad. Since he was her only son, he was the only other interested party. Not my uncle."

"But isn't it true that you hid your grandmother's principal asset? The inventory you filed when you opened her conservatorship didn't accurately reflect the full picture of her worth."

"What do you mean?"

"Well, what I mean … isn't it convenient that you withheld a check totaling two million dollars? That had it been properly deposited in your grandmother's estate account sixteen years ago, or wisely invested, it would have earned a substantial amount of interest."

"I didn't know about the check. I only discovered it when I removed floorboards in the bathroom for a remodeling project."

"And only after you were told your grandmother only had a few months to live. How convenient."

"Objection," I said. "Argumentative."

"Sustained, Mr. Einhorn. Let's stick to the facts."

"Of course, they're telling enough, aren't they? I have no further questions for Ms. Paul."

"Ms. Leary?"

"No, Your Honor," I said. "Nothing more from us."

"All right, you may step down. Look. This isn't a formal trial. So, I'm not interested in hearing closing arguments. You've both submitted lengthy Memoranda of Law. It is my intention to take the rest of the week, review the testimony and evidence presented over the past two weeks, and render an opinion on the merit of the petitioners' request. For today, that is all."

Wentz banged his gavel. Zoe got to her feet. She stayed regally rigid as she walked past Einhorn's table. Bradley Paul gave his daughter a searing stare. Pure hate. As she got to me, I wrapped my arm around her and led her out of the courtroom, away from him.

Chapter 32

THE PARKING LOT was empty as I led Zoe to my car. She couldn't go home. I worried someone might have followed me this morning to pick her up at her friend's house.

"I want you to stay at my place for a few days," I told her. "I don't want you going back to your house at all. For anything. Not for a little while."

"Are they doing this?" she said. "My father? My uncle? Did they break into my house?"

"Zoe," I said. "There are some things I need to share with you. Things that don't have a direct bearing on what's going on in court. But they have a direct bearing on you. But I don't want to talk about it out in the open. Come on. Let's go to my place. I have tons of room."

"I need some things," she said. "I need to tell my work I won't be in."

"Anything you need you can either borrow from me or buy. My house is set up for guests. It's quiet. Tucked away. There's the lake."

She looked so gaunt and tired. I hoped a few days and the lake air would do her good. She climbed in the car and stared straight ahead as I pulled out of the lot.

"What's going on?" she asked. "You know what they ... whoever they are ... were looking for, don't you? They think there's more money hidden in the house. Are they going to tear it apart?"

"Nobody's going to do anything at the house again," I said. "Eric's got patrols set up watching it. And no. They weren't looking for money, Zoe. They were looking for documents. Evidence I believe your grandmother had compiled."

"Tell me. I need to know everything."

As concisely as I could, I explained what I'd found on Marilyn's CD and my theories about it. It took me all the way back to my place to explain it all. When I finished, I'd just made the turn into my driveway. I parked in the garage. Zoe stared straight ahead, unmoving.

"Do you understand what I'm telling you?" I said. "We believe your grandmother was gathering evidence against her employer. We have some rather big pieces to connect, but it looks like Valentine Pizza was a front for some criminal activity perhaps. Money laundering."

"She was a secretary," Zoe said. "She made appointments and answered calls for Tim Valentine. Grandma didn't handle the books as far as I know."

"Maybe not. But assuming she's the one who made the copies of those ledgers, she at least had access to them."

"The two million dollars. You think it was part of all of this?"

"I know there was a lot of money going through that business. Double entries that represented hundreds of thousands of dollars every month. The pizza place did well, but not that well."

"She was scared of something," Zoe said. "You said Hal Dolenz told you that. Frieda said something too. We *were* arguing a lot more in those last few months. She was just constantly on at me about being independent. About making sure I had some kind of plan in place. Cass ... is this what happened? Did someone try to kill her?"

"If they did, we'll probably never be able to prove it. The eyewitnesses to her accident saw her swerve to avoid hitting that squirrel. There was nothing wrong with her brakes. She wasn't under the influence of any drugs or alcohol. It's still entirely possible she just got very unlucky. But ... as I've told you, I believe someone broke into your house looking for those discs. Someone knew she had evidence that could be used to hurt Valentine and whoever they were working for."

"What am I supposed to do?"

"For now? Sit tight. Detective Wray is helping me. We need to find out who the Valentine Corporation was working with. But Zoe, this doesn't involve you."

"It does though," she said. "I found that money. They're going to think I know what my grandma did."

I wanted to tell her she was worrying for nothing. It would be a lie and an insult to her intelligence.

"Can we destroy the discs?" she asked. "Can we just burn them or something? I didn't know about them until you told me. I swear to God. I didn't know about that money until I found it three months ago. I wish I never had."

"Zoe, I think it's too late for all of that. We've found evidence of a crime. I can't just destroy it. I'm an officer of the court. Detective Wray has a duty to uphold the law as well."

"It's cursed," she said. "That money is cursed."

"There's something else," I said. "I have reason to believe Chad Einhorn might be on the payroll of whoever's trying to find those discs. They may well be using this probate case to ferret out whatever information you or your grandmother had. It may not be about the money at all."

"It is to my dad and uncle."

She went very still. The hardest fact stared her right in the face. Slowly, she turned to me. "Cass ... they don't care, do they? My family. If you're right. If Einhorn's connected to whatever my grandmother was involved in. They sided with the devil against me, didn't they? What if I'd been home when whoever that was broke in? They don't care if I get hurt. They don't care if my grandma gets hurt."

I wished I could tell her something different. I couldn't.

Zoe buried her face in her hands. The weight of everything I'd just told her bent her back. She doubled over.

"Come on," I said. "Let's get you settled inside."

Behind me, Joe pulled up, startling Zoe.

"It's okay," I said. "He's a friendly. It's just my brother Joe. He's staying in the apartment over the garage. I've got another guest room inside. Let's get you set up."

I quickly introduced Joe and Zoe. As Zoe walked into the house, I mouthed to my brother that I'd talk to him in a minute. He looked puzzled, but didn't follow us in.

"It's really beautiful here," Zoe said, looking out the living room windows at the lake beyond. It was quiet today. No boats. A pair of geese landed just in front of the seawall. My two dogs, Marbury and Madison, sprang into action. They came racing around the side of the house to chase them off.

"Good dogs," I said. "Those things poop everywhere. Do you like dogs? I forgot to ask."

"Yeah," Zoe said. "They're a couple of cuties."

"Go on out and meet them," I said. "I've got some clothes that will fit you. My sister's always leaving things here."

Finally giving me a smile, Zoe walked out the back porch. Marby and Maddie came running toward her, ready to bestow doggie kisses in exchange for belly rubs.

Behind me, Joe came in through the garage.

"Find another stray, did you?" he asked.

"More or less. You think you can keep an eye on her? Without … acting like you're keeping an eye on her?"

"She in trouble?"

"She might be. It's just not safe for her to go back to her house right now. So, keep it under your hat that she's even here."

"Got it. Is it safe for you for her to be here?"

"Nobody's gonna get in or out of here without me knowing," I said. "Or you knowing. Hopefully this is a temporary situation."

Joe waited for me to explain more. When he saw my expression, he realized I wouldn't. He gave me a terse nod and made his way back out to the garage.

"Thanks, Joe!" I called after him. I pulled an extra change of clothes from the hall closet and put them on the guest room bed. From the window, I watched Zoe play with the dogs. Madison led her over to the edge of the water. The geese kept their distance.

My phone rang. I slipped it out of my pocket and frowned at the caller ID. It read "unknown caller."

I sat on the edge of the bed and answered.

"This is Cass."

For a moment, I was met with dead silence. Then finally, "You don't know when to quit, do you?" My deep throat. She sounded breathless. I heard rushing sounds. Wind. She was outside.

"Where are you? We need to meet," I said.

"No way. Not now."

"You listen to me. I've let you jerk me around for weeks. You don't hold all the cards anymore. I know what you've been hiding. I know what Marilyn was trying to do and I think you were either helping her or she told you about it."

"You don't know anything," the woman shouted.

"You told me to follow the money. I did. But so did Marilyn, didn't she? She was following it for weeks. For months. Maybe longer. She was methodical. She documented it all."

Silence.

"How am I doing?"

Silence.

"Suppliers being double billed. Cash going out that wasn't coming in. Deposits and receipts that don't line up. There were two sets of books at Valentine Pizza. Marilyn had proof."

"Marilyn was so stupid. I told her. She wouldn't listen."

"Who are you?"

"Dead. I'm dead."

"Not if you let me help you. I can get you in touch with people who will listen. Who can keep you safe."

"You can't. No one can."

"So why did you reach out to me in the first place? It's Zoe, isn't it? Did Marilyn ask you to look out for her? Did she know something bad might happen to her?"

My caller started to cry softly on the other end of the phone.

"Did she drag you into it? Or did you drag her into it?"

"She thought she was smarter than everybody. I told her. I warned her. I said these people don't mess around."

"Who was Valentine working for? Who was he laundering money for? Who is paying Einhorn's legal fees?"

"These people don't let people like me or you get away with this kind of thing."

"Lady, you don't know who I am. You think you know something about Chad Einhorn. Well, maybe you should have done your homework about me. I'm not afraid of him. I'm damn sure not afraid of whoever Valentine was in bed with."

"Then you're a bigger fool than Marilyn was."

"Did you look into me? Did you bother finding out who I worked for before I came back home to Delphi? Look up the Thorne Law Group. And trust me. Whoever Valentine was laundering for, they weren't bigger or badder than Killian Thorne."

"He's not going to protect you anymore though, is he? I heard he's off the board."

"Why did you call me? The first time. Now? If you're just going to throw vague threats my way, I'm no longer interested. Time to put up or shut up. I'm close to putting the pieces together without your help. You're a distraction. Goodbye. And don't bother calling me again."

"Wait!"

I stayed on the line but didn't say anything.

"All right," she said. "All right. You're right. Listen to me. I made a promise."

"To whom?"

"To Marilyn," she said softly. "She said if anything ever happened to her, she wanted me to look out for Zoe. So, I have been. She's okay. She did okay. But she's going to get hurt. She's going to become collateral damage. These people will do whatever it takes to keep that evidence you're talking about from seeing the light of day. Marilyn trusted all the wrong people."

"Are you going to tell me who Valentine was working for or not? Because right now, that's the only thing I'm interested in hearing from you."

Silence. Then, she sobbed.

"I can get you to people who can protect you. If you come forward and tell the police what you know …"

The call dropped. I stared at my phone screen. Had she hung up? Or had someone else been listening in?

"Who are you?" I whispered.

Zoe came back in with both dogs close behind. "It's beautiful here," she said.

"Thanks. I think so too." I decided not to tell her about my cryptic phone call. It would only make her more skittish. I showed Zoe where she could find everything. She thanked me and asked if she could take a shower. I shooed the dogs out of the guest room and headed outside with them.

The sun began to set as I walked out to the end of the dock.

My phone rang again. This time, it was Eric. "You okay?" he asked.

"I'm good. I got another call from lady deep throat. I think she was working with Marilyn at Valentine. Which narrows down the candidates considerably. I'm betting it's either Eileen Maguire, Jean Francis, or Holly Billings. I'm going to get some pictures together and take them over to Mindy, Judge Wentz's clerk, in the morning. She was in the courtroom for every single hearing. I know this woman was there at least once. Mindy never misses anything. It's worth a shot anyway."

"Good thinking. But Cass, I think I'm onto something. I don't want to talk about it over the phone, but I've had some luck chasing down more intel. I'm on my way over."

"I'll meet you at your place," I said. "Zoe's fragile. She's still processing everything I told her."

"All right. I'll see you in an hour," he said. "Do me a favor and watch your back. You know how to make sure nobody follows you?"

I smiled. "I learned from the best. See you in an hour."

Chapter 33

I PULLED into Eric's driveway ten seconds after he did. He opened the garage door of his condo and motioned for me to park beside him. Puzzled, I did as he asked.

"Is this overkill?" I asked as I stepped out of my car.

"I don't know. Maybe. It's just ... come on inside. We've got a lot to talk about. Bring your bag."

"My bag?" I reached across the driver's seat and grabbed my weather-beaten messenger bag and foisted it over my shoulder. Eric held the door for me, and we walked into his kitchen.

He'd downsized. Last year, Eric sold his three-thousand-square-foot house. It had been the place he'd built for his wife, Wendy. Fifteen years ago, he thought they'd raise kids there. It never happened. Instead, Wendy cheated on him, then got into a horrific car crash on the heels of hiring a divorce lawyer. Eric had stuck by her until the end. When it was over, he couldn't stand looking at the house anymore.

Eric went straight to his liquor cabinet in the living room and poured himself a shot of bourbon. He unclipped his badge and tossed it on the low coffee table in the center of the room.

"Should I ask you to pour one for me?"

He downed his quickly and poured a second.

"Ah," I said. "So, it is going to be that kind of conversation."

I went back to the kitchen and opened his fridge. I took out the bottle of Moscato he kept for me and poured myself a glass. Eric was sipping his second bourbon. As I joined him, he slid his service weapon out of its holster and set it on the table next to his badge.

"All right," I said. "What did you find out?"

Eric rubbed his forehead and took another sip of bourbon.

"Eric?"

"You have to get away from this one, Cass."

I leaned back and adjusted the couch pillow behind me, settling in.

"I'm listening."

"Walk away. Just ... withdraw from the case."

"You know I can't do that. I have an obligation to Zoe. Hell, I have an obligation to law enforcement at this point."

He let out a great sigh. Of course, he knew this would be my answer.

"When are you going to take my advice and just spend your time doing real estate closings? Or maybe take a teaching gig at the community college?"

"Me? Teaching? How about this? I'll do it if you do it. Come on. It might be fun. They're always looking for adjuncts in the criminal justice department."

Eric rolled his eyes. Worried as he was, he couldn't suppress a smile.

I leaned across the table and touched his arm. "Come on. Tell me what you found out. If it's a problem, we'll work it out together."

"It's not a problem. It's a civil war."

"Valentine Pizza was laundering money for whom? The Russians? I know it wasn't the Irish mob. I would have heard about that. So, who?"

"The Pagano family," Eric said. He set his rocks glass down. "You've heard of them?"

"Only by reputation. The Thornes didn't have much to do with them. Different business model."

"Yeah," Eric said. "Some business. Cass, these guys are as dangerous as they come. At one time, they were responsible for the largest supply of coke coming in from the Eastern Seaboard."

"How?"

"You know how, you've seen the same cooked books I have."

"No. I mean, how did you make the connection between Valentine and the Paganos?"

Eric's face hardened. He'd finished his bourbon and eyed the liquor cabinet.

"Eric ..."

"I poked the same bear as before."

"Corbett," I said. "He told you all of this?"

"No. Corbett isn't answering his phone anymore. I took a ride out to his house and his car's gone. His wife's too. The neighbors said they haven't been home for days. He dropped his dog off with one of them."

"Corbett's in the wind? Christ. Eric. He's involved then. He knows you're digging into him."

"It could be a coincidence."

"You know it isn't. And you still haven't told me how you made the connection."

Eric leaned forward, resting his elbows on his knees.

"Corbett retired years ago. You know what I found out about his finances. So, I started looking at the kinds of cases he was clearing before he turned in his badge."

"You said it was mostly property crimes."

"It was. But I checked into a few of his registered informants. One in particular he had meetings with quite a bit in the years before he left the force. A kid named Bud Durante. He got popped on a few larceny charges twenty years ago. His big one was car theft. He did time for that. Anyway, he helped Corbett on some robberies back in his day. A few of Corbett's biggest collars came from the intel he got from Durante. But then in the last few years before Corbett retired, things were static. Durante's name didn't show up on any of the cases Corbett was clearing."

"But you said he kept meeting with him. Frequently."

"That's the thing," Eric said. "It just didn't track. I saw call after call. Meetups logged. But Durante seemed like he'd dried up as a useful source a while before that."

"Did you talk to him? Durante?"

Eric nodded. "Yeah. I tracked him down at this strip club he haunts. The guy's a mess. Strung out. But he was willing to talk to me. Twenty years ago, Durante was a runner for the Paganos. Sold dope out of his car. Small time. Somehow, he managed not to get caught for that. But Corbett knew it. Durante leveraged what he knew about the Paganos' organizational structure to get himself out of the worst of his charges. But ... after a few years, Durante started sampling too much of his own product and lost his usefulness."

"Except to Corbett."

"Except to Corbett. When I pressed Durante on that, he got skittish. I thought he was gonna clam up on me. But he didn't. I couldn't get him to shut up."

Now my head was starting to pound. "All right. So, you've got the Pagano family running cocaine out of Detroit all the way through Delphi and points beyond. You're telling me Valentine is laundering one vein of their cash flow for them."

"That's the gist of it."

"Did Durante know how Valentine got hooked up with the Paganos?"

"Vaguely. Nothing concrete yet. But Tony Valentine ran with a rough crowd as a kid. He's not from here. His family's from Detroit originally. Valentine did some time for an assault when he was in his early twenties. I'd bet money his involvement stemmed from there. Once he got out, he was a changed man. Never got so much as a parking ticket from that point on."

"I can look into the corporation itself," I said. "Valentine Pizza has only been in existence for what, twenty-five years? I'd bet money that if I dig deep enough, I'll be able to find his initial investors were connected to the Paganos."

"That'd be a pretty safe bet, yes."

I set my now empty wine glass next to Eric's glass. "And they're still in business. For all we know, they're still doing the same thing they were doing when Marilyn worked there."

"And someone knows you're poking around. Cass, this is what I'm trying to tell you. This case? It's not worth it. Two million bucks? This means nothing to these kinds of people."

"What about Corbett?" I asked. "Eric ... how did you find out Durante's name? Do you mean to tell me that kind of information is just laying around in some police department database for anyone to go look at?"

Eric's face changed. His posture stiffened. A sick feeling came over me.

"Eric," I said.

"It's better you don't know."

"Eric ... I know you skirted the line when you investigated Corbett's pension information. You told me you ran into a wall with command. If Corbett's dirty ... if he was on the take with the Paganos, is it possible someone in the department was covering for him or protecting him?"

"I don't know."

"This whole time you've been trying to warn me off this case I don't think I'm the one who's in danger. I think you are."

"I can handle myself."

"And we don't know how high this goes up. God. Eric ... I didn't ask you to do this. Not this way. I never wanted you to expose yourself to this kind of trouble."

"I told you, I can handle it."

I vaulted to my feet. Adrenaline rushed through me. "You can't handle it. You said yourself, the Paganos are dangerous. If they have some kind of foothold within the Delphi P.D. ..."

"I don't have any reason to think it went any higher than Ned Corbett."

"Don't lie to me. It's what you suspect. There's a reason you were warned not to keep looking into Corbett."

He didn't answer.

"Can they hurt you?" I asked. "Are you in danger of losing your job over this?"

Still no answer.

"Stop," I said. "Don't make it any worse for yourself. Promise me."

"All you have is a disc full of spreadsheets," Eric said. "If we can't connect Valentine to the Paganos, then this goes nowhere."

"Twenty minutes ago, that's what you told me you wanted. You begged me to withdraw from the case."

He wouldn't look at me. It was then I knew what he meant to do.

"No," I said. "No way. You're not flying solo on this one. We're in this together. You need Marilyn's discs to prove Valentine's business dealings. And I may need Bud Durante to testify as to the connection to the Paganos."

"Cass ..."

"This is bigger than both of us."

"I told you, I can handle this."

"No. You can't. And neither can I. And you have to stop. Right now. You can't say another word to anyone at the police department about what you suspect. You can't trust anyone there. But you can trust me."

"There's something else ..."

My stomach churned. "What? What else?"

"Jason Mackin, that attorney who just showed up saying he represented Marilyn. I looked into him like you asked. Years ago, he had his own issues. Got caught up in a prostitution sting one of the task forces put together."

"There's no record of that," I said. "He's had no disciplinary actions filed against him by the bar."

"Because the charges against him didn't stick. His name was in the report, but he wasn't indicted. The thing is ... on a hunch, I double-checked the names of every law enforcement officer involved in that particular task force. One was a detective from Delphi P.D."

"No," I said. "Corbett?"

"Yeah. It's not a smoking gun per se. But there's a connection. If Corbett made Mackin's charges go away ..."

"Then he might have had Jason Mackin in his back pocket. Ned Corbett could have been pulling the strings with Zoe's family. Eric, we have to talk to Mackin. If he knows we put this together, he might change his tune. Admit that he's lying."

"Yeah. I thought of that. So, I went to pay him a visit."

"What did he say?"

"Not a word. Cass, Mackin's dead."

"What?"

"His landlord found him hanging from the rafters in his garage. He hung himself. About twelve hours after he testified in your probate hearing."

"My God."

Eric met my eyes. "Cass ..."

"This has gone far enough. I know what I have to do. It's probably what I should have done the second I found those discs. I'm taking this to the feds."

"Cass ..."

"Lee Cannon," I said. Long ago, he'd been my handler when I planned my exit strategy from the Thorne Law Group.

Eric closed his eyes. "All right."

Two words. They took me off guard. I expected Eric to push back. Slowly, I sank back to the couch next to him.

"All right," I repeated. "I'll set up a meeting. We can trust Cannon."

"I agree." A muscle jumped in his jaw.

"Let me make the call. Are you sure you can trust Durante if we need him?"

Eric gave me an ironic smile. "No."

"Well, one step at a time anyway. I'll make the call. There's just one more person I need to talk to. I told you, I have a hunch of my own who my mysterious caller might be. I'll let you know if I'm right."

"Cass, be careful."

I crossed my heart and leaned in to kiss Eric. "Always."

Chapter 34

PROBATE COURT CLERK Mindy Price didn't miss much and that was the thing I counted on. I caught her between hearings the next morning and plied her with copious cups of coffee at the diner across from the courthouse.

"Take your time," I said as I put five 8x10 photographs in front of her. One I'd pulled from social media. Two I'd screengrabbed from the Valentine Pizza corporate website.

"And these women have what to do with your client's case, exactly?"

"Maybe nothing. At this point, I'm just trying to figure out which one of them might have been in the courtroom for a couple of the hearings."

Mindy picked up each photograph in turn. "I know her," she said. "Jean Francis. She goes to my church. I wouldn't say I know her very well. But I'd have recognized her if she was sitting in on one of your hearings."

Mindy put Jean's picture facedown and stared at the others.

"The woman I saw," she said. "The one I think you're looking for. She didn't want to be recognized. That's why I noticed her in the first place. It was eighty degrees outside and she showed up with this knit scarf over her head and half of her face. Dark glasses. She took them off though. Kept her head down."

Mindy put another of the photos facedown, leaving one left.

"Her," she said, picking up the last photograph. "I think it was her." She handed the picture to me.

Holly Billings.

"Are you sure?"

"Is it something I'd need to be sure enough to testify about?" Mindy took another sip of coffee. The woman had to have a bladder of steel. I couldn't fathom how she could sit through hours of Judge Wentz's hearings with the amount of caffeine she drank.

"Would it make a difference if I said yes?" I asked her.

"I think I could. That's the woman I saw in the courtroom. She was there the day Bradley Paul testified. She sat way in the back, and came in after your witness had already been sworn in. She stayed in the seat right by the door. I think she wanted to leave herself an out. She scooted out right before you finished your cross."

Mindy's account tracked. I received a call from my mysterious informant right after that hearing. I looked at the photograph.

Holly Billings. Eileen Maguire told me she was the office administrator when Marilyn worked as Tim Valentine's secretary. She might have had access to almost all the financial information Marilyn had stored on those CDs. What I didn't know was whether Holly Billings had given those discs to her or if Marilyn had made the copies herself.

"She seems like a good kid," Mindy said. "Zoe Paul."

I nodded. "I think she is."

"I hope everything works out for her. You know it's not appropriate for me to talk about the case with you."

"And I would never ask you to. But this is helpful. Thank you."

"You should watch your email today," she said. "I will say I think the judge is getting very close to issuing a ruling. You might hear something by the end of the day."

"Thanks for the heads-up. I really appreciate your time and insight with this."

"He's not so bad, you know."

"Who?"

"Judge Wentz. I know the way he runs his courtroom is a little unorthodox, but he'll issue a fair ruling."

"I have no doubt," I said.

"Well, I better get back. He's taking testimony in a wrongful death action today. A rough one. Little girl who drowned in her grandmother's bathtub."

"How awful. Thanks again, Mindy. I'll let you know if anything comes of this. If I need you to prepare an affidavit or any type of formal statement about this woman being in the courtroom. For now, I'd appreciate it if you'd maybe just keep this conversation between the two of us."

"I won't lie," she said.

"I wouldn't dream of asking you to."

"But ... I don't see why I have to volunteer any info. And I don't see why anyone would come out and ask me. If they do, I'll let you know."

"I'd appreciate that too. More than you know."

I put a twenty on the table and walked Mindy out of the diner. She waved goodbye and crossed the street, headed back for the courthouse.

"Holly Billings," I said. A quick browser search on my phone brought up an old LinkedIn profile. No address or phone number. I knew if I had just two seconds to hear her voice, I'd know for sure if she was the one who had been calling me. But it also might spook her.

I walked to the next block and took a seat on a park bench in the courtyard of the government building. I stared at the reflecting pool; in the center of it was a large statue of Apollo. Today, he would be the only witness to the next call I had to make.

I took my cell phone out of my bag. Then, I opened the messenger app and texted Special Agent Lee Cannon.

He might ignore me. He may have gotten rid of this cell phone number. Or he might decide I was no longer worth the effort. All I could do for the moment was wait.

Three blinking dots stared at me from the cell phone screen.

"Come on, Cannon," I whispered. "Prove to me you're not a liar."

A minute went by. Two. After ten, my heart sank. I slipped my phone back into my bag and started the three-block walk back to my office. I made it halfway before my cell phone rang.

Finding shade beneath a large elm off the sidewalk, I answered.

"This is Cass."

"Hey, Leary." Cannon's deep voice poured through me like liquid velvet. He was an old friend and so far, a loyal one.

"Are you safe?" he asked. The man had plenty of reasons to be angry with me. It meant a lot to me, that was the first question he asked.

I looked around. Across the street, two deputies walked back toward the public safety building. A pair of women on bikes whizzed past me.

"I'm safe enough," I said. "But there's a case I'm working on. Certain aspects of it have become ... complicated. I could use your expertise."

"Complicated. Shit, Leary. I know what that means when you're involved. How big of a mess are you in this time?"

"This one's not my mess."

"Why don't I believe you?"

"It isn't. I swear. It's just ... Lee, I might be in over my head on this one. You of all people know how hard that is for me to admit."

He laughed softly. "Yeah. I do."

"I'm not asking for any favors. Depending on your point of view, I may be doing you one with the information I have."

"What do you want from me?" he asked, his tone turning sober. I suppose I couldn't blame him. He had plenty of reasons not to trust me.

"A meeting," I said. "No more than an hour of your time. Then you'll be free to act on what I have ... or not."

"Is that all you're going to give me?"

"I don't think it's the best idea to say more over the phone."

He let out a sigh. "Cass, I got in a lot of trouble after what you pulled last year, dragging me into your last case. And Killian Thorne is still out there somewhere. Still made of Teflon."

"I'm sorry," I said. "If there had been any other way to protect my client, I wouldn't have involved you."

"Yes, you would have," he said. "There were plenty of other ways to protect your client. I was just the most expedient."

"You got what you wanted," I said. "Killian Thorne has been neutralized for now. You got to put one in the win column. And I promise you. This? What I want to talk to you about? It has nothing to do with Thorne or any of my past ... um ... entanglements. But I have a client who may be in real trouble. And I have information I think the FBI might be interested in. The kind that could make your career. If you want me to beg ... consider this me begging, Cannon."

"Neutral territory," he said.

"Of course. You pick the place and time, but the sooner the better."

"I'm not that far away from you, as it happens."

"See? It's fate."

"There's a rest stop off northbound 23, the one near Coleson. Do you know it?"

"I know the exit. It's right across from a fireworks outlet."

"That's the one. I'll meet you there around six. I'll text you when I'm close."

"I'll be there," I said.

"I'm driving a silver Explorer. Government plates."

"I won't be able to miss you," I said.

"See you then."

"Thank you. I know I owe you. Hopefully ... what I have to show you will be a big step toward paying my debt to you."

"I won't hold my breath."

I deserved that, I supposed. "Thanks," I said.

"Leary?"

"Yes?"

"You sure you're okay?"

"Yeah. I am. Promise."

"All right. See you soon." He clicked off before I could say goodbye or thank him again. I held my phone to my chest for a moment. Then I called Eric.

"We're on," I said. "I'm meeting Cannon at the rest stop near Coleson."

"Do you want me to come with you?"

"No," I said. "But there's something else you can do for me. There's someone I need you to track down."

"What've you got cooking?"

"I think I might know who my lady deep throat is. Mindy, Judge Wentz's clerk, gave me a positive ID off a photograph of a woman named Holly Billings. B-I-L-L-I-N-G-S. She worked at Valentine when Marilyn did. Mindy confirmed she was in the courtroom during Bradley Paul's testimony a few weeks ago."

"Cass, that's not a lot to go on."

"I know. My gut mostly. But I don't want to run the risk of her disappearing like Corbett. Or Jason Mackin."

"Do you have an address?"

"I don't. I pulled up a LinkedIn page. Do you think you can work your mojo and try to find her? Make up any excuse you need to. I'm just afraid if I'm right ... if I figured out who she is ... someone else might."

"I'll find her," Eric said.

"I'm sorry," I said. "Here I am, expecting you to drop everything on another one of my capers. Where are you right now?"

He didn't answer.

"Eric? You're not ruffling any more departmental feathers, are you?"

"You really want me to answer?"

"I guess not."

"I just want to talk to Corbett again. I've got a lead on where he might be."

I didn't like how cagey he was being. "Just be careful. Promise?"

"You too."

"Okay. We'll meet back up at my place tonight. I might be a little late."

"Just keep in touch."

"You too."

I clicked off the call and adjusted my bag. I could feel the weight of the smaller black bag inside where I'd tucked Marilyn Paul's CD and hopefully the key to this whole case. I just hoped Lee Cannon would come through.

Chapter 35

THE COLESON REST stop was only about a half hour out of town. I got there early. An hour before we were supposed to meet. I waited. He might not believe me. He might not even show up at all. Whatever happened in the next hour, I knew this might be one of the last slots on my punch card with Special Agent Lee Cannon. I only hoped the information I was about to give him would put me back in his good graces for a while.

The rest stop off 23 near Coleson wasn't one of the nicer ones. State budget cuts had left it in disrepair. The roof leaked. The dog path had become overgrown. Most people tended to bypass it, heading for the deluxe plaza twenty miles north with the fast-food court and barber shop. Today though, it was perfect. The only trucker in the lot pulled out as I was pulling in. He gave me a wave from his cab as I slid into a spot at the very end of the row.

The minutes crawled by. I watched car after car whiz by. Cannon said he'd text me when he was a few minutes out. I put my phone on the magnetic holder Joe had affixed to my dashboard, then jumped as it rang.

Zoe.

I hit the accept call button and let the Bluetooth speaker kick in.

"Hi, Cass," she started. "I'm so sorry to bother you again."

"It's okay."

"I'm at the hospital. They transported my grandmother about an hour ago. She's been having a bad reaction to her medication. She had a seizure that lasted almost twenty minutes."

"I'm so sorry," I said. "Are you okay? Is there anything you need?"

"No. It's just ... I'm probably going to be here all night. I wanted you to know in case you heard anything from the judge."

"I don't think we'll hear anything today. But his clerk promised to give me a heads-up when he's got a ruling. Did you go to the hospital straight from Maple Valley?"

"Yes."

"Let me send a text to Jeanie. She can swing by the house and pack a few things for you if you're going to be spending the night there."

"Cass, you don't have to do that."

"Zoe ... you don't have anyone else. And Jeanie lives for this type of thing. Let us help you."

She made a choked sound on the other end of the phone, and I knew she was holding back tears.

"Thank you. Cass, they're telling me she might not leave the hospital this time. This might be it."

"Okay. Okay. One day at a time. Remember?"

"Yeah. I'm sorry to bother you. I know you've got a million other things going on."

"Just the one," I said. I watched from my rear-view mirror as cars zipped by on the freeway. None of them slowed. It was after six now. Cannon would pull up any second.

"I'll let you go."

"Zoe," I said, beginning to feel uneasy. "You're going to stay at the hospital all night, right?"

"Yes," she said.

"Okay. Please do. If you need to leave, let me know. I just don't want you to go back to your house yet. Not until I have things sorted out with my contact at the FBI."

"I know, Cass. I'm being careful. I won't go anywhere alone. I won't take any calls from my deadbeat family. I promise."

"Okay," I said. "I know this is trite, but just hang in there. We're going to have this wrapped up for you soon. Then you can have your life back."

I resisted the urge to add that I could have my life back too. Zoe thanked me and apologized for the umpteenth time for calling me even though I told her I never minded. The sun was beginning to hang low.

"Any minute now, Cannon," I said. I could wait, but my bladder couldn't. Another trucker pulled into the lane behind me. I grabbed my phone off the stand and headed into the restroom.

A custodian had just put a wet floor sign in front of the women's room, blocking the door. I looked behind me. The trucker hadn't come out of his cab.

"Screw it," I said, heading for the men's room. I was in and out as quickly as I could, hearing the custodian whistling behind the next wall.

Exiting the men's room, I pulled out my phone and looked at the last message from Cannon. He said he'd be driving his government-issue silver Explorer. I looked out the front windows. The trucker had already begun to pull out again. Odd.

"I'm here," I texted Cannon. "I'll wait for you inside if you're close."

Three blinking dots, but no response.

The custodian came out of the women's restroom. He gave me a smile. "Sorry," he said. "Didn't mean to hang you up."

"It's okay." I smiled back and pointed to the other restroom. "I'm all set."

He gave me a wink and moved the wet floor sign in front of the men's room then disappeared inside.

My phone vibrated.

"You're inside where?" Cannon texted back.

"The rest stop off 23 near Coleson like you told me," I answered. "The place is deserted. It'll be plenty quiet to talk. Let me know when you're a few minutes out."

The chemical smell from whatever the custodian was using to mop the floors made me sneeze. Violently. I walked outside to get some fresh air.

My car was only a hundred yards away. There was no one in the lot, but my spine began to crawl. I'd left the discs in a bag under the passenger seat. Stupid, I thought. Even though I kept the doors locked, someone could have just taken them.

Cannon texted back a question mark. A moment later, he sent a picture text, but it didn't have a chance to download. I only had a single bar. Then my phone rang again.

Eric.

I answered.

"What's up?"

"Cass," he said. Immediately, I knew something was wrong. "Are you alone?"

"What?" I asked.

"Is Cannon with you?"

"No. He's running late, I think. I'm trying to text with him …"

"Cass, get out of there. Drive away as fast as you can."

"What?" The call cut in and out. I walked away from the building to the end of the sidewalk, trying to get a better signal.

"Cass, listen to me. He knows. Corbett knows. He's put … spoof … right here … all … whole time … way … fast …"

"Eric, what? Say that again. Corbett knows what?"

Eric was shouting into the phone, but he kept breaking up. "Come home … twenty …"

I heard a car pull in behind me. Turning, I expected to see Lee Cannon's silver Explorer. Instead, it was a rusted-out black Buick. The driver's side window rolled down.

My senses reached my brain in the wrong order. First, I heard a crack. My fingers seemed to stop working. My phone dropped to the pavement.

Heat spread through my hand. I saw the black barrel of the gun through the small crack in the Buick's window.

Finally, from far away, I heard Eric's voice telling me to run.

The second shot flew right past my head. Missing me by millimeters. The Buick revved its engine then barreled straight for me.

Chapter 36

BLOOD. My blood. It leached out of me in a trail of stinging heat. For a moment that seemed to stretch forever, I stared at my hand. My right pinky hung down at the wrong angle. Bits of bone poked out.

A voice came to me. My own.

Run!

I already was.

The shooter blocked my route to my car. I was on my own. I bolted left, ignoring the pain in my hand.

The next shot hit the glass door behind me, shattering it. I thought of the man inside. The custodian. I found myself praying he wasn't hurt. Wishing I could shout out a warning. Hoping the shooter didn't see him.

The dog trail was to my left, overgrown with weeds and branches. Beyond it was the woods.

Cars sped by on the highway. There was no way to get to them. They were going far too fast. They would not stop. I was more in danger of being run over than shot.

I hit the trail, hopping over a rotted branch, my feet nearly tangling in the thick, thorny vines that wrapped themselves around every tree trunk here.

I screamed for help. At least, I think I did. The trucker. Where was the trucker?

Gone. Gone. Gone.

Another shot; this one went wide, hitting the tree to my right, splintering its bark.

I flailed my arms over my head, hoping someone would see. That they would stop. That they would call 911.

But it would be too late.

The Buick went into reverse; almost spinning backward, he blocked my route to the highway. There was only one way to go.

I raced to the woods, hoping the thick brush would hide me. There were houses back there. Maybe a half a mile back, I remembered seeing a junkyard with old school buses and hubcaps everywhere. It might as well have been fifty miles away.

Another shot. This one rang by my left ear. A split second before, my right foot landed in an uneven patch of ground. It was just enough to make him miss the shot. Otherwise, the bullet would have exploded inside my skull.

"No!" I shouted.

I reached the tree line. He was no more than fifty yards away.

At top speed, something sliced through my shins. I hit a small, nearly invisible wire fence meant to keep passersby from trespassing on whoever's land this was. I pitched forward, tumbling over the fence and landing face first, my legs tangled in the wire.

I heard a car door slam. Footsteps.

"No. No. No."

I fought against the wire. It cut through my jeans. My right hand wouldn't work. I kicked out for all I was worth.

I got one leg free. But my left was hopelessly ensnarled.

I saw him. Big. Burly. He wore a dark knit cap though it was eighty degrees out. He passed under a streetlamp that had just turned on at dusk.

I knew him. Horror heated my blood. Fighting past the pain in my hand and legs, I pulled at the wire.

Ned Corbett came closer and closer. He raised his gun, aiming it straight for my head.

Begging wouldn't help. Calling for help wouldn't do any good. He knew. Somehow, he knew why I'd come here. The only way to stop me was to kill me. For a moment, I thought I was already dead.

He had a smile on his face even as his eyes held no emotion. He was a hunter. I was nothing more than prey.

Did I say something? Did I scream? I saw myself as if I existed outside my body. This was it. Game over. I watched myself freeze.

But it was false. A nightmare. One I knew would haunt me for the rest of my life if I had one beyond this moment.

The skin on my palms seemed to peel away as I struggled with the wire fencing. Ned Corbett held his gun out two-handed; he aimed it at my head.

Then, the wire gave out. I kicked out with both legs. Just before the shot rang out, I rolled hard to my side.

He would have killed me then, even as I'd freed myself. But something happened. His weapon jammed. A merciful God intervened perhaps. Blood pouring from my hands and my shins, I managed to claw through the grass and get to my feet.

Pain didn't matter. Breath didn't matter. Time didn't matter. Distance. That was my only defense. I ran for the thickest part of the woods, praying there would be no more fencing. Pleading with God to help me hide.

"You don't have to run!" Corbett yelled.

Part of me almost laughed. He was crazy. Or I was. I pushed my way past the brush, struggling to stay on my feet.

Keep going. Keep going. Keep going.

I couldn't hear the highway anymore. Couldn't see lights or houses or anything at all. There were only the trees and the darkening sky. I swear I could hear Ned Corbett's breath in my ear, though I knew that wasn't possible.

My heart felt as if it would explode inside my chest. That my own body would betray me far before Ned Corbett's bullets could rip me in two.

Ahead of me, a group of blackbirds took flight. Crows perhaps. Were they biding their time? Waiting for the next death that would keep them alive?

Not today, you assholes, I thought.

Another shot. This one to the right of me. He was close and getting closer.

I changed course; this had to end. There had to be a place to go.

Dark. Footfalls. Every shadow seemed to hold a monster inside of it. Every noise could be the last thing I heard.

Pain seared through me. I wasn't bleeding that badly, but with every panicked beat of my heart, I felt it drain me.

I was tired. So, so tired.

Keep going. Keep going. Keep going.

I tried to get my bearings. I'd been past this stretch of land a thousand times heading north on US23. It was nothing more than a mile marker. A patch of woods where deer might jump out if you weren't paying attention. Now, these woods meant life or death.

I chanced a look behind me. Around me. Would he come from the side? If I found a place to hide, would he run right past me? Was he a hunter who knew how to track? Were those lights ahead of me? How far?

I kept going, changing course, I headed for an even thicker part of the woods. There was farmland up ahead, I was sure of it. But for me, that could mean death. With flat, open ground, Corbett could pick me off at his leisure.

I had to find my way back to the road. Surely, I could hide long enough for there to be a break in the traffic. I could cross the highway, head out into the open. Corbett couldn't possibly gun me down on a busy highway in full view of cars going in both directions.

Could he?

But the farther I ran, the harder it became to orient myself. Had I gone in circles? I knew I'd passed that tree with the bulbous knot in its trunk before. There were road sounds to the left of me, but also to the right.

I had to stop. I had to catch my breath. My lungs burned. My muscles were on fire.

I took a chance. A moment. I pressed my back against the thickest tree trunk I could find. Looking up, its gnarled branches formed a network, stretching and connecting to all the trees around it.

If I could climb high enough, I might be safe. But the nearest branch was too far above me. It was a foolish notion. A fat crow sat on a branch and stared down at me with his big, yellow eyes. His head twitched. At that moment, I would have given anything to be like him.

Give me wings, God, I thought. Let me fly.

The next bullet seared past me with the sound of a missile.

I didn't scream. I didn't move. It came from directly behind me. Corbett was close. He had followed my path.

Slowly, carefully, I sank to the ground in a crouch. I reached out, clawing the ground with my good hand looking for something. Anything.

My fingers closed around a large rock. I let out a silent breath. My head pounded. I couldn't hear anything but the rush of my own blood through my veins.

As quietly as I could, I straightened my legs and stood upright.

1-2-3.

Then I threw the rock as hard as I could in the opposite direction. It smacked against another tree, rustling leaves in its wake.

Another shot. The crow screamed a warning as it took flight.

I ran to my right, pushing through branches, hoping like hell I didn't twist my ankle and pitch forward face first.

"Dammit!" I heard a voice. Had he fallen? God. He seemed so close. He seemed like he was everywhere.

I kept running. Kept praying. Bit my tongue past the urge to scream and reveal my position.

Then, abruptly, the woods fell away. I burst through a clearing; ahead of me stretched acre upon acre of flat farmland. Rows of soybeans, and in the distance, I saw a white farmhouse with black shutters. The lights were on.

Could I make it? Would Corbett risk shooting me out here in the open? There could be witnesses even though dusk had come. There were a few outbuildings to the east of the barn. I heard machinery. Movement.

It could be my salvation or seal my doom.

A choice. A split second. Run for help or hide.

He was coming. I heard branches breaking behind me and to my left. In another few seconds, he would reach the clearing too.

Corn, I thought. Why couldn't this be a cornfield or something else tall enough to hide me?

I decided to run. Staying hidden in the tree line, I made my way toward the edge of the field, toward the house.

Would he kill me in front of witnesses if I made it there? Or was I putting the lives of whoever was in that farmhouse in danger too?

I kept going. Every second I lived was a victory. It gave me another second to decide what to do.

I could make it. I had to make it. I almost did.

Then ... my knee exploded in pain as I tripped over a rotted branch. I stayed on my feet. I would have kept going.

Something jerked me backward. Corbett's hot, fetid breath brushed against my cheek. He smelled of sweat and marijuana.

"Gotcha," he said.

He came from nowhere. From everywhere. The farmhouse seemed like a mirage as Corbett yanked me backward into the woods.

He flung me down to the ground. On pure adrenaline, I tried to scramble to my feet.

"There's no use," he said, raising his gun again. "There's nowhere else for you to go."

"You don't have to do this," I said. "Corbett. We can work together. You know who I am."

He had a sadistic smile on his face.

"Corbett!" I yelled, my heart pounding. My brain felt like mud, but I had to think. I had no weapon. I only had my words.

"Corbett. You know who I am. If you kill me, you're going to bring Killian Thorne and the Irish mob down on your head."

Pure contempt filled his eyes as he advanced on me. "You're a snitch. I know who you were waiting to meet. You're in bed with the feds. No one's going to care about me taking care of a rat."

"I can give you the money. You want Marilyn Paul's two million dollars? I can tell you where it is. If you kill me, you'll never get your hands on it. And the evidence I've got ... Marilyn's evidence. I made copies of everything."

"You mean this evidence?" he said, holding up the black bag I'd left in my car. "No. No. I don't think you did make copies."

"Is that a chance you're willing to take?" I said. "You've cut corners before, haven't you? Trusted people you shouldn't have."

My mind raced as I tried to put the last pieces in place. What did Corbett know? How did he know it? "Roy Lockwood, Marilyn's brother, you tried to use him before, didn't you? Did you send him to Marilyn's house after her accident to try and find what she stole? Did you promise him a cut of the money if he found it? Zoe said he tore the house up. But he didn't find anything. And Marilyn can't talk. You thought you had everything under control for Valentine, didn't you? I know that's who you're working for. They're gonna find out how sloppy you are, Corbett. Then what? They'll kill you."

"Shut up!" he said, but I could see fear in his eyes. I'd hit on something.

"I know you bankrolled Chad Einhorn. I have proof," I lied. "I've had an informant, Corbett. Holly Billings. She's been feeding me information this whole time. She knows you're involved. She's talking to the police as we speak. It's over. Killing me is only going to add to your problems. They'll know it was you. You won't be able to hide. There's nowhere far enough for you to run. You'll have the feds, the state police, and the Valentines, all wanting you dead, Corbett. No safe harbor."

He hesitated. His step faltered. He was worried.

"Ask yourself," I said. "You know who I am. Who I'm connected to. I can help you. I'm the only one who can. You should have come to me first instead of Lockwood or Bradley Paul. We could have worked together." Would he believe me? I tried to crawl backward. If I could get to my feet. Slowly, I clawed at the ground, trying to find something else I could use as a weapon.

"She was stupid, wasn't she?" I said. "Marilyn could have had everything. But she got greedy. Or she got self-righteous. You told her all that, didn't you?"

"Yeah," he said.

"She couldn't even handle getting into a car accident the right way," I said. "Couldn't just die outright."

He snorted, laughed.

"It's over, Corbett. There's no walking any of this back. Marilyn's evidence is already with the police. My contact at the FBI is going to come looking for me. Eric Wray knows that you're mixed up in this. I get it. You're a fixer. But there's no fixing this. I'm the only one who can help you now. But not if you kill me."

"Yeah. I should have killed Marilyn. I'm not leaving you to chance."

I saw lights up ahead in the opposite direction of the farm. Something familiar. Something close.

Corbett ran forward. He reached down and grabbed me. I punched for all I was worth, kicking, flailing, biting.

My eye seemed to explode as he hit back with a closed fit. I fell to my knees.

Cars. I heard cars. Had I run in a circle? Was that the highway just up ahead again?

"End of the road, counselor," he said.

I tasted blood in my mouth. I tried to get my legs to work. My brain. All I could see was the barrel of Ned Corbett's gun as he aimed it straight at my head.

"They'll hear you," I said, spitting blood out. In some dark corner of my brain, I found myself wondering how I was still conscious. He'd hit me as hard as he could. My ears rang.

"They'll hear nothing," he said.

"Please," I whispered. "Don't."

Corbett tilted his head to the side. I saw his finger twitch on the trigger. I turned, crawling forward. He might shoot me in the back, but I would not sit there and wait for it. I found my way to my feet.

One leg in front of the other. Lights ahead of me. I could hear him take a breath.

Then ...

Pow!

Cold death. Darkness. The final sound of the gunshot.

Chapter 37

"Cᴀss! Cᴀss!"

A disembodied voice reached my ears through the pounding of my own blood. Someone came toward me. Running. I turned back, looking for Ned Corbett.

He was gone. No. He was on the ground. I took a step forward. Then another. Until finally, I stood over him. He lay on his back, his right eye blown out. In its place, blackness. Slowly, blood seeped out behind his head.

"Cass!"

Arms came around me, pulling me back. Taking me away.

Eric. Strong. Sure. Angry. He ran forward, crouching over Ned Corbett's body. He kicked the gun away from Corbett's lifeless hand.

"Is he alone?" Eric shouted.

"What?"

Eric turned back, his eyes wild. He held his service weapon out and downward.

"Cass! Was Corbett alone?"

"Yes," I gasped as the fragmented events of the last few minutes began to reform into a chronology that made sense.

Corbett raised his gun to shoot me. There was a shot. But it had come from Eric's gun. He was here. Somehow. Impossibly. He was here. Then I looked in the direction from where he had come. The lights. The familiar lights. They were from the rest stop. I'd run in a nearly complete circle.

Eric pulled his radio out of his pocket.

"Dispatch, this is Unit 128. I'm out at the rest stop near Coleson on US23 northbound. Shots fired. Suspect down. Need medical code three. Alert command and send crews to the scene. Repeat suspect down."

Eric pocketed his radio and came to me. He holstered his weapon and pulled me to him. The blood started to flow to my limbs again. The pain came with it.

"Cass," he said. "You've been hit. Where have you been hit?"

We were on the move. I took a step. Then I tried to take another. Then Eric picked me up as if I were lighter than air. He took me through the clearing back to the parking lot of the rest stop.

He sat me down on the curb where the light was brightest.

"My hand," I said, raising my mangled right hand.

"That's all?" he asked, alarm draining the color from his face.

"Isn't that enough?" I tried to joke.

"God," he said, his voice cracking. He sank to a crouch in front of me. "I was afraid I wouldn't get here in time."

I smiled. I took my good hand and touched his cheek. "You always get here in time." Then. "How did you get here in time? How did you know?"

Eric's face fell. "Cass, he knew. He's known every step you've taken. Corbett had a tracking app on your phone. On his computer, he had the thing mirrored. He could see every call you made. Every text you wrote. Your GPS. He's had your office bugged too. He knew you were going to meet with Cannon. He knew when and where. He was able to use a spoof app to send a text to Cannon that looked like it came from you."

"He said something," I said. "Cannon. I called when I thought he was late."

"As far as Cannon knew, you texted to cancel the meeting about twenty minutes after you set it up. It was a trap, Cass. Corbett was lying in wait."

"The discs," I said, trying to rise. "Corbett had them. They should be around here somewhere."

"I've got them. We'll worry about all that later," he said. In the distance, I could already hear the sirens coming.

"Eric," I said. "How? How the hell did Corbett get access to my phone?"

"It's not just your phone," Eric said. "I told you. He also bugged your office. He's been listening in on every meeting you took on Zoe Paul's case since almost the beginning. Cass, it's how he knew about the discs being at Zoe's. That day, when we were in your office looking at them, Corbett heard the whole thing."

"My God," I said. "Zoe. He ransacked Zoe's house looking for them because of us?"

"It looks that way. It's over," he said. "It's all over. Ned Corbett isn't going to hurt you or anyone else ever again."

The sirens came closer. Then three marked patrol cars careened into the rest stop parking lot. They were followed close behind by a silver Explorer. Lee Cannon was behind the wheel.

"I want to stand up," I said, reaching for Eric. He offered me his hand. I tried to take a step but felt the world start to spin. Eric put an arm around me and helped me to his car. He opened the back door and had me sit inside.

"I called Cannon," Eric said. "I didn't know which one of us would get here faster."

I smiled at him. Cannon parked next to my car and got out, his face bloodless, his eyes wide.

"Is she ..."

"I'm okay," I answered. "More or less in one piece. But it took you long enough."

Eric shouted directions to the responding officers. A moment later, an ambulance pulled into the lot.

"She's over here!" Cannon yelled.

"Everything's on those discs," I said to him. "Eric, show him."

Eric walked over with the black bag containing all of Marilyn Paul's CDs. He handed it to Cannon.

"It's all here," Eric said. "A paper trail going back twenty years. The Paganos' main money launderer in this region. I've got a witness tucked away who will testify to the connection between them too. Merry early Christmas, Cannon."

Cannon couldn't take his eyes off me. Dumbstruck, he took the bag from Eric and slid it over his shoulder.

"Pleasure doing business with you," I said. "Though next time, let's pick a nice, public place in the middle of the city. A coffee shop. Or maybe even a bar. Yes. A bar. I think I'd like a drink right about now."

The EMTs closed in, blocking my view of Eric and Lee Cannon. It was then that I let myself feel the pain.

Chapter 38

Forty-eight hours, one hand surgery, and one CT scan later, I sat in a wheelchair in the lobby of Windham Hospital waiting for my ride. I didn't want to make a fuss. Matty and Tori had enough on their plate. So did Joe and Vangie. If I weren't under driving restrictions on account of my hand and mild concussion, I would have quietly slipped out of here alone. But when Eric pulled his car around, I found myself very glad to see him. He came out and helped the patient porter wheel me to the passenger side.

"I've got it," I said. "I'm okay. A little banged up and worse for wear, but ..."

"Shush," Eric said. "You were shot, Cass. And you look ..."

He couldn't finish the sentence. I climbed into the seat and pulled down the visor, opening the mirror.

"Horrible," I said. No amount of make-up would hide the ugly bruise covering the entire left side of my face. The doctor told me I was lucky Corbett hadn't shattered my cheek or orbital bones around my eye. As it was, a blood vessel had burst, turning the white of my eye completely and shockingly red.

"Ugh," I said, quickly flipping the visor up.

Eric slid behind the wheel. "I'm staying with you for a couple of days if you don't mind."

I wanted to tell him I was fine. I was. But everything hurt. So instead, I looked at him and said, "Thank you."

We drove in silence for a moment. I sensed something in him. Something he wasn't telling me. It felt like more than worry.

"Okay," I said. "What happened?"

He sucked in a breath. "I shouldn't even say. I should just drive your ass straight home and make you get into bed and rest like the doctors want you to."

"But ..."

"But Cannon called a half an hour ago. Last night, they picked up Holly Billings at a train station in Jackson. Your instincts were right. She was your deep throat. Cannon's got her in protective custody."

"Is she all right?" Two days ago, when I went to what I thought was my meeting with Cannon, Eric had tried to track Holly Billings down. She'd disappeared. Until now. I had feared the worst after what happened to Jason Mackin and what almost happened to me.

"She's in one piece. Scared to death though. She knows what happened to you. She knows Corbett is dead."

"It's only a matter of time before the Paganos figure out she's the one who snitched. Eric ... she's been reckless. She marched herself into that courtroom. Einhorn could have seen her. If I put two and two together, someone else will too."

"They already have," he said. "Your calls with her were all accessible to Corbett."

"God. But she's okay?"

"She's safe. For now. And she's talking. Cannon managed to get the U.S. Attorney on board. They're offering her full immunity, witness protection. The whole deal."

"Will she take it?"

"She's waffling. She's already told Cannon enough to launch a full-scale investigation. There will be indictments against the major players at Valentine, but Cannon's hoping he can flip someone even higher up than Holly Billings. But ... he needs her too. She's asking for you."

"Where is she?"

"The Bureau has put her up in a hotel in Ann Arbor."

"He's with her now?" I asked.

"He is."

"We could be in Ann Arbor in twenty minutes," I said. "You know exactly where they are, don't you?"

"Cass," he said.

"You knew I was going to want to go. You could have just kept it to yourself. Given me my pain meds and waited until I went off into la la land again."

"Then I know you'd have killed me."

"You're right," I said, pointing to the next road sign. "Pay attention, you'll miss your exit."

Eric grumbled but didn't argue. I tried to smile, but my face hurt too much. Instead, I laid a hand on his arm. "I love you, you know."

"I love you too," he said, his voice sounding thick. "I just wish you'd pick a different line of work."

"Come on," I said. "This was Probate Court. Didn't you ask me to switch to that specialty because you thought it would be boring?"

He growled again, but things settled between us for the rest of the drive. Twenty minutes later, Eric pulled into the lot of a Best Western off I-94.

Cannon's silver Explorer was easy to spot. Eric parked in the space next to it.

He pulled out his phone and checked a text.

"Cannon says we can go on in," he said.

Eric got out first and came around to open the door. He held a hand out for me. It hurt to move. Every muscle in my body ached, even the ones Ned Corbett hadn't abused.

Eric's growl seemed to become a low, constant vibration.

"We're not staying long," he said.

"I'm fine," I assured him.

Eric led me inside and down the hall to Room 217. He raised a hand to knock but Cannon swung it open. He took one look at me, and his face fell.

"You should see the other guy," I joked.

Now it was Cannon's turn to growl out his concern. I put a hand on his chest and gently moved him aside. Room 217 was a suite. Two female agents stood in the sitting room area. To the left of them, an alcove opened and Holly Billings sat on the bed looking more pained than I felt. When she saw my face, she started to cry.

"I'm sorry," she sobbed. "So sorry." Ah. That voice. Had there been any doubt, those two words clinched it for me. Holly Billings had been the one feeding me information since this whole thing started.

"I'm okay," I said. "But you're doing the right thing."

Eric sprang into action. He found a chair and pulled it over to me. Before I could protest, he gently guided me into it.

"Cass is lucky, Mrs. Billings," Cannon said.

"Lucky? She was trying to get to you," Holly said. "This is what they did to her for trying to tell you the truth? What do you think they'll do to me?"

"This is why you need federal protection. Agent Cannon can protect you. He's good at what he does. All these agents are."

"I've told you what I can," she said, addressing Lee.

"Mrs. Billings has corroborated everything you found among Marilyn Paul's things. The double ledgers, every payment going in and out. She even had direct contact with members of the Pagano organization. With her testimony, the records you found, and what we seized from Ned Corbett's house and computer, we have enough to make a real dent in their organization. Mrs. Billings, you're going to help us take a massive amount of illicit drugs off the street. Your testimony will save lives. You need to know that."

She wrung her hands. The woman looked ready to collapse.

"I never meant for any of this to hurt Marilyn's family," she said. "I knew Zoe. When she was younger, Marilyn used to bring her into the office. She was the sweetest, smartest little kid. I always thought what Marilyn was doing, taking her in for that deadbeat son of hers, was noble. I don't know if it's something I could have done."

"Holly, how did Ned Corbett fit into all of this? How did Marilyn get mixed up with him?"

"The Valentine brothers had him doing security for them," she said.

"Side projects," Eric said. "All authorized by the department. We figured that's how they met."

"Exactly," Holly said. "So he could wear his Delphi P.D. uniform while he was patrolling the restaurant and surrounding buildings after hours."

"We think that's how he got in with the Valentines, at least initially," Cannon said.

"Marilyn trusted him," Holly said. "She trusted everybody. Especially Tim Valentine. Look, I knew something was going on. We were taking in far more money than we should have been. The pizza place was doing well. Just not that well. And I heard some things over the years, you know? Rumors and such. Anyway, I needed that job. I had kids to feed. Bills of my own to pay. My husband got laid up and I was the one with the health insurance. I looked the other way."

"Marilyn didn't," I said.

"She was my friend. She started asking a lot of questions. She was looking over the books. She said Tim asked her to. I don't know if that's true or not. Anyway, Marilyn came to me one day with the copies she'd made of the book entries. She asked me if I knew anything about it. I tried to play dumb. I told her. I warned her. Stay out of it. For a while, I thought she listened to me. Then ... she said she knew what Valentine was doing was illegal and she had a plan to prove it."

"Did you know that she and Ned Corbett were close? That she was talking to him about it, too?" I asked.

Holly shook her head. "I knew they were friendly. But she kept that relationship from me. I think she knew I'd tell her to watch out for him. I never liked him. I thought he was a letch. Always staring at the younger girls' behinds, that sort of thing. Anyway, Marilyn asked me to help her. She wanted access to the company check book. She said she wanted to see the register."

"You gave her access?" I asked.

"Yes. She was relentless. She said she had a plan to make sure that if anything went wrong, we'd be taken care of. It was little by little. A hundred dollars here and there at first. Reimbursements for office supplies, mileage, company trips and lunches that we never really took. Nobody noticed. Over time, she got bolder. I wasn't keeping track, but now I know. She took millions. She was doing it for Zoe. Marilyn was worried what would happen if she ever got caught. Or if things didn't go how she planned. She wanted to have enough money so Zoe would never have to worry."

Cannon had printouts of all the spreadsheets and ledger entries we'd taken from Marilyn's CDs. Holly Billings pointed to deposits into a single account at Delphi Savings Bank.

"These were Marilyn's," she said.

"It adds up to two million dollars," Cannon confirmed.

"So she skimmed money for herself while she was compiling evidence of the laundering scheme against Valentine," I said.

"I told you. She said it was her insurance policy," Holly said. "If anything happened to her, she wanted to be able to survive. For Zoe to survive. And she ... I'm sorry. I regret all of this now. But this account here, this was for me."

"She funneled a half a million dollars your way," Cannon said.

"Over time. Yes."

"She closed the account," I said. "She had the bank cut the balance to her in a cashier's check and hid it under her bathroom floorboards."

"I didn't know she did that, I swear. At least ... I didn't know she was ready to follow through. All that stuff Zoe's family has been saying. It's all lies. Or they've twisted it. Marilyn wasn't trying to get rid of Zoe. She wasn't afraid of her. She was trying to make sure Zoe would be taken care of if Marilyn had to disappear for a little while. She was trying to figure out how to cash that money without being caught or drawing attention to herself. She got really scared. Afraid that if she cashed it then they'd be on to her. She was trying to get her exit strategy in place. And then ..."

"The accident," I said.

"As far as I know, that's all it was," Holly said.

"That's what Corbett thought too," Eric said. "My informant, Durante, confirmed it. Valentine didn't know Marilyn was skimming from them or compiling this evidence. By the time they figured it out, Marilyn had already crashed her car. Corbett let them think he'd taken care of the problem."

"Yes," Holly said. "Corbett came to me. He threatened me. He said he knew what Marilyn was up to and that she'd given me money too. He said he'd let me keep it and Valentine would be none the wiser. I think he was afraid I'd be the one to slip and tell Valentine what Marilyn was doing. He'd be in big trouble then because he was supposed to be their fixer. Their inside guy with the cops. It was all about to get away from him and then poor Marilyn just klutzed her way into a car crash."

"Luckiest thing that ever happened to Ned Corbett," Cannon said.

"And then Zoe found that check," I said. "And Corbett's little problem resurfaced."

"I was afraid to leave my house. Afraid to *stay* at my house," Holly said. "I knew Corbett would come looking for me. I've been staying with friends. In motels."

"We think Corbett has more or less been acting alone," Lee said. "We're still going through his phone records, his computer. But he had several meetings with a member of the Pagano family in the last few weeks. When your probate case made the news, they started getting suspicious."

"Corbett probably assured them he had everything under control," Eric said.

"He got lucky," I said. "A squirrel handled the job he couldn't."

"Looks that way," Cannon said.

"He had a burner phone on him when I shot him," Eric said. "His last text was to Lou Pagano. He's second-in-command for the entire organization. He was assuring him that he was about to neutralize you."

I felt sick. Physically sick.

"He would have killed her," I said. "Or tried to. If Zoe's grandmother hadn't gotten into that accident, she'd be dead anyway."

"I told her," Holly cried. "I warned her. It wasn't worth it. No amount of money was worth that. I was afraid all this would happen. That's why I reached out to you. Tried to warn you. These people don't mess around. They're killers. Trained killers."

"Einhorn," Eric said. "You started this whole thing telling Cass you thought Einhorn was on the Paganos' payroll. Is there any truth to that?"

"Yes," Cannon said. "He's done some defense work for a few of their associates. We're looking into it. For the moment, it doesn't appear he's done anything illegal. My suspicion is that the Paganos decided not to put all their eggs in Ned Corbett's basket. Having Einhorn represent Zoe's father gave them an insight into what was happening in court. So he would be privy to whatever you found out about the source of those funds, Cass. They probably never cared whether Zoe won or lost that case."

"I'd seen him a few times coming out of Tim Valentine's office," Holly said. "I recognized the name. When I saw he was representing Zoe's family against her, I knew they were behind that lawsuit somehow too."

"You took a big chance, Holly," I said. "It was dangerous for you to show up in court. What if Einhorn had recognized you? What if Corbett was waiting for you?"

"I wanted to see for myself. He doesn't know who I am. I'm sure of it. I wanted to see Zoe. That day ... I thought maybe I would just warn Zoe myself. I couldn't do it. I just couldn't do it. I got scared."

"Corbett more or less admitted to me that he was using Roy Lockwood, Marilyn's brother," I said. "He moved into Marilyn's house in the months right after her accident. I think he promised Corbett he would find whatever evidence or money she stashed there. He just never did."

"We've found payments from Corbett to Jason Mackin," Cannon said.

"He paid him to lie in court about Zoe and Marilyn's last wishes," I said. "Do you think his death was suspicious? Could it have been murder?"

"We may never know," Eric said. "There's no evidence of foul play. No one was seen coming or going from his house on his security footage. It may well be that Mackin was scared enough about being found out after Corbett pressured him to lie under oath."

"He's a victim in this too, either way," I said.

"Definitely," Cannon said.

"Einhorn has blood on his hands too," I said. "I just don't know if I can prove it."

"I'll be looking into him too," Cannon said. "If I find something that can stick, I'll let you know."

"You're doing the right thing, Holly," I said. I just wished she'd done it sixteen years ago. There was no point in saying that now.

"You have what you need?" Eric said to Cannon. "I need to get Cass home. She needs to rest."

"I'm glad you're okay," Holly said. She came to me. Gently, she put her arms around me and hugged me. "Tell her for me, will you? Tell Zoe I remember her. Tell her her grandmother really loved her. She did the wrong things, but she wanted what was best for Zoe. Now she can have it. Zoe can put that money to good use and maybe Marilyn can finally be at peace too."

I exchanged a look with Cannon.

"I'll tell her," I said. "Take care of yourself, Holly. And you can trust these agents. You're going to be okay."

I only hoped that she would.

I said goodbye. Cannon followed Eric and me back out into the hallway. I turned to face him.

"The check," I said. "Marilyn Paul's two million dollars. No matter what happens in my case, her family isn't going to be allowed to keep it."

Cannon gave me a tight-lipped smile. "Likely not. It'll probably be part of my seizure order. I'm sorry, Cass. Mrs. Billings is right about one thing. Marilyn's granddaughter didn't deserve any of this. This is one thing I might be able to do for her. There are a lot of moving parts though. I better not commit to anything just yet."

"Thank you," I said. "To be honest, once Zoe understands the full scope of this, I don't think she's going to want to have anything to do with that money."

"I predict when her leech of a family realizes they won't get it either, they'll crawl back under the rocks they came from," Eric said.

"You're probably right."

"Roy Lockwood at least may be facing criminal conspiracy charges," Cannon said. "If you can prove he perjured himself on the stand, you can bring state charges."

"It's not my case now, but we'll look hard at it. Come on," Eric said. "Time to get you to bed."

"You sure you're okay?" Cannon asked. "You really do look awful."

I laughed. "I'll survive."

Cannon looked at Eric. "Take care of her, Wray."

"I have been," Eric said. "And don't take this the wrong way, Cannon. But I really hope I don't see you again anytime soon."

Cannon gave him a half-hearted salute. "Understood."

"Let's go," Eric said, gently nudging me back down the hall. It was in me to protest. But the moment we started walking, I realized how tired I really was.

"I like how you take care of me," I said as Eric helped me adjust my seatbelt. It was harder to do with my left hand than I anticipated.

He kissed me. Even that hurt.

"So you know," he said as he pulled out of the motel parking lot. "None of it was my idea. When you get mad, remember that."

"None of what?" I asked.

"Your coming-home party. Vangie cooked it up. I managed to put them off until this evening, hoping you'd be able to get a good nap in. But that's all I could do. Your whole family is waiting for us at the house."

I leaned over and put my head on Eric's shoulder as he drove. Yawning, I told him, "It's okay. I know exactly who to blame. And who to thank."

I couldn't help it. I laughed. It was agony. At the same time, I realized maybe I didn't mind so much. They were big. Loud. Chaos agents. But they were mine and I loved them.

"I'm just glad this is finally over," Eric said. "You need normal and boring for a while."

"That sounds like heaven," I said. Then I stopped myself from saying something else. This wasn't over. There was still one last thing.

Chapter 39

THREE DAYS LATER, Judge Wentz issued his final ruling. I stood in the courtroom bruised, battered, broken, but feeling strong. Beside me, Zoe Paul had been broken in a different way. But I knew in my heart she would emerge just as strong.

"Where is he?" Judge Wentz asked. Though the hearing had been scheduled to start ten minutes ago, Chad Einhorn was a no-show. So were both of his clients.

"Your Honor," I said. "I haven't heard from Mr. Einhorn."

"We called his office," Mindy Price said. "They said he hasn't been in and isn't answering his cell phone."

I had my suspicions. Arrest warrants had been issued for Tim Valentine, and several high-ranking members of the Pagano family. Einhorn had likely been told to cut and run or taken the initiative himself. There was also a warrant out for Roy Lockwood in connection with his embezzling Marilyn's fundraiser money. It may be too late to prosecute, but Eric wanted to try. Bradley Paul had completely vanished. The prosecutor wanted to question him too about a potential perjury charge. I had a feeling both he and Uncle Roy would never set foot in Delphi again.

"Well, I guess we don't need him for this," Judge Wentz said. "If you're okay with proceeding with the petitioners in absentia ..."

"We are, Your Honor," I said.

"All right. I'll file a written order and memorandum later today. But I find the petitioners' motion to be without merit. Despite several days of testimony and at great cost, I do not believe the petitioners have made a showing by a preponderance of the evidence that Zoe Paul has failed to act in her grandmother's best interests. Therefore, I am denying the request to have her removed as Marilyn Paul's guardian. Likewise, I see no misuse of funds or self-dealing in any of the accountings Ms. Paul has filed in this conservatorship. Therefore, on the petition objecting to her annual accounting, I find in favor of the respondent, Ms. Paul. As for the issue of the will contest, that presents far more thorny legal issues. Respondent filed a will on her grandmother's behalf over fifteen years ago. Petitioners were notified of its existence and have only just now seen fit to object to its validity. I also find the testimony of Jason Mackin to be specious at best. Regardless of whether Mrs. Paul intended to change her will or write a will disinheriting her granddaughter, she never did. At such time as Marilyn Paul becomes deceased and the will is presented for probate, we can revisit these issues then. For now, I'm ruling against the petitioners without prejudice on the matter of the will contest. That is all."

Judge Wentz banged his gavel, rose from the bench, and turned so fast his robe twirled.

"What just happened?" Zoe asked as soon as the judge left the room.

"Well," I said. "You won. Mostly. He's saying he's not removing you as your grandmother's guardian and conservator. He's not sure about the will but won't rule on it now. But Zoe, it's likely going to be a moot point. You understand the FBI isn't going to let you keep that money anyway."

She smiled and hugged me. It still hurt.

"Oh, I'm sorry," she said.

"So am I."

"No. I don't care. Not about the money. Not really. It's drug money. Isn't it?"

"It really looks that way."

"Drugs took my mother away from me," she said. "And they were always what my father cared most about until recently. I don't want to profit from that kind of misery. If that money can be used to put dealers and other evil people like that behind bars and keep more people from getting hurt, then I'm happy. Truly."

"You're a special person, Zoe. Has anyone ever told you that?"

She teared up. "One."

My heart caught in my throat as I realized who she meant. Marilyn. I couldn't help but wonder what might have happened if Marilyn herself hadn't let greed take over.

Zoe paused for a moment as we walked out of the courthouse. It was almost as if she'd read my thoughts.

"It's cursed, anyway," Zoe said. "That money. I believe my grandma's accident was just that. But ... I don't know. Maybe she was extra distracted thinking about everything that was happening with the Valentines. What she was doing. What she knew. Maybe all that was on her mind when she got behind the wheel. I don't know. I just believe in my heart that things would have turned out differently ... better ... for both of us if she'd never gone to work for Valentine. If she'd never taken that money in the first place."

Zoe grew silent as she walked with me to my car. As I slid behind the wheel, she stared out the window, pensive.

"Are you sure you're up for this?" I said. "You don't have to be involved. I can handle it on my own."

Zoe blinked back a tear. "No. I need to be here for this. I need to be in the room when you tell her. I need to see her face."

"Okay," I said. "Then let's do this." I put the car in reverse and took Zoe Paul to do perhaps the hardest thing yet.

Chapter 40

When we got to the hospital, my heart dropped to my knees. In just one week's time, Marilyn Paul looked as if she'd wasted away to nothing. She was receiving only food and hydration now. The final round of chemo had done nothing but make her worse. Zoe had signed the papers, terminating further treatment for the cancer that ravaged her grandmother's body. She wasn't expected to live for more than a week or two.

We walked into the room together. I squeezed Zoe's shoulder as Marilyn's visitor turned and offered Zoe a smile through tears.

"Hi, honey," Frieda Jones said. She crossed the room and pulled Zoe into a hug. Her own tears fell freely now.

"She's been agitated today," Frieda said. "I tried to get her to eat some chocolate pudding. I know that's been her favorite. But she just doesn't have any interest anymore. I put on her favorite soap opera. That held her attention for a while. I just don't know how much of her is in there anymore, poor thing."

"We just came from court," Zoe said, taking the seat closest to her grandmother. I hung back against the wall. Frieda busied herself tidying up the room. She poured ice chips into a cup and brought them to Marilyn. She slid one between her gray lips.

"There you go, honey," Frieda said. "She likes that."

"I won my case," Zoe said. "Uncle Roy and my dad didn't even bother showing up. But it's okay. Nobody's going to try and keep me from taking care of Grandma again."

"Good. I'm so glad," Frieda said. "I knew you'd win."

"She didn't win everything," I said. "Marilyn isn't going to be able to keep the two million dollars Zoe found."

"What?" Frieda said. "How could they give it to those deadbeats?"

"It's part of a government seizure," I said. "Marilyn stole it. It's drug money, Frieda."

Frieda sank into the chair near the window.

"Even if Roy and Bradley had been successful with everything they sued for, they wouldn't see a dime of that money either."

"All that waste," she said. "It was for nothing, huh?"

"Did he tell you he'd give you a cut?" I asked. "How much was it? A hundred thousand? Two hundred thousand? Ten percent?"

Frieda kept her eyes fixed on Marilyn. Marilyn was partially awake. She had a dreamy smile on her face as Zoe took her hand.

"My office was bugged," I said. Zoe kept very still, focusing on Marilyn. "My phone too. See, the thing is, Ned Corbett was never in my office to my knowledge. No plumbers. Handymen. HVAC people. Not even any cleaning people; we do that ourselves. Not a single person had access to my office that I didn't know about. Just my staff. My clients. And witnesses I interviewed."

I took another step toward Frieda. "You spilled your coffee," I said. "Remember? I almost didn't. But you were there. I left you in my office for what, four or five minutes? Got you a towel."

"I was clumsy. I still feel bad about that," Frieda said, though her voice had gone an octave higher.

"Four or five minutes. That's all the time it would have taken to place that tracker app on my phone. It was on the table between us. That's where they found the bug too, stuck under that table."

"Why are you telling me this?" Frieda said.

"Because it was you," I said. "Corbett gave you the bugs and sent you in there with instructions on how to place them. He put you up to it. So, what I'm asking is, what was the price for my life? For Zoe's? For Marilyn's?"

"No," Frieda said. Her eyelids fluttered wildly.

"My dad and uncle didn't have access to my house anymore," Zoe said. "But you did, Frieda. You've always had a key. Even after I changed the locks."

"Corbett heard me talking to Detective Wray when we found Marilyn's evidence on those CDs. In *my* office. You were just down the street. Plenty of time to scoot on over and turn Zoe's house upside down looking for more discs."

That was the cue. Behind me, two sheriff's deputies appeared.

"You don't understand," Frieda cried. "You don't know how dangerous things got. I told Marilyn she was playing with fire. I told you. He would have killed me. You know what Corbett was capable of now, Cass. You've got the bandages and bruises to prove it. He came to me. He was going to kill me. Kill members of my family if I didn't help him."

"You could have told me," Zoe said. "I've trusted you my whole life. You were like a second grandmother to me. Cass could have helped you."

"No. No. You don't know what these people are like!"

"I hope that's true," Zoe said. "I hope it was fear and not greed that allowed you to betray me, Frieda. Betray my grandmother."

The deputies came into the room. One of them began reading Frieda Jones her Miranda rights. "Ms. Jones you are under arrest on suspicion of conspiracy to commit murder, illegal wiretapping, breaking and entering ..." They rattled off a few more charges. Frieda sobbed as they put the cuffs on her and led her out of the room.

"You okay?" I said to Zoe. "That was brave."

"I'm okay," she said as she rubbed lotion into her grandmother's hands. Then she dabbed her cracked lips with some salve. Marilyn reached up and touched her granddaughter's face.

"Special," she whispered to her.

"I love you, Grandma," Zoe said.

Then, Marilyn Paul looked at me. The clouds in her eyes seemed to lift and she stared at me with the coolest, keenest expression. For just that instant, I could have sworn she knew exactly what was going on. A second later, the haze seemed to return. She sank back against the pillow and smiled at Zoe.

"I'll be here in the morning, Grandma," Zoe whispered. "Sleep tight."

Zoe pulled the covers up to Marilyn's chin then walked out into the hallway with me.

"It's just the two of us now," she said. I put my arm around her.

"Not quite. Zoe, you know … even though this case is over … you can call me. You're more than my client. I'd like to think we've become friends. Okay? If you need anything. Someone to talk to. Someone to go with you to any of your grandmother's appointments. If … when … she takes a turn."

Zoe smiled. "Thank you. I think I'll take you up on it."

"There's something else," I said. "Something I didn't want to say in front of Frieda. I got a call from Agent Cannon about an hour ago. He wanted to make sure everything was in place, that he'd gotten the approval from the powers that be. But … the money …"

"It's okay, Cass. It really is. I'm not sad about not being able to keep it. Truly."

"No. The two million dollars will have to be turned over to law enforcement. But there's something else. A federal narcotics reward program for individuals who provide information leading to the arrest of major drug traffickers. Zoe, you qualify. Agent Cannon put in the paperwork. It's been approved."

"H-how much?"

"Two hundred and fifty thousand dollars," I said. "And it's payable directly to you. Not through your grandmother's estate."

"I c-can't … I can't breathe."

I hugged her. "It's a good thing you did."

"We did it," she said. "Cass ... if it weren't for you ..."

"Just remember what I said. You're not alone. I'm here for you, Zoe."

"Thank you. For everything. But mostly for being my friend."

I gave Zoe one more hug, then turned on my heel and headed for the lobby doors. Eric texted me as I did, reminding me I was about to be late for dinner.

Chapter 41

LATER, as the sun began to set over the lake and Vangie prepared her famous meal of pizza delivery, cake, and ice cream, Matty got the pontoon ready so we could all take a ride. I helped in the kitchen, collecting the empty pizza boxes. It was then I noticed as I carried them to the fire pit.

"You didn't," I said to my sister as I read the label on the top box.

"What?"

"Valentine Pizza?" I said.

She smiled. "Well ... I mean they do still make the best pizza in town."

I shook my head. "Funny. Real funny."

I turned. The others were making their way down the dock. Matty was already behind the wheel. Tori climbed aboard. Behind her, my niece Emma held baby Sean in her arms. She handed him to his mother then stepped onto the platform. Vangie's daughter Jessa came up behind her, cooing and talking baby talk to Sean.

"He's got himself a couple of built-in babysitters, hasn't he?" I said.

"I can't believe Jessa's old enough already."

"She's twelve," I said. "I wasn't much older when I started taking care of you and Matty by myself."

Eric stood on the porch, watching the others. He'd just got off work and still wore his uniform. Joe touched his arm, handed him a fresh beer, then moved past him. He looked happier today. I'd actually seen him smile a few times. He caught my eye and headed over to the fire pit, carrying a lighter.

"See you on the boat," Vangie said, kissing my cheek. "I'm glad you're feeling better. I mean, you still look like shit and all ... but ..."

"Stuff it!" I teased. She scooted away as Joe came up to me.

"You sure you're feeling better?" he said.

"Good as new," I said, holding up my bandaged hand. I had at least one more surgery ahead of me, but the orthopedic surgeon assured me I'd be good as new after that and some physical therapy.

"Damn," Joe said. "And that's your nose-pickin' hand, too."

I swatted him but missed.

"I love you, you know," he said. It took me off guard. I hadn't realized how much I needed to hear it from him.

"I know," I said. "But you can be a real pain in the butt."

"I know that too. I'm sorry. Most of the time."

"Are you going to be okay?" I asked. "Really?"

He looked out at the boat. They were laughing at something the baby did. Tori beamed as she held her tiny son.

"Yeah," he said. "I think we're all going to be okay one way or the other. Today helps."

"Yeah," I said. "It does. Thanks for planning it."

"What?" He feigned indignation. "This was all Vangie."

"No, it wasn't," I said.

His face grew serious for a second, then split into a grin.

"No. It wasn't. Are you coming?"

"In a sec," I said. Eric started to walk toward me. Something had kept him late at the office today. Something ... His eyes held darkness in them. Joe saw it too.

"We'll wait for you," he said, then cleared his throat as he left me and headed for the dock.

"Sorry I'm late," Eric said.

I went to him, sliding my hands around his shoulders. He sank into me. I felt tension in his whole body.

"You wanna talk about it?" I asked, pulling away.

He didn't answer at first. The boat's horn blared. Jessa had Sean in her lap. She was playing with the steering wheel. The baby flailed his arms and squealed with delight.

"I had my meeting with IA today," he said.

"Ah. A formality though, right?"

"It didn't turn out that way."

"What are you talking about? Eric, they can't blame you for what happened with Corbett. I would have died if you hadn't shot him. He was trying to kill me."

"It's not that. I've been cleared. It was a clean kill. It's just ... I've been reprimanded for how I went about collecting evidence against Corbett. I went off book."

"Reprimanded. If you hadn't done what you did, Corbett would have killed me. Probably Holly Billings too. And the FBI wouldn't be about to bring down one of the most notorious organized crime families in Detroit. How can they reprimand you for any of it?"

"Well, they did. Somebody somewhere still thinks cops shouldn't investigate other cops, even retired ones. So ... as of this morning, I've been relieved of my assignment with the Detective Bureau. If I go quietly, I can have a nice, cushy job in records sitting on my ass for the next eight years until retirement."

"Oh Eric, I'm so sorry. We can fight it. That's not right."

"It's over," he said. "I told them where they could stuff their new assignment. I turned in my badge and gun, Cass. I'm finished."

It was only then I realized he wasn't wearing either. His side holster was empty. "Are you okay?"

He smiled. "I'm unemployed."

I took his hand in my good one. "No. You're not. Eric, what you did? I don't care what the department says. That was some fantastic investigative work. It saved my life. It probably made Lee Cannon's career. You can do so much more outside the Bureau. You can do it with me. I've asked you before. Come to work with me. You're a born investigator. I could use you."

He smiled. "You sure about that? I'm going to be expensive."

There was a lightness about him as he said it. I realized that at that moment, he'd decided. My heart raced with excitement and new possibilities.

The horn on the boat blared again. This time, it was Matty. "All aboard, that's coming aboard!"

"Keep your shorts on," I yelled. "Come on," I said to Eric. He squeezed my hand and led me down the path to the dock. To my family. My big, loud, dysfunctional family. As we stepped on board and Eric threw off the ropes, I knew he was part of it. We would all sink or swim together and I wouldn't have it any other way.

UP NEXT, when Cass inherits the practice of an old legal mentor, his client list is more than she bargained for. The resulting murder trial has all the twists and turns you've come to expect from a Robin James thriller. Don't miss The Client List!

https://www.robinjamesbooks.com/tcl

DID YOU KNOW?

All of Robin's books are also available in Audiobook format. Click here to find your favorite! https://www.robinjamesbooks. com/foraudio

Newsletter Sign Up

Sign up to get notified about Robin James's latest book releases, discounts, and author news. You'll also get *Crown of Thorne* an exclusive FREE bonus prologue to the Cass Leary Legal Thriller Series just for joining. Find out what really made Cass leave Killian Thorne and Chicago behind.

Click to Sign Up

http://www.robinjamesbooks.com/newsletter/

About the Author

Robin James is an attorney and former law professor. She's worked on a wide range of civil, criminal and family law cases in her twenty-five year legal career. She also spent over a decade as supervising attorney for a Michigan legal clinic assisting thousands of people who could not otherwise afford access to justice.

Robin now lives on a lake in southern Michigan with her husband, two children, and one lazy dog. Her favorite, pure Michigan writing spot is stretched out on the back of a pontoon watching the faster boats go by.

Sign up for Robin James's Legal Thriller Newsletter to get all the latest updates on her new releases and get a free bonus scene from Burden of Truth featuring Cass Leary's last day in Chicago. http://www.robinjamesbooks.com/newsletter/

Also By Robin James

Cass Leary Legal Thriller Series

Burden of Truth

Silent Witness

Devil's Bargain

Stolen Justice

Blood Evidence

Imminent Harm

First Degree

Mercy Kill

Guilty Acts

Cold Evidence

Dead Law

The Client List

With more to come...

Mara Brent Legal Thriller Series

Time of Justice

Price of Justice

Hand of Justice

Mark of Justice

Path of Justice

Vow of Justice

Web of Justice

With more to come...

Audiobooks by Robin James

Cass Leary Series

Burden of Truth

Silent Witness

Devil's Bargain

Stolen Justice

Blood Evidence

Imminent Harm

First Degree

Mercy Kill

Guilty Acts

Cold Evidence

Dead Law

The Client List

Mara Brent Series

Time of Justice

Price of Justice

Hand of Justice

Mark of Justice

Path of Justice

Vow of Justice

Made in the USA
Middletown, DE
21 April 2023

29252035R00217